LIES

Also by Patrick Dillon

TRUTH

LIES

PATRICK DILLON

MICHAEL JOSEPH
LONDON

MICHAEL JOSEPH LTD
Published by the Penguin Group
27 Wrights Lane, London w8 5TZ
Viking Penguin Inc., 375 Hudson Street, New York, New York 10014, USA
Penguin Books Australia Ltd, Ringwood, Victoria, Australia
Penguin Books Canada Ltd, 10 Alcorn Avenue, Toronto, Ontario, Canada M4V 3B2
Penguin Books (NZ) Ltd, 182–190 Wairau Road, Auckland 10, New Zealand

Penguin Books Ltd, Registered Offices: Harmondsworth, Middlesex, England

First published 1997
1 3 5 7 9 10 8 6 4 2

Set in 11/13.25pt Monotype Bembo
Printed in England by Clays Ltd, St Ives plc

A CIP catalogue record for this book is available from the British Library

ISBN 0 7181 4170 9

Truth and reality begin when one no longer understands what one is doing or what one knows . . .

HENRI MATISSE: *Jazz*

In her photograph, June Donaghy looked just like anybody else: quite pretty, quite happy, not ready to die.

The photograph was held six inches from my nose, between her mother's thumb and forefinger. Mrs Donaghy was a neat-looking woman in her fifties with a white blouse that had been ironed that morning and a big gold cross hanging down over her chest. She touched the cross each time her lips puckered up, which was whenever I asked her a question, or she had to say her daughter's name. Her eyes were moist behind National Health glasses which trailed a fine gold chain around the back of her neck. Every few minutes she blew her nose on a folded-up Kleenex she took from the sleeve of her cardigan.

Mrs Donaghy got her voice back from somewhere and said, 'I can still see her sitting there. Sitting in the chair you're in now. Every evening we sat here together. We were never great ones for television.'

The room was bare, with cheap carpet on the floor and an unlit gas fire filling the hearth. The furniture was designed for thrift not comfort. From the walls a dozen photographs of June Donaghy watched her mother cry. In the right place, under the right lights and with the right music playing, someone would have found June Donaghy beautiful. She had tiny freckles on her cheeks, in the photograph taken on the beach, and a nice smile in front of the Eiffel Tower. On moorland, in a blue anorak, her eyes were like her mother's: blue, cold and determined.

'June and I were everything to each other. She took me to Paris one year. From what she earned.' A smile perched itself lopsidedly on Mrs Donaghy's mouth. 'Have you been to France, Chief

Inspector? Our hotel was very expensive. You should have seen the bathroom — all the little towels. That was last Easter.' She looked down at her lap and her fingers touched the big gold cross. 'The one thing I'm glad of is what you told me — that she didn't know anything. I hate to think of my June being frightened or in pain. The thought that she didn't know anything . . .' She looked up at me. 'That's a comfort.'

I shifted in my chair. The photographs of June Donaghy eyed me accusingly from the wall. 'That's what the doctor said,' I lied.

It was the sort of lie Mrs Donaghy needed just then. I watched her fingers playing with the big cross, twisting it around on the chain as if she was trying to wring tears out of it.

I looked at more photographs of June Donaghy; there was nothing else to look at except for a black piano with the lid down and a straight-backed armchair with a middle-aged woman in it who didn't know how to cry but was learning fast. Some of the photographs showed another woman as well: a blonde with a hard, amused mouth who was taller and prettier than June had been. There were no photographs of the blonde woman by herself, and no pictures of any men. At least Mrs Donaghy wasn't going to turn the house into a shrine to her younger daughter: it already was a shrine. The mantelpiece carried a formal graduation shot of June Donaghy with candles on either side of it as if she was a twenty-year-old saint with a mortarboard for a halo.

Mrs Donaghy looked up at me. 'Who would do a thing like this, Chief Inspector? My daughter had so much in front of her.' What June Donaghy had had in front of her would have been too much for any mother. Mrs Donaghy frowned at the carpet again; I could see her lips moving.

'She was a lovely girl,' I said.

June Donaghy had stopped being a lovely girl sometime the night before, somewhere near where Blackfriars Bridge arched over the riverside walk on the south bank of the River Thames. By the time the patrol found her, her body had stiffened on the mud banks. The tide was already creeping towards her. Another few hours and it would have drawn her away under the bridges and out to sea.

By the time I got there daylight was just starting to take over from the police arc lamps they had set up on the riverside walk. On the far side of the river, lights were winking on in the office blocks of the city. Blackfriars Bridge was thick with early commuters, a stream of tiny figures pouring across the river into work. Not many of them stopped to watch. Maybe they couldn't see what we were doing on the river bed, or maybe they didn't want to see. It was six o'clock on a Monday morning in March. Maybe that was all the tragedy they could cope with.

Out on the river a police launch was doing just enough against the current to keep level with us. A yellow oilskin figure in the stern was hunched against the spray thrown up by a sharp wind along the river.

Baring's red face was taut with exhaustion. 'Phone call, sir. Man's voice. Twelve-oh-eight. Hysterics.'

'Did he leave a name?'

'Something about a car, that was all. Registration number. Then he slammed the phone down.'

'Is there a call box near here?'

'End of the alley, sir. We've taken prints.'

June Donaghy's body had caught on pilings just below the embankment. That was what had saved her from the falling tide. In landing she had trapped one leg between pilings and twisted it around behind her. From above it looked as if she was dancing. Figures in brown waders had churned the mud around her into a quagmire.

From the shoulder bag a policeman had found in the alley we learned that she had a clean driving licence, no cards and a cheque account with the Abbey National. She tied her dark hair back, usually, and had a slight squint when the light caught her in the eyes. She kept small change apart to put in the charity box. From her Filofax we learned that she kept a record of all the numbers she'd played on the lottery, and didn't have enough friends. Her hair was cut by someone called Max. The rest of her bag told us she liked *Gone with the Wind* enough to have read it more than once, and bought her lunchtime sandwiches from Boots. Either she believed in God, or someone close to her had given her a bookmark with the prayer of St Francis of Assisi on it, and a key ring in the shape of a crucifix. She earned enough money to have three taxi receipts and to wear Ysatis, but not enough to get the strap of the bag fixed. Either that, or she'd been too busy to get it fixed; or else she'd had a premonition that she was never going to need a new strap. That was something that the bag couldn't tell us.

'Anything on the body?'

'Nothing, sir. She wasn't touched. Clothes as they were. Lucky she hit the pilings or we'd have lost her.'

The police doctor said, 'Can't have had time to think about it, can he? Just heaved her over. Otherwise he'd have checked where the tide was. Silly cunt.'

The doctor was a cheerful type in a padded ski jacket which made him look like an electric blue snowman. He grinned at me through glasses smeared with river spray.

'How did she die?'

'Bang on the head. Might have been the glass there. Don't know yet.' His hand indicated the back of the river walk, where policemen were crouched around a shop front which had been smashed, either by June Donaghy's head or by some other lifeless object. 'Get her back to the lab, we'll tell you when she last washed her hair. Tell you what she had for supper last night. Tell you what kind of toothpaste her boyfriend used. You leave it to us.'

There was nothing else to show why anyone would kill a girl who liked *Gone with the Wind* and had her hair cut by someone called Max. A row of policemen was crawling towards us on their knees, hands caressing the river walk. From beyond the cordon, a small crowd watched them searching. A woman jogger in a grey tracksuit and headphones kept running on the spot as if she was trying to escape from killers in a nightmare.

The doctor said, 'Wouldn't have let her come out here late at night if she'd been my girl. If I was her boyfriend I'd have told her to take a taxi. Paid for it. Or her dad. That's what I say to Josey, after ten-thirty you take a cab. I mean, you'd rather pay than worry, wouldn't you? Any dad would.'

Up on the bridge a double-decker bus was crawling slowly through traffic. Its windows were yellow with condensation.

Baring looked at me. 'Bet you wish you hadn't come back, sir. Day like this. You could have stayed out of it.'

He was wrong about that. I'd tried staying out of it and it hadn't worked. It was a cold morning in March and quite soon I'd be looking at the face of a girl who'd died in the wrong way, then looking for the person who'd made her die. I'd still rather have been doing that than walking across Blackfriars Bridge towards the same computer screen and joke mug I'd stared at the day before, and knowing that this evening I'd cross it the other way, a little older and not much richer, and still not notice what was happening down on the river bed.

I knew that no one up on Blackfriars Bridge would have changed places with me either.

In the end we had to drop ropes over the embankment and get her up that way. June Donaghy's body came up out of the mud slowly, as if there was a part of her which didn't want to leave it at all. The wind caught the stretcher and made it twist against the ropes. It was twenty minutes before we set it down on the river walk and I could see properly what someone had done to June Donaghy's face.

By ten o'clock the bridge was empty and the ambulance was gone. June Donaghy's death was just an ordinary tragedy, not enough to stop either of the tides: the Thames flowing under the bridges, the city workers pouring over them. But then, it was Monday morning and everyone had other things on their minds.

Out on the river the police launch was already disappearing into the mist.

Mrs Donaghy straightened her back and twitched her mouth back into shape. She didn't look as if she'd ever done much crying and she didn't like doing it in front of me. Neither the tears nor her glasses managed to hide the cold blue chill of her eyes. Something about the set of her face reminded me of the pictures of martyrs I had seen in prayer books as a child. They could have put Mrs Donaghy over the same fires and her eyes would have stayed cold.

I said, 'You told me June had some trouble at work. What was that about?'

5

'It wasn't important.'

'Was she happy there?'

Mrs Donaghy touched her nose with the folded Kleenex. 'It was only a little trouble with Mr Thacker. If it wasn't for that she would have been happy. It was a good company.'

'What was the trouble with Mr Thacker?' I asked.

I got the same response I had got the last time I asked that question: a slow stiffening of the neck without any answer to go with it. Mrs Donaghy stared defiantly past my shoulder. She was the martyr and I was the inquisition and she could have held her silence for ever.

I sighed. 'How long had June worked for PTI?'

'Ever since she left college. She wanted to go into the city.' Mrs Donaghy frowned: a remembered disappointment in a career she was proud of. 'It was the recession. They weren't taking people on, not even girls like June, with her degree. Did you know she had a degree?' It was only the fifth time she had mentioned it. 'She decided to become a personal assistant instead, and work her way up.' Her voice was defensive, scared that anyone would think her daughter had accepted second best.

'And did she?'

Mrs Donaghy frowned. 'I don't understand.'

'Work her way up.'

'Oh, she became Mr Thacker's assistant soon enough. He kept saying . . . He kept *saying* . . .' Her voice turned bitter and then died. It didn't come back to life again.

'When did June stop enjoying her job?'

'She did enjoy it.'

'What did Mr Thacker keep saying?'

'That she'd . . . that one day . . .' She turned her pale, determined eyes on me. 'He was the reason why she never got promoted any further, Chief Inspector. It wasn't that she wasn't good enough.'

'I'm sure it wasn't.'

'She had a BA. Business Management. She was going to do history but she thought it wouldn't lead to anything.'

All Business Management had led to was a row of pilings under the Thames embankment. June Donaghy hadn't been told that

6

when she filled in her UCCA form. Maybe history would have been a better choice.

I said, 'So what stopped Mr Thacker promoting her?'

Mrs Donaghy twisted the cross viciously at the end of its chain and stared at the photograph on the mantelpiece. She didn't say anything. I looked at the photograph with her. June Donaghy smiled back at us from under a mortarboard that didn't quite fit her neat brown head.

'Did your daughter have a boyfriend, Mrs Donaghy?' That was another question I had asked before. Mrs Donaghy's eyes narrowed. I said, 'It would help if you told us everything.'

'I have told you everything. Everything that matters.'

'Were you close to June?'

She turned pale eyes on me and answered a different question. 'She was everything to me.'

'Did she have any close friends?'

'She was too busy for that kind of thing.' She spoke as if friendship was only a step away from premarital sex, mortal sin and unwanted babies. 'June's work mattered more than anything to her.' Her fingers touched the cross on her chest. 'Almost anything. June had a sense of duty. Ten o'clock, eleven, she'd work to, some nights. Yesterday wasn't the only Sunday. She'd call me from the office. I used to make things for her supper that wouldn't spoil. Things you could heat up in the oven. She'd call me and say, "Mum . . ."' Mrs Donaghy's mouth opened as if she couldn't get enough air to breathe, then tightened again into an unyielding straight line.

'What about her sister?' I nodded towards a photograph of the blonde woman giving June a strained smile in front of a table-top Christmas tree.

Mrs Donaghy's back stiffened. 'What about her?'

'Was June close to her?'

'They hardly saw each other.' Mrs Donaghy's voice sounded dismissive.

'Her father?'

Mrs Donaghy's lips tightened. Anger brought more colour into her cheeks. 'My husband isn't with us.' She didn't tell me who he

7

was with – God or another woman. I waited for her to go on. 'He left us.'

'How long ago?'

'Fifteen years.'

'Did either of your daughters stay in touch with him?'

'I didn't want them to.' She paused and added, 'My husband didn't understand his responsibilities.'

'Do you know where he is now?'

'I don't want to know.'

'When did you last hear from him?'

Mrs Donaghy's chin turned and rose, killing the answer. From the same position she said, 'He walked out on us without any warning. Two little girls and a woman by herself. He never sent us a penny; I had to pay for everything. There weren't any holidays. I put both of them through school. I paid for June all the way through college.' She must have realized early on that God was the only one on her side. Mrs Donaghy stopped and turned her eyes towards me, considering what kind of impression she had made. 'It wasn't all hard. I made sure they had fun as well.'

'What kind of fun?'

She had to think about that, looking across the room at a photograph of two little girls in matching dresses which were tied tightly about their waists, as if to stop them running away. 'We were a happy family,' she said finally.

There were footsteps in the hallway outside and the door opened. I turned to see a tall woman with blonde straight hair framing a face that must once have been prettier. She had aged since the last photograph had been taken with her sister. When I looked back at the straight-backed chair, Mrs Donaghy's face was set in the expression of a martyr, hands gripping the chair, eyes towards heaven.

The blonde woman looked at me and said, 'I'm Sarah.'

'Sarah *Rider*,' Mrs Donaghy said, stressing the surname as if it made the blonde woman less of a daughter, less of a rival to June.

'I thought you might want more tea, Mum.' The hard edges in Sarah Rider's voice were only just kept under the surface. She didn't come any further into the room.

'I'll get it myself if I need it.'

I heard the door close. Mrs Donaghy's face was aggrieved, as if she couldn't understand why God had taken the favourite daughter and left her this one. The fingers of her left hand tried to tease an answer from the cross on her neck.

There was a pause. We seemed to have come to a dead end again. June Donaghy had been an ordinary girl, quite pretty and quite happy, whose mother probably loved her too much and probably spent too much time fingering the cross around her neck. None of that was a reason for anyone to kill her. There didn't seem to be a reason for anyone to kill her. The only cloud on June Donaghy's horizon – apart from living with a martyr – was some trouble with her boss. And that was the one thing her mother wouldn't tell me about.

I said, 'What exactly does Mr Thacker do at PTI?'

'It's his company. Him and his brother. It used to be called Thacker Construction until they changed the name.'

'When did your daughter start to argue with him?'

'They didn't argue.'

'When did she stop enjoying her job?' I could hear the weariness in my own voice.

Mrs Donaghy's neck stiffened.

I shouldn't have gone on, but it was the only direction I could think of to go in. Maybe it would hurt Mrs Donaghy's feelings; but her feelings were already beyond any healing I could offer. I said, 'Did your daughter have an affair with Mr Thacker?'

I shouldn't have said it. Mrs Donaghy's eyes froze over. Her fingers dabbed at her forehead then tapped each shoulder in turn. Anger made her back straighter and put an extra yard between us. The silence between us slowly filled up with Mrs Donaghy's anger. It looked like something she was good at – something she'd had practice at. She seemed to have an inexhaustible supply of it. Once again the world had failed to show enough respect for her daughter. I was no better than the rest of them.

'June was a pretty girl,' I said, as if that was going to get me forgiven.

'Of course she was a pretty girl.' Mrs Donaghy's voice was

resentful. 'It doesn't mean she went running off after men. Not all the girls these days are like that, you know. Some of them are just decent, ordinary girls. Not like . . .' Mrs Donaghy's lips tightened just in time to stop her telling me who June wasn't like. She turned her face to one side again, as if staring at photographs of her daughter for long enough would make everything else go away, including me and the fact that June's body had just been found on the mud-flats of the River Thames.

'But Mr Thacker wanted her to have an affair?'

'I don't want to talk about it.'

'It might help.'

'It can't bring June back.' She started to cry.

'No,' I said. 'But it might help us find out how she died.'

'Do you think there's a connection?'

'I don't know until you tell me more about it.'

Mrs Donaghy took the folded Kleenex from her sleeve and pressed each eye in turn. 'He . . .' She gave a deep sigh, as if she was too tired to fight any longer. Her mouth twisted out of shape as she swallowed. 'Mr Thacker made suggestions.'

I nodded. 'Is that what went wrong with her job?'

'Yes.'

'How long had it been going on?'

'Ever since she started working for him. She worked for somebody else first. A Mr Price. As soon as she moved to Mr Thacker's office . . .' She stopped.

'What did June say to him?'

'She told him . . .' Mrs Donaghy frowned at the difficulty of describing things she didn't know how to express and had probably never experienced. 'She made it clear she wasn't interested in his . . . in what he wanted.'

'But that didn't make him stop.'

Mrs Donaghy shook her head. 'She had to go to a conference with him. In Scotland. She had to have dinner with him. Smoked salmon and fillet of beef. He tried to get into her hotel room afterwards.'

'Did your daughter tell anyone about it? Complain to anyone?'

'She said . . .' Mrs Donaghy voice was high and strained. 'She said she'd thought about telling the newspapers. It was the only way. There were other things she didn't like about him. She wasn't sure he was always honest.'

'Why didn't she leave her job?'

'She might not have got another. Because of the recession.'

'She could have tried for another position inside the company.'

'She did. Mr Thacker held her back. He said if she didn't . . .' Tears filled up her eyes suddenly and kept on flowing, as if something inside her had broken. 'He said, if she didn't do what he wanted she'd lose her job. He'd make sure she didn't get a job anywhere else either. That's what he said to her.'

Mrs Donaghy blinked at me across the threadbare carpet. Her face was drained of all colour. She looked exhausted.

I closed the notebook on my lap. There were other questions I could have asked her, but Mr Thacker would probably give better answers than the woman in front of me. Mrs Donaghy wanted me to go away now. She wanted to be left alone with her crucifix and the pictures of her daughter. I stood up.

Mrs Donaghy stayed in the straight-backed chair; her blue eyes followed me. I couldn't tell if she was seeing me or a brown-haired girl setting off for work in the morning.

As I reached the door she asked, 'What sort of person would do a thing like this, Chief Inspector?'

She made the question sound simple and professional, as if we kept a list of people who did things like that at Kennington Police Station. I didn't have an answer for her. I didn't know what sort of people they were, except that they lived in the same city as the rest of us, breathed the same air, shopped in the same stores – and that would hardly have been much comfort to anyone.

I looked back at her. 'Do you know of any reason why anyone would have wanted to kill your daughter?'

'There are a lot of evil people in the world.' She didn't need to tell me that, and it wasn't an answer anyway.

I left her staring at the photographs of her daughter.

2

I found Sarah Rider standing in the kitchen with one hand on an old-fashioned kettle on the gas stove. Her lips acknowledged me with a look that didn't quite dare to be ironic. She had her mother's hard mouth; the rest of her face came from somewhere else.

'Have you finished?'

'For the moment.'

'Tea? I'm making some anyway.'

I said, 'I'm sorry about your sister.'

'Yes.' Sarah Rider looked down at the kettle. 'Well.'

The kettle started to blow steam. She took it off the hob without waiting for it to whistle and slopped hot water into an old brown teapot. The teapot was the only thing marring the kitchen's clean surfaces. Everything else was locked up behind cupboard doors.

I watched her searching through the cupboards for mugs. Sarah Rider's clothes had been chosen carefully that morning: a knitted blue top, a miniskirt she must have put on before she heard about her sister. She had long fingers tipped with red nail varnish. Brown roots were starting to tell stories about the blonde hair.

'Are you going to stay here long?'

'I don't suppose so.' She glanced at me, then quickly back down at the kettle. A little water had spilled on the surface. 'Mum and I . . .' She left unsaid what was wrong between her mother and her. Maybe the only thing wrong was that she wasn't June and she was still alive while her sister's body was lying in the police mortuary. 'I'm looking after a friend's place at the moment.'

'When did you hear about June?'

'First thing this morning. Mum called me. I knew something must have gone wrong when she called.'

'Will your mother be all right?'

'Of course not. You've seen the sitting-room.' She shook her head. 'How does anyone get over something like this? Mum won't. She doesn't know how to forget things.'

'Were she and June very close?'

'Yes.' There was a slight hesitation in the way she said it. She looked frankly up at me to cover it. 'Closer than she was to me. Milk and sugar?'

I told her neither and watched her spill brown water on the kitchen worktop and down the side of the mug.

Sarah went on, 'June was Mum's favourite.' She shrugged. 'Didn't make any difference to me. She was more like Mum than I am. I'm more like Dad.' Her lip curled ironically. 'That's what Mum tells me, anyway.'

I took the mug of tea and sipped it. For the sake of saying something that wasn't about her sister, I said, 'Do you remember him at all?'

'Remember him? Course I do. I still see him. Comes over every couple of years, doesn't he? Comes to borrow money from me.' She made a face. 'Don't know why he bothers. I haven't got any.'

'Did he see June as well?'

She shook her head over the top of her mug. 'Dad doesn't have anything to do with this, if that's what you're thinking. You probably think we're all nutty, don't you? A nutty family who started killing each other. We're not that bad.'

'I didn't say you were.'

Sarah looked up at me again and her eyes stayed on me. At any other time, in any other house, I would have thought she was sizing me up. Maybe she was, or maybe she just didn't know any other way to look at men. The fine lines around her mouth had been filled in expertly with powder. It was a good repair job but it wouldn't have fooled an expert. Her looks were going and she knew it.

She grimaced suddenly and said, 'She must sound nutty enough. When she starts going on about . . . you know. Mum thinks

Dad's possessed by the devil. She thinks I am, too. She told me once.'

'What did you do wrong?'

Sarah started to laugh, then cut it off abruptly when she remembered this was the wrong house to laugh in and today was the wrong day. I liked how the beginning of the laugh sounded. It was open and frank, and didn't have a cross hung round its neck. 'I got married. It wasn't only that. You'd never know I used to be the blue-eyed girl, would you? When I was a kid. I used to be Mum's favourite. I was the pretty one.'

'Did you mind when that changed?'

'Not enough to push her in the river, if that's what you mean.' She'd said that without thinking and it came out all wrong. She flushed and buried her face in the mug of tea.

Through the kitchen window I could see a sparrow searching in vain for food between two cracks in the concrete paving. The garden was surrounded by tidy wooden fencing creosoted to an even mud brown.

I said, 'What would June have been doing on the south bank late last night?'

'I don't know.' Sarah's voice was wary.

'We got a call from someone who saw a car there. A man. Was she meeting someone there?'

Sarah Rider's fake blonde head moved from left to right.

'Did she have friends near there?'

'Not that I know of.'

'Your mother said she didn't come home that way. She hadn't arranged to meet anybody. Why else would she go there?'

Sarah Rider shrugged. 'Search me.'

'Did June have a boyfriend?'

She sipped tea and looked at me. 'What did Mum say?'

'She said June didn't have time for that kind of thing.'

'Then she didn't. Mum never tells lies. She told me so, once.'

'She might not have known about it.'

Sarah shrugged again.

'Were you and June close?'

'Used to be. Close about some things.'

14

'Men?'

'She didn't have time for men.'

'What about her job?'

Sarah put the mug down on the worktop. 'What about it?'

'Did she ever talk about it?'

'It was a good job. She earned good money. More than I ever did.'

I said, 'Your mother told me she had some trouble with her boss.'

'Barney Thacker? He was always chasing her, if that's what she meant. June told me about that.' She shook her head. 'Mum's nutty about sex. I don't suppose it meant anything. I mean, it was still worth it, wasn't it? The boss's hand up your skirt . . . any girl can stand that, the amount she was paid.'

'She said June was thinking about going to the papers. She thought he was dishonest as well.'

'She was probably just moaning. Bad day at work . . . People are always moaning about work.' One red fingernail scratched a pattern in the pool of spilled tea on the worktop.

'When did you last see your sister?' I asked.

'Week ago. We met up for a drink.'

'Your mother told me you never saw each other.'

'She didn't know. June thought it might piss her off. Mum's a pain to live with when she's pissed off. She sulks.'

I looked at her hard, pretty face. I said, 'How did you feel when you heard about June this morning?'

For a moment Sarah Rider looked shocked, then she started to laugh again. She had to put the mug down on the worktop so she could laugh properly. 'Is that the sort of question coppers ask these days?' She shook her head and looked straight at me. 'If you want to know I felt glad. Only for a moment – it didn't mean I *was* glad. It was what I felt. I was jealous of June. Who was the one everyone thought would do all right? Me. Who was the one ended up with the smart job and the money? My kid sister.' Suddenly Sarah Rider was crying. She put the back of her hand against her nose as if that would be enough to catch the tears. She said, 'Don't listen to me. I say stupid things.'

15

'I'm sorry.'

'What have you got to be sorry about? You're only a copper.' She turned her back on me for a moment. Her shoulders went up, then slowly dropped. When she turned round she had set her face again in the hard, amused look I had seen in the photographs.

'It wasn't what I really felt.' Her lip curled at me. 'Feel. Have you been to see Barney Thacker yet?'

'Why?'

'I was wondering what you were going to say to him.'

I was starting to wonder that myself. I took the address where Sarah Rider was staying and watched the woman police constable who'd come with me feel discreetly through the pockets of June Donaghy's coat and blue anorak. Mrs Donaghy wouldn't let me go upstairs alone. It only took five minutes to work out that June Donaghy's bedroom belonged to an ordinary girl in her mid-twenties who spent too much time at work and all the rest of her time at home. The decorations came from ten years before, when a teenaged girl had liked flowers and a flounce around the bed and hadn't wanted to send her teddy bears to the attic. The books by the bed were costume romances sitting on a leather bible with the marker in Revelation. In the flap-down desk I found nothing but brown envelopes full of work papers. The clothes in the wardrobe were chosen for work not play. Mrs Donaghy told me the yellow check dress with the button-up collar had been bought for June's graduation. She also told me that Sarah had worn a miniskirt and brought shame on the family. She didn't like me opening the chest of drawers or feeling under the pillow. When I left the room she was still smoothing down the flowered eiderdown, as if to pretend that no one had ever been in to disturb it.

Outside, the police car was waiting for me. Across the street, a terrace of severe Victorian houses frowned at passers-by and ignored the three tower blocks which showed above their rooftops. If I hadn't looked up I might not even have noticed the tower blocks were there. I guessed that anyone who lived in Renshaw Road was good at not looking up. The copper on the doorstep looked like he'd had enough of people watching him from behind net curtains.

I gave the driver the address of June Donaghy's office, and didn't look up at the tower blocks.

3

The office where June Donaghy had worked was a glass box hovering over the rooftops of Bloomsbury like a spaceship that couldn't decide whether to land or not. The lift she'd used every morning played soft music at me, then opened its doors on to a reception full of rubber plants and modern furniture. Beyond it I could see a glass roof pouring colourless light over rows of desks, white columns and robots toiling over computer screens. A gallery looked down on the desks from above. Framed pictures on the wall of the reception area showed motorways cutting through green fields and profit charts ascending into the clouds.

The robot behind the reception desk smiled. It didn't mean she was pleased to see me; it was the smile they'd programmed into her at the factory.

'I want to see Barney Thacker.'

'Mr Thacker isn't available right now.'

I looked at her. The powder covering her cheeks had blotted up all expression from them; her vivid gold hair looked like strands of fine wire. 'It's about June Donaghy.'

Her red mouth formed an O without making the noise that went with it. 'I'll see if he's free.'

While she dialled I looked at the other pictures on the reception walls. A boardroom photograph showed two men in suits on either side of a conference table – I remembered Mrs Donaghy telling me the firm was run by two brothers. I failed to find June Donaghy in a group shot of staff grinning up at a photographer on the gallery.

'Will you come this way, please?'

I followed the receptionist to a staircase that led up on to the gallery. From above, the workers looked like rows of ants.

That must have been the way the Thackers saw them. The receptionist led me along the gallery towards an open door at the end.

As we approached it, a young woman came out of the door backwards with a pile of folders clutched to her chest. She might have been a pretty girl when she left for work that morning. Now her blouse had become detached from the waistband of her skirt and her lipstick seemed to have slipped on one side.

She was saying, 'I know, Mr Thacker. I'm sorry. I know you told me to check. I'm sorry, Mr Thacker.'

As she turned to pass us she stumbled on her stiletto heels. There were grey half moons of sweat under her arms.

The receptionist glanced at me, then knocked on the door and went in without waiting for an answer. I followed her. Inside was a conference room with a big mahogany table almost the same length as the room. Two men were sitting at the table – the same men I had seen in the photograph in reception. Behind them a young blond man in a tweed suit was hovering with an open notebook.

It wasn't hard to guess which of the brothers had been the boss June Donaghy hated. Aggression came off Barney Thacker like a bad smell. He was thick-set and muscular with a fringe of ginger hair cut square across his forehead and unhealthy white skin that made him look like he was recovering from a disease. His feet were drumming up and down under the desk as if someone had plugged him in to an electric current. Red fists were balled on either side of a blotting pad covered in angry doodles of stick men.

He didn't wait for me to reach the table. 'We heard about the Donaghy. They told me this morning. Bloody shame. She was a damned good secretary.' Barney Thacker's voice was big and harsh with a jeering edge to it.

His brother didn't seem to like it any more than I did. His lips pursed fastidiously. He stood up as if he needed to put distance between himself and Barney. 'It was shocking news, Chief Inspector.' He put out one hand. 'Peter Thacker.'

Either Peter Thacker was younger than his brother, or he'd spent more time taking care of himself. He was tall and well-groomed with flashes of grey hair over his ears and an evenly tanned face that made him look like a saloon-bar singer. His handshake was cold and soft; it felt like shaking hands with an empty silk glove. He had humorous brown eyes which stayed detached from the smile he gave me, as if someone in the background was telling him a joke no one else could hear. 'I wrote to Mrs Donaghy as soon as we heard. I've offered her whatever help we can give. I understand she depended on June's support.'

I said, 'That was generous of you.'

'We do what we can. June Donaghy was a highly valued employee.' He gestured towards a chair and sat down again, pulling his own chair an inch further away from his brother's. 'Can you tell us what happened?'

'She was attacked down by the embankment. We don't know who did it.'

'It's a tragedy.' Peter Thacker picked the word carefully, like someone choosing the best cake off a plate. 'Did she know the attacker? You can sometimes tell that, can't you?'

'We don't know anything yet.'

'Did anyone see it happen?'

'A man. He gave us the number of a car he saw near there, then rang off. We haven't heard from him since.'

'How odd.' Peter Thacker frowned. 'It sounds as if . . . as if it was just one of those things, doesn't it? It seems a dreadful thing to say. A senseless attack.'

'Nutter.' Barney Thacker's voice was a short, decisive bark. 'Let them all out of the fucking hospitals two years back. Shouldn't have done it. Fucking nutters wandering around the streets all night. What do they think's going to happen?'

I said, 'Why was June Donaghy at work yesterday?'

'We're a busy firm.' It was Peter Thacker who answered. 'We often work on Sundays. Yesterday was no exception.'

'What time did she leave?'

'You'd have to ask Alf that.' He showed white teeth. 'Our security man. Alf would have seen her go out.'

'What hours did she work normally?'

'As long as it took her to do what I wanted.' Barney Thacker was leaning forward over the table, trying to bore holes in it with one broad white finger. 'When she'd done everything I wanted she could go home. If it took her all night then she worked all night. That's the way we do things here.'

I didn't tell him how tough that made him. Maybe that was a mistake. I said, 'How long had June been working here?'

'Ages. Didn't always work for me. Worked in some shit-hole dead end in the accounts department. I picked her out.'

'Why?'

Barney Thacker chewed slowly on his lips and regarded me as if he was wondering what kind of a meal I'd make. 'Because she was efficient. She wasn't always running around after damned boys. Didn't spend the whole time touching up her fucking make-up. She was a damned good secretary, the Donaghy.' He fell back in his seat and his voice dropped to a low growl. 'Not like the tramp who's taken over from her. Told her half an hour ago, you fuck up once more, you spend the rest of your life in the fucking typing pool. What does she do? Starts crying all over the carpet. Fucking useless.'

The pause was filled by the sound of Barney Thacker's feet drumming up and down beneath the table.

I said, 'Tell me something about the company, Mr Thacker.'

'Of course.' Peter Thacker's voice was smooth and assured. 'We work on civil engineering contracts. Large works. Motorways.' One hand brushed opposition aside. 'And so on. We're specialists.'

'Do you own the firm yourselves?'

'It used to be family owned. We've been a public company since 1987.'

Barney Thacker slapped three white fingers against the edge of the table. 'Only construction firm in the black last year, whole UK sector. Five years' profits, rest of 'em still stuck in the recession. When Dad retired they were digging fucking car parks. Didn't even own our own fucking diggers.'

'Did June Donaghy have anything to do with running the company?'

'She was my brother's personal assistant.'

'Secretary,' Barney Thacker interrupted. 'Course she didn't

have anything to do with running it. She was a fucking secretary.'

Peter Thacker's smile looked brittle. The humour was gone from his eyes. 'We try to give all our employees an opportunity to rise,' he said.

I looked at Barney Thacker. June Donaghy's opportunity had depended on sleeping with him in a conference hotel somewhere in Scotland. She'd chosen to stay where she was.

'Did June have any close friends in the company?'

Peter Thacker looked at his brother warily, as if he hardly trusted him to speak. Barney was tapping his fingers impatiently on the table top. He shook his head. He looked bored.

'Is there anything else we can help you with, Chief Inspector? If there's anything at all . . .' Peter Thacker opened his hands above the mahogany table. 'We'd do anything possible to help clear this up. I wondered about a reward. It seems odd this witness hasn't come forward yet. Do you think a reward would help persuade him?'

'It might.'

'I suppose if June Donaghy was attacked at random it makes it harder to find them. Unless they leave some evidence behind.'

Barney Thacker's chair scraped on the wooden floor. There was an odd gleam in his eyes. He said thickly, 'Did they fuck her?'

From the corner of my eye I saw Peter Thacker freeze. The smooth smile had gone rigid on his mouth. One hand hovered over his gold tie pin. Behind him the male secretary's face was stiff with shock.

I let the gleam in Barney Thacker's eyes wear off a little, then I said quietly, 'No. Did you?'

Barney Thacker moved slowly, the way people move when they can afford to take their time over it. His fists moved from the table to the arms of his chair without unclenching. His smile didn't disappear; it grew wider. He said, 'There's always one, isn't there? Put 'em all in uniform, there's always one thinks it makes him king of the fucking castle. Like that fucking traffic warden this morning. Yellow band on her hat, she thinks she's fucking Napoleon. What is it with all you little people?'

I didn't tell him what it was with us little people. I kept my eyes

22

on his face and wondered how long it had taken June Donaghy to start hating her boss.

Barney Thacker's shoulders dropped. He sighed, as if I wasn't a meal worth eating anyway. 'Why else would anyone kill the Donaghy? She was a nice little thing. Course they fucked her.' His voice held the weary false knowledge that that was all men wanted and all women were good for.

Peter Thacker said, 'We mustn't take any more of your time, Chief Inspector . . .'

I didn't let him finish. 'This morning June Donaghy's mother told me she wasn't happy with the way the firm worked. She didn't like knowing she'd only get promoted if she went to bed with her boss.' I kept my eyes on Barney Thacker. 'With you.'

'That's a damned lie.' Barney Thacker's lips were twisted. 'The old woman's lying to you. I never told her that. The Donaghy was a mouse. I never laid a damned finger on her.'

'Her mother said she was planning to go to the press about it.'

'Chief Inspector . . .' Peter Thacker was trying to interpose long brown hands between us.

His brother ignored him. 'The trouble is, they give them a little bit of power, they start to enjoy it. They start to think being a Chief Inspector is something fucking wonderful. What did you say your name was?'

I told him what I'd said my name was.

'Havilland.' He made a show of storing it away in his memory. 'Did you ever spend time on the beat, Havilland? Yes? You must have. Did you enjoy it?' His short white finger stabbed at my face. 'You want to go back there, then you're going the right way about it. Understand? It's going to be a pleasure. Havilland. I can ask you for directions next time I'm driving through fucking Kennington.' His voice rose at the end until he was shouting. I couldn't tell whether he was putting it on or not. Shouting made his forehead clench like a boxer's fist. It was a face June Donaghy must have got used to.

For a moment we stared at each other. Peter Thacker's voice broke the tension. It sounded tired. 'We seem to be straying from the point.' I looked at him. 'The point is to clear up this tragedy. Obviously we'll give you any help we can, Chief Inspector.' From the corner of my eye I could see Barney Thacker still glaring at me. His glare was a blue glint through red eyelashes. 'The way my brother treated Miss Donaghy may have been unfortunate. We'll make that up to her family in whatever way we can. This firm is fully aware of its responsibilities.'

Barney Thacker's chair scraped noisily on the floor as he stood up. His brother didn't look at him; his face was still set in an amused half smile.

Barney Thacker said softly, 'Why don't you fuck off?'

Nobody moved until the door had closed behind him. The blond secretary was studying empty pages in his notebook. I wondered how many scenes like this he had witnessed before.

Peter Thacker said, 'He's upset by this. It may not be the way everyone would show it . . .' He rubbed his chin ruefully. 'Barney feels things very strongly.'

'Did you know how he'd been treating her?'

Peter Thacker's hand stopped moving on his chin. 'I made it a point of principle not to get involved. Unless I had to.' He sighed. 'To be honest with you, Chief Inspector, something like this had happened before. Another secretary. He got the girl pregnant.' He shrugged. 'It got into the papers. I'm not telling you any family secrets.'

'Who told the papers?'

'Her father.'

'You mean you weren't generous enough?'

Peter Thacker's lips twitched. He said drily, 'He was a man of principle.' He glanced over his shoulder at the secretary. 'You might leave us alone for a moment, Charles.'

The blond man nodded and started walking towards the door. Peter Thacker waited until he reached it. 'How many people has Mrs Donaghy told about my brother's indiscretion, Chief Inspector?'

'I don't know.'

'It could be very difficult for us – for the firm.' He frowned at his brown hands. 'Companies can be affected by this kind of thing

more than you think. Share prices . . . It would be most unfortunate if a story like this reached the press again.'

I started to get up. It wasn't my business what reached the press.

Peter Thacker looked up at me. 'I know it's the last thing on
your mind at the moment. We both know how it can happen,
though. Junior police officers talk. They all know people in the
papers.'

I said, 'Thank you for your cooperation, Mr Thacker.'

One hand lifted off the table, trying to detain me. 'It's important
that we go on cooperating, isn't it?' Peter Thacker's eyes glinted as
if he was telling an amusing story. 'I've already said we might
consider a reward. We could be generous to you as well, Chief
Inspector – to you *personally* – if the firm's name stays out of any
publicity. I think you know what I mean.'

I looked at him. I knew what he meant. I said quietly, 'Barney
wasn't the only thing June didn't like about the firm.'

'I'm sorry to hear that.' The humour had vanished, leaving only
a hard veneer of charm. 'My brother is a difficult man to work for.
It's hardly surprising Miss Donaghy should feel *bitter*. The whole
situation was most unfortunate.'

It wasn't as unfortunate as where June Donaghy had ended up.
I turned and started walking towards the steel door. Peter Thacker
didn't try to stop me. Down in reception, a group of office
workers was gathered around the coffee machine. Barney
Thacker's new secretary was sitting wanly by herself, sipping at a
Diet Pepsi. As I waited for the lift I looked at a photograph of
concrete piers stamping across green hills. In the foreground
Barney Thacker in a yellow hard hat was stabbing his finger at a
folded drawing. His elbow blocked out the face of a girl who
might have been June Donaghy.

The opening of the lift doors was a relief.

4

Tottenham Court Road was full of young men in anoraks staring into hi-fi shops at stacks of machines and the covers of dirty videos. Maybe they were hoping that if they could fill their bedsits with enough machines and enough dirty videos they'd never have to talk to another real person again. I found the car waiting for me in Store Street. The driver had the first evening paper open on his knees. June Donaghy's death was a small paragraph at the bottom of the page, under a picture of a television actor grinning at a litter of golden retriever puppies.

We crossed Trafalgar Square through afternoon traffic. Secretaries were hunting the first spring sunshine around the fountains. By Westminster Bridge tourists were pointing cameras at Big Ben through the windows of their coaches. A policeman in a yellow cape held back the traffic to let a long black car pull out of the House of Commons.

The river was at high water. It looked bright and innocent, as if there was nothing in it that we didn't know about and nothing buried in the mud that would cause anyone any pain. A tour boat was turning against the current just opposite the Houses of Parliament. If we hadn't got to her in time, June Donaghy's body would be flowing up and down under these bridges by now, hair waving in the muddy river water, hands white, flowing out to sea on the ebb tide and back in on the flood until her body finally drifted against the pier of some bridge and came to rest. Instead she was in a police mortuary somewhere with doctors' hands prying deep inside her to find secrets that someone didn't want us to know, and maybe June Donaghy didn't want us to know herself.

In the incident room I found two policemen poring over a large-scale map of the river. The air smelled of cigarettes. It was a long room with a table down the middle of it and a pin-board on the wall with nothing on it but a photograph of June Donaghy – the one from her security card which gave her a squint and the surprised look she must have been wearing when the killer first approached her; before surprise turned to fear, and then to the expression she died with. In the background a voice was reading back the times of tides to someone on the phone.

Baring was in an interview room to one side, talking to a kid in a brown leather jacket with files of mugshots strewn over the table between them. When he saw me, he got up and came out of the room, closing the door behind him.

'We got something on the car, sir. Traced the registration.' He screwed up his face. 'One number wrong but it must be the same one. Silver and blue Cortina. Registered to a bloke called Mark Mitchell. Just off the Old Kent Road.'

'Is that him?' I jerked my head towards the interview room.

'No. I went round to Mitchell's place, talked to his mum. He sold the car last Wednesday. Needed cash for his holiday. Flew off Thursday to Torre . . .' Baring couldn't pronounce Torremolinos. He shook his head and said, 'Spain. Chap in there's the bloke he sold it to. Puma Motors – used-car dump on the Old Kent Road. His name's Jimmy Bolan.'

'What does he know?'

'Says he doesn't know anything.' Baring glanced through the glass panel in the door. 'Says he sold it the same afternoon. Took cash – he doesn't know the name. He's given us a description.'

I pushed open the door. Jimmy Bolan looked up with an eager expression, as if I was someone he'd always wanted to talk to. He was a handsome boy with a big lock of greasy hair hanging down over his forehead in a way that girls probably found romantic. A gold ring in his ear was supposed to make him look like a gypsy or the hero in a pirate movie.

'Can I go now?'

I pulled back the chair on the other side of the table and sat down. The eager expression on Jimmy Bolan's face faded. He frowned at the file of photographs in front of him as if it was a difficult exam paper with questions he hadn't revised for. 'He isn't here – the bloke I sold it to. I'd know him again. I already told him.' He nodded towards Baring.

I said, 'Tell me about the car.'

'I already told him,' Jimmy Bolan repeated.

'So tell me.'

'It was . . .' He shrugged. 'Cortina. Silver and blue. Nothing special.'

'When did Mark Mitchell bring it in?'

'Wednesday.'

'What did you pay him for it?'

'Fifty quid.' Jimmy Bolan shrugged. 'Wasn't worth more than that. It sounded terrible.'

Baring said, 'His mum told us three hundred.'

Jimmy Bolan shook his head. 'It was only fifty. Scrap. Only had MOT through to April. Maybe he didn't want his mum to think he'd been had.'

'By you?'

'When he bought it.'

'What were you going to do with it?'

'Parts. Scrap. I'd have got my money back.' Jimmy Bolan sounded cocky and confident, a man who knew how to get his money back.

'So what happened?'

'I had it parked outside. This bloke came round.' His dark face grew serious with the effort of remembering details. 'Black guy. Said he was looking for a banger. Nothing flashy. Car you wouldn't notice.'

'Did he say why?'

'I didn't ask.' His shrug told us it wasn't his business to ask.

'Did he know about the MOT?'

'I gave him the papers, didn't I? I hadn't filled them in yet. I just gave everything to him. Let him deal with it.'

Baring said, 'That's why he never got the lad's name.' He looked at Jimmy Bolan. 'You could get in trouble for that.'

Jimmy Bolan tried to look contrite but didn't succeed. He knew it wasn't bad trouble.

I said, 'How much did he pay for the car?'

A grin split Jimmy Bolan's dark, handsome face. 'Five hundred. Cash.'

'Have you still got the notes?'

'Took 'em down the bank. You don't want to keep too much in the office.'

'Did you think it was strange he paid that much for it?'

Jimmy Bolan blinked. 'Course I did. Black guys want flash cars. Mercs. BMWs. Cortina's a white boy's car.'

I shifted my weight off the table and stood up. 'What did he look like?'

Jimmy Bolan thought about that by rubbing his fingers over cheeks darkened by stubble. 'Skinny. A little beard. He had a purple jacket on. Leather.'

'Have you ever seen him before?'

He shook his head. Baring said, 'We've put out a description, sir.'

He followed me out into the incident room. Jimmy Bolan was frowning down at the photographs again, making a show of thinking about them.

Baring said, 'What do you think, sir? Shall we keep him in?'

'Does he have a record?'

'Trouble with some MOT certificates last year. Didn't get to court. There isn't anything else.' He shrugged. 'I think he's told us all he knows, sir. The guy who bought it . . .' He shrugged. 'He's the one we need. Must have wanted a car in a hurry. Why else would you pay five hundred for an old Cortina?'

I nodded. 'Let him go. We can always pick him up again. Has anything else happened?'

'We got the doctor's report, sir.' Baring pulled a beige folder towards him across the table. 'It was the bang on the head that killed her. No water in her lungs. She was dead when he put her over the wall.'

'Anything else?'

'No prints, no hair, no blood. None of *his* blood, anyway. No sign she was messed about with. A lot of long words. Don't know why they can't just say a bang on the head.'

I looked at Baring. He was a bulky man with a red square face under white hair which he brushed sideways to hide how little of it he had left. He'd been working in rooms like this, on cases like this, for thirty years now and somehow he'd managed to stop it from getting to him. About the time I had come out of nursery school he was taking his sergeant's exam for the first time. While I had been sitting in a student's room listening to jazz records, Baring was patrolling the high-rise blocks behind Kennington Road. Somehow he'd managed to stop that from getting to him either.

'Has anything turned up on the phone call?'

'Not yet. We got a transcript. Man's voice. Smart. Told the girl he'd seen someone being attacked. End of story.' He shrugged. 'Nothing else to say, is there? Not without a name.'

There wasn't anything else to say. Someone had killed a girl down by the river. They hadn't raped her or taken her money. There wasn't any reason for anyone to want her dead. No one had seen it happen except a man with a smart voice and no name. End of story.

Baring was frowning at the photograph of June Donaghy. He said, 'I hate these ones. Makes me think of my girl. I mean, you never know when it's going to happen, do you? Could be walking back from the tube one night. Could happen to anyone. Same age as my girl, too.' He shook his head. 'Sometimes I wonder why you came back, sir.'

He made it sound as if I ought to have an easy answer to that; as if I could tell him what we were all doing there, sitting in a long room under neon lights with a dead girl's photograph on the wall and six million people tramping the streets outside, one of whom was a killer.

In a different voice Baring went on, 'Chief Superintendent Mason's been after you, sir. Said he wanted to see you soon as you came in.'

'Have we got anything to tell him?'

'Only the guy who bought the car.' Baring shrugged. 'It's a good start, but it's all we've got. We carried out a search round there. No one heard anything. That building's all offices – up to the top floor, anyway. No night guard and the flats on the top floor are all empty except one – they didn't manage to sell them before the crash. Old lady at the end said she went to bed at ten. Took sleeping pills. Said she's never been able to sleep since a bomb landed next door when she was a kid.'

Maybe I could tell Mason about an old lady who always took sleeping pills.

Baring looked at me. 'Chief Superintendent Mason did say it was important, sir.'

I started walking towards the stairs. Just as I reached them I remembered what it was I needed to find out. I turned back towards Baring. 'Does the doctor's report say whether she was a virgin?'

'A *virgin*? Doesn't say, sir.' Baring's frown said that was nobody's business but June Donaghy's. He would have been right except that June Donaghy was dead now, and we were minding the shop for her.

I said, 'Call them for me.'

5

Mason was sitting behind his desk in shirtsleeves with a pile of papers stacked up on the desk in front of him. A uniform jacket was hitched over the back of his chair. When I came in he had his fingers pressed in to his eyes; his glasses were lying on the stack of papers. When he looked up his steel-grey eyes were bloodshot, with dark rings under them.

Since I'd first met Mason ten years had passed and he'd aged twenty. The lines on his face were about the difficulty of persuading the eighty thousand people who lived in Kennington not to kill each other, or steal each others' television sets, or fight each other when they got drunk. They were about flats barricaded with security shutters, and women calling the station in the middle of the night, and shops which kept guard dogs because that was the only way for a man alone at night to feel safe. The rings under Mason's eyes said that he'd been losing for ten years and it felt like twenty.

Mason put a flat hand on the stack of papers. He said, ' "Inter-Area Liaison Group Preliminary Findings". They keep sending me the stuff. God knows when they think I'm going to get time to read it.' He shook his head. 'Come in, George. Sit down. I wanted a word.'

I sat down. Mason kept smiling at me but that was only because he was too tired to take the smile off his face.

'Is it about June Donaghy?'

'In a minute.' He picked up a polystyrene cup from the desk, sipped cold coffee and made a face. 'I was up at the Yard this morning. Inter-Area Group meeting. They've got a filter machine up there. What's wrong with us?'

A brass plaque behind Mason's head said that in 1962 he had passed out top of his year at Hendon Training College. Others told me about commendations and promotions along the way. Sometime between the last plaque and now Mason had turned from champion of the righteous into an old man waiting for his retirement. I had a plaque like the first one in my own desk somewhere, along with the other documents and papers that went with being a policeman. I wondered what the plaque would look like in thirty years' time. I wondered what I would look like.

'I've been meaning to have a word with you for a while, actually, George. Haven't been able to make the time. God knows where it all goes. I meant to have this lot finished by lunchtime.' He shook his head at the stack of papers. 'I've been meaning to ask you how it's all been going.'

'You mean June Donaghy?'

'You know I don't.' A flash of shrewdness appeared in his tired eyes. 'It's a year, isn't it? A year since you came back into the force. Or don't you believe in anniversaries?'

'Not this one.'

'I don't know why not. It's been a good year, George. You've done good work. Don't know how we managed without you.'

'You managed.'

'Bloke at Scotland Yard this morning . . .' He laughed. 'You remember Bob Cayman? Chief Inspector, now. Same rank as you. Said he could never understand why I pushed to get you back in. Said you were bound to cause us trouble one of these days. He ought to know – he used to be your sergeant, didn't he?'

I nodded.

'He's a smart boy. He's been noticed. Noticed in the *right* way. I told him about Ronnie Whelan.' He grinned. 'That made him look a bit thoughtful. It's been a good year. I know Ted Baring wants to go on working for you. I told Cayman that as well. He said you must have changed.' He looked up at me. 'I told him you had – in some ways.'

He left a pause for me to agree with him. I didn't say anything.

'You're still an arrogant sod, aren't you? All the same . . .' His voice tailed off. He was thinking of something else. 'Even so, you've got a battle on your hands if you want to get anywhere – you know that, don't you? The Yard don't like people walking out on them. They think it's a job for life . . . brave boys staying at their posts – you know the stuff. There are people who can't forgive you for walking out on us after we caught Mattie Hill.'

'That wasn't why I walked out.'

'Anyway. It's something to watch out for – it's as well to have them on your side if you ever get into a scrape.'

'I'll try not to.'

'Will you?' Again the grey eyes were shrewd. Mason picked up his coffee cup and turned it round in his fingers without drinking from it. He said, 'You wouldn't tell me what you did, those two years after you walked out. Why was that?'

I shrugged.

'Job?' After a moment he said, 'Have it your own way. If it's a secret.'

'It isn't a secret. There's nothing to tell.'

'Have it your own way,' Mason repeated. He put the cup down. 'Is Mary well?'

'She's fine.'

'Still singing, is she?'

I nodded.

'She's a nice girl. You're lucky, George. Most of the wives sit home all day worrying whether their bloke's going to come home all right. The girlfriends, whatever. I never like the sound of that. Mary's got her head screwed on.'

Mason sighed, picked up his glasses and perched them on the end of his nose. Glasses made him look like a schoolteacher with too many reports to write. 'What can you tell me about June Donaghy?'

It didn't take long to tell him when she died, and how she died, and that we didn't know who had killed her.

'What family did she have?'

'Her mother's religious. The father left home when she was a child. She's got a sister she wasn't close to.'

'Boyfriend?'

'No.'

'Good Catholic girl, eh? Did they tell you anything else?'

I said, 'Nothing that matters.'

Mason's fingers tapped the pile of papers in front of him. Something was bothering him. He said, 'John Harlow had a word with me about it when I was up at Scotland Yard. I didn't realize who June Donaghy worked for.'

'Does it make any difference who she worked for?'

'Not to the case, no.' Mason frowned. He wasn't looking at me any more. 'It's an important company, PTI. The Thackers are important people. Did you ever see that profile in the *Sunday Times?*'

I shook my head.

'I can't see them wanting their name all over the papers. John Harlow was keen on that, too. You know the score. Tell the press she worked for a temp agency. Blah blah. If that's the way John Harlow wants it . . .'

I said, 'You want me to lie to them?'

Mason looked pained. 'I wouldn't call it that.'

'What would you call it?'

He looked up at me. 'I'd call it common sense. We need people like the Thackers on our side. No point making life harder for ourselves than it has to be. Anyway, what does it matter who she worked for? You said that yourself. If June Donaghy had worked for some little office on the corner no one would even bother to report it. Just because she's PA to a big industrialist . . . We'd have the press all over us, George, and we don't want that. Got enough on our hands as it is. And John Harlow all over us because he's cross with us for not playing it the way he wants. None of us need this, George. None of us.'

I looked at his troubled, defensive face. 'The evening paper hardly mentioned it,' I said. 'A pretty girl killed in the middle of London and they hardly mentioned it. Is that because of the Thackers?'

'Probably. If you ask me, you ought to be grateful to them. Keeping the papers off your back . . . A whole day and no one arrested yet. They'd be shouting for your head in a week.'

I said quietly, 'I went to see the Thackers this afternoon. Peter Thacker offered me a bribe if I kept their name out of the papers. Barney Thacker threatened to make trouble for me if I didn't.'

'There you are, then. It matters to them.' Mason frowned angrily. 'I'm not saying I condone . . . the way they did it. It's the way they are, George. These people are used to getting what they want. You won't do yourself any favours by annoying them.'

'You mean I should have taken the bribe?'

'Of course I don't.' Mason fiddled with his pen. Once again he had stopped looking at me. He went on, quietly, 'That's not all I heard, George. I heard you went in there threatening to cause trouble for them. That was the other thing Johnnie Harlow said. He asked me if you were the right man to deal with the case.' He looked up at me. 'Barney Thacker had been on the phone to him. They know each other somehow. Play golf together . . . I don't know.' His face was troubled, the face of a man caught in the middle.

'Did John Harlow tell you what they're trying to keep out of the papers?'

'It's just publicity, isn't it? The big companies don't like it.'

I leaned forward over the desk towards him. 'This morning June Donaghy's mother told me something about Barney Thacker. He'd been giving her daughter trouble at work. Harassing her. He told her that unless she slept with him he'd make sure she never got another job. She refused. That's what they're scared is going to come out.'

Mason's shoulders dropped. He didn't say anything for a long time. His hands lay idle on the desk in front of him. 'I'm not saying . . .' he began slowly, but didn't go on. After a moment he tried again. 'I'm not saying I like them, George. I don't like the way they work. I don't like the way they treat people. That isn't our business, though.' He looked up at me. 'Barney Thacker may be any kind of monster you like. He may bother his secretary. He may try to threaten coppers.' One hand lifted off the desk. 'I don't like any of it any more than you do.' Mason's chair scraped on the floor. He stood up and stretched. There was an ink stain on the cuff of his uniform shirt. 'Listen, George, June Donaghy was killed by some nutter. Kids, some nutter, I don't know. Could easily have been a kid these days, the drugs they take . . . The point is, it doesn't make any difference who she worked for.' He turned away from me, looking out of the window at shoppers and idlers passing along the Kennington Road. 'You learn something if you've been doing this as long as I have. You learn that it's hard enough to fight the battles you have to fight without taking on the rest of the world as well. You learn that our job's difficult enough already without us making it harder for ourselves.' He rubbed his hands over his mouth and blew out air. 'I thought you were starting to learn that for yourself. All right, so it's a compromise. I know you hate compromises. But sometimes, just *some*times . . . Oh, for Christ's sake, George, it's not a big issue. It's not going to stop us finding the bloke who killed her. Just do what I'm telling you, all right?'

I stood up. Mason turned round. 'I hope I've made this clear enough, George. John Harlow wants the Thackers left alone. No more interviews. No trouble about Barney Thacker. We do what we can to keep them out of the papers. Do you understand?'

I said, 'Is that your advice, sir?'

Mason's eyes flashed angrily. 'No.' His voice was curt. 'It's an order.'

I stopped in my office on the way back downstairs. For a moment I sat at the desk and stared at the pin-board in front of it without thinking of anything. After a while I focused on a small photograph half buried under memos and reports. I reached across the desk and pulled it off the pin, tearing one corner. It showed a man sitting on a chair holding a trumpet. He was wearing a green shirt open at the neck and his gaze was challenging. It was the picture Miles Davis had used for the cover of *Milestones*. In the photograph Miles was holding the trumpet as if it was something precious: something full of riffs that hadn't yet been blown and tunes nobody had played before. Something that would never tell him lies.

I let a few notes of its first track drift into my head – 'Dr Jekyll'. I remembered a day in the canteen during my first spell in the police. It was just after I had come to Kennington and someone told me that jazz was music for poofs, and college boys, and niggers who thought they were clever. His friend told me he was drunk, and that I shouldn't take any notice. The copper shook him off and took a swing at me. From inside his head it was hard to tell how far away I was. All he did was pour hot coffee over my ear before I laid him out. When Mason sent him in to apologize the next morning, he made his apology to Miles Davis, pinned a foot above my head. His face said that Miles was just another clever nigger, and I was just another college boy and, for all he knew, a poof as well.

Jazz wasn't the music of the canteen. It was one of the things that had made me different and wrong, like the fact that I'd gone to college, or the fact that I didn't drink enough beer. It had never worried me in those days. I'd been proud of being different, and hadn't much cared what anyone else thought of me anyway – anyone except my brother and Mary. Jazz had floated me through days that were too long and nights when I didn't get far enough away from the police. Jazz was the music that sounded like what I saw every day: the music of cold streets and late nights; music that was hard and aggressive on the outside but showed pain as soon as you were alone with it. For five years I'd fuelled myself on coffee, jazz music and a belief left over from childhood that I could set the world right without any help from anyone else. But when the crash came, jazz hadn't been enough to pull me out of it.

I reached forward and pinned the picture of Miles back on the board. These days, even though I was living with Mary again, I didn't listen to so much jazz, and I didn't talk about it in the canteen. I talked about the things that other policemen talked about. Gradually the picture of Miles was being buried under police memos.

I took my jacket from the back of the door and headed out of the police station. The stairs were full of officers hurrying off to the pub or the sports club. From the door of the canteen came a gust of laughter and the smell of food. The auxiliary on the desk nodded at me without taking her attention from an old man who wanted her to know that Japanese soldiers on bicycles were coming up the road from the Elephant and Castle. Kennington Road was jammed solid with cars. The cars were on their way back to neat houses in Surrey which had patches of lawn at the back and satellite dishes trying to grope dreams out of the air overhead. I walked down to the bus stop and queued alongside tired secretaries and mothers hurrying home to their families. I could have waited for a police car that was heading in the right direction but I needed to be by myself. I watched the faces behind the windscreens. Bored, mostly; or just glazed; or laughing at something on the radio. When the bus came I followed a fat black woman upstairs. Her stockings had slipped and her shopping bags caught on the corner of the stairs: it had been a long day. I found a seat next to a boy whose knees were moving in time to whatever was playing on his Walkman. The sky was turning dark behind dirty glass.

For the first time in a long time I thought about the two years I had spent outside the police force. I had tried two jobs and found that both of them needed somebody smarter than me, or not so smart; or tougher, or not so tough. Either way, they didn't need me. I had walked away from a dozen other chances to save myself from finding out the same thing. Two years was a long time in which to learn that the rest of the world was no cleaner or more straightforward than the police force had been. I had walked out at the end of the Hill case because I didn't like the compromise Mason was asking me to swallow; outside I found that everybody else was making compromises every day without even noticing them. I had walked out because Mason had wanted me to hide the truth about someone; and I'd already discovered for myself that the mud you get on your hands in burying the truth stays on them for ever. It wasn't a bad reason; the trouble was that running away from something wasn't the same thing as beating it. I'd kept my own hands clean; but the traffic kept building up on Kennington Road every night, and the Thames kept flowing under the bridges; children were born to grow up into saints or villains, or something in between the two; on Saturday nights I could still hear the police sirens wailing across Hyde Park. I hadn't made the world a better place. I had just walked away from it.

I had phoned Mason two months after I moved back in with Mary. Maybe she'd known all along that I wasn't fit for anything else. It was the police force which had broken up our relationship before, but this time she didn't even complain. The day I started work again she kissed me and remembered not to ask what time I would be home. We slipped back into the routine of strange hours and stolen evenings which we had lived in the old days. Mary's singing career was starting to get somewhere – as far as a jazz singer's career ever can – and sometimes it was she who came in at two in the morning and tried to get into bed without waking me. Maybe that made it easier. Whatever the reason, the old arguments didn't start up again. Maybe we were both wiser, or just older and more scared of being alone. Or maybe we both knew that this was a last chance. Most people stay together, during the bad times, because they can't imagine being apart. We could imagine it. We'd been through the arguments, and the slow rages that burned for days, and the bush fires that kept flaring up when you thought you'd stamped them out. Somehow we'd managed to leave that behind and get back together. But we both knew that if things went wrong again, it would be for the last time.

The bus crawled forward, the top deck nosing against the branches of trees. Shop signs along Kennington Park Road splashed garish colours across pavements thick with people hurrying home. Outside a petrol station a row of kids was sitting on a wall, waiting for the world to come to them. Two office workers were flirting at the back of the bus; nobody else spoke. In an evening paper in the row in front I could see football scores. Somewhere, a mile or so away, Mrs Donaghy was praying for her daughter; and somewhere else the man who had killed her was drinking a pint, or buying the evening paper, behaving just like any of the rest of us. Outside the windows Brixton arrived in a blaze of light, pavements crowded, shops full. I stood up and started fighting my way to the back of the bus.

Lights were shining in the windows of the flat. I unlocked the door, hit the hall light switch and reminded myself, the way I had every evening for a month, to put a new bulb in the socket. The stairs smelled of Don's Jamaican café next door. I groped the carpet for mail and made my way upstairs by instinct. Through the door of our flat I could hear jazz: the rattle of drums, horns braying and Louis Armstrong's growl preaching to the Brixton night.

Mary was slumped in the sofa, eyes closed, only the tapping of her foot showing that she was awake. She didn't even open her eyes when I kissed her.

'Did you have a good day?'

'So-so.' I kept my voice neutral.

'Then you can go and get me a drink.'

I stood up. 'Were you rehearsing?'

'Eight hours. It's crazy playing so much just before a gig.'

'So tell Charlie.'

'You know what Charlie's like.'

In five days' time Mary had a date on the support bill at Ronnie

Scott's. After ten years playing to old men in pubs, singing too loud because the juke box was playing next door, trying to keep her mind on the beat over the jingle of cash in the bar till, Ronnie Scott's seemed to her like the Festival Hall. She'd hardly stopped working in a fortnight.

'Why are you listening to this?'

'Charlie's idea. He wants us to do it.'

Louis Armstrong hit a low note and grumbled over the sound of traffic outside.

> I see trees of green, red roses too
> I see them bloom for me and you
> And I think to myself
> What a wonderful world

Mary opened her eyes. 'It's not bad. We can do something with it.' Jazz purists would have called it pop music, but Mary had never been a purist. She started laughing and picked up a cushion to throw at my head; then the laugh died. 'What's the matter?' Her face was serious.

'Nothing.'

'Yes, there is.' She rolled her eyes. 'Come on, George. There's something bothering you.'

I shook my head. One of the rules between us was that I didn't bring work in off the street with me.

'Go and get me a drink.'

I went into the kitchen, took the cork out of a bottle of wine and poured two glasses. Back in the living room Mary was sitting up, frowning at the rug on the floor. She took the wine without saying anything and sipped at it.

'There is something wrong.'

'It's nothing that matters.'

'Tell me.'

I closed my eyes. Superimposed on the darkness I could see June Donaghy's body spread-eagled on the black river mud. 'They found a girl's body down by the river last night. I'm running the investigation.'

'That's horrible.' I opened my eyes. Mary was staring down into

42

her wine glass as if the red liquid had suddenly soured in her mouth. 'Do you know who killed her?'

'Not yet.'

She shivered, maybe seeing herself on the bank of a river. 'Will you catch them?'

'I don't know.'

'They never do, do they? Mad guys. There's nothing to go on. They just . . .' Her grey eyes stared at me over the rim of her glass. 'Did they rape her?'

I shook my head.

Mary nodded. 'Is this what's bothering you? The girl who was killed?'

I didn't answer for a long time. I looked into my wine glass and remembered old arguments.

'You might as well tell me, George.'

'The man she worked for . . .' I stopped and looked up. Mary's face was tense, composed for whatever I might be about to tell her. 'She worked for a man called Barney Thacker. A businessman. Her mother told me he tried to have an affair with her. He said if she didn't sleep with him . . .'

'Was it him who killed her?'

I shook my head. 'He doesn't have anything to do with the murder.'

A faint frown crossed Mary's face. 'Go on.'

'This afternoon I went to see him. He told me that if anything about him got into the papers he'd do what he could to make trouble for me. He has friends at Scotland Yard. His brother offered me a bribe . . .'

Mary's face turned suddenly away from me. She stared bleakly across the room. 'He obviously doesn't know you.'

'When I spoke to Mason this afternoon he ordered me to leave them alone. He told me to do what I could to keep their name out of it.'

I stopped. Mary's lips were moving, almost as if she was reciting the words of a song. 'What did you say?'

'I didn't say anything.'

'What are you going to do?' She looked back at me.

'I don't know.'

'Is there anything you can do? He didn't break the law, did he? This man?'

'Maybe. I don't know. I don't like the idea of helping him to cover it up.'

'Of course you don't.' Mary sucked air in through her teeth. She got up suddenly and went over to the hi-fi. The noise from the speakers grew louder, then faded away. 'Do you really think they could make trouble for you?'

'Probably.'

'Mason thinks so.' She turned round. 'That's why he told you, isn't it? Told you to leave them alone.'

'Partly.'

'So what are you going to do?'

When I didn't answer she came towards me. Her hands were cold, the fingers long and strong. She held my head and looked at me for a long time. There was a nick in her left eyebrow, a tiny scar from some childhood fall. I wondered how many times I'd looked at it.

Her grey eyes searched my face. 'You don't need any more trouble, George.' After a moment she prompted, 'Do you?'

'No.'

'Neither of us does. It's not as if you have to do anything about that man. You could just do what they tell you.'

'I know.'

Mary looked at me for a moment longer. Slowly her face hardened. 'But you won't. Because they're the sort of people who got away with everything last time – in that case with Mattie Hill.' Her voice had anger in it.

'What are you saying?'

'I'm saying . . .' She wriggled backwards off the sofa and stood up. 'I'm saying it's time you put something else first.' Her voice was quiet and determined. 'Not just fighting battles. There are other things that matter as well, George. I can't . . .' She raised one hand to stop me interrupting. 'I can't face all of that trouble again. What you went through with Mattie Hill. You refusing to talk to me, and not . . . not . . .' Suddenly she was crying. I put one hand forward to touch her but she shook it angrily away. 'I'm not going to go through all that again, George. It isn't fair. I want you to promise me.'

'Promise you what?'

'That you won't . . .' She wiped the back of her hand angrily across her eyes. 'That you won't stir up trouble with these people. That you'll do what Mason wants, leave them alone. George?'

I closed my eyes. There was space between us now, a no man's land littered with the minefields and rusting barbed wire of old fights. I remembered arguments we had had years before. Mary had never asked me to sacrifice anything for her before. Now she was asking.

'George?'

I looked up at her. Her broad forehead was creased with worry; there was trouble in her grey eyes. I put one hand up and touched her forehead.

She brushed it to one side. 'Promise me, George. Promise me you'll leave those people alone.'

I said what she wanted me to say.

We went to bed early. Mary lay with her back to me, pretending to sleep. From outside, the streetlights threw an orange glare on the ceiling. I thought of June Donaghy's body lying sprawled on the river mud; of her mother fingering the gold cross on her chest; I thought of Barney Thacker's face. I thought of the last time Mary had left me, and of what had made it happen. She had started an affair with someone she met at a gig: someone who didn't bury things away from her, and who didn't come back late at night with the loneliness and fear of the streets still wrapped around him like a shroud; someone who made sacrifices for her. She had got sick of that in the end and come back to me. She had never asked me to sacrifice anything for her, except this.

Her body moved beside me. In the half light I could only make out the shape of her hip; her face was still turned away from me.

It was a long time before I got to sleep.

7

The voice on the phone was a man, smart, maybe with a trace of a Northern accent.

It said, 'I should have called you before. I know that. I'm sorry.'

'Why didn't you?'

'I don't know. I suppose I was . . . frightened?' He made it into a question, although he was the only one who could answer it. 'I wanted to get away from there . . . from what I saw.'

'What did you see?'

He didn't answer that. I heard his breath come and go on the other end of the phone.

I said, 'What's your name?'

'Harvey. Michael Harvey.' He said it as if I was supposed to recognize it. 'I should have called you yesterday, shouldn't I? I should have made a statement straight away. Will I get into trouble for that?'

'Not if you make a statement now.'

'Of course. Can you come to my house?' He read out an address in Notting Hill Gate.

Mechanically I wrote it on the pad next to the phone. 'Why can't you come to the station?'

'I'd rather not.' Some anxiety was gnawing at his voice. 'There's something else you ought to know.' He took a deep breath. 'I'm a politician. A Member of Parliament.' He waited for me to say something about that. I didn't say anything. 'I'd rather . . . my name was involved as little as possible.'

He wasn't the only one who wanted that. 'Is that why you didn't call us yesterday?'

'Partly. It was stupid of me. I can see that now. I've been a fool.'

'You don't have anything to worry about. Not if you were just a witness.'

'But it wasn't only that. You see . . .' Michael Harvey's voice was scared again – scared and strung-up. 'I was the one June Donaghy had gone to meet.'

Michael Harvey's address was a street full of cherry trees that had just come into blossom. Behind the trees were iron railings and steps leading up to stucco porches; beneath them expensive cars were parked along the kerb. The only noise came from children playing in back gardens. Michael Harvey's house was like the others in the street: tall and stuccoed, with windows showing curtains neatly looped back at the sides and antique furniture behind the curtains. A security camera watched me climb the steps to the front door.

A girl opened the door. She had a slender white face and black hair cut short at the neck. Her eyes were a startling cornflower blue. They watched me coolly for a moment before she said anything. Her demure cotton dress belonged to Sunday School, and not to the look she was giving me.

'Yes?'

'I'm looking for Michael Harvey.'

'Have you got an appointment?'

I gave her my name.

'Oh. I thought you might be a constituent. Daddy's upstairs. He hates seeing constituents at home. He's in his study.'

She turned and led me down a hall furnished in the mixture of antique furniture and bad taste that signalled old money and plenty of it. I wondered how that fitted in with the trace of Northern accent in Harvey's voice. The girl opened a door on the half-landing. Through a window at the back of the room I could see trees.

Michael Harvey was sitting behind an antique desk. He was a young-looking man with a wave of brown hair and a thin, intense face that seemed slightly familiar. He didn't look old enough to have a daughter that age. Tortoiseshell glasses and a severe haircut were supposed to make him look older but only succeeded in

47

making him look like a clever college student. His handshake was practised and meaningless, a politician's handshake.

I sat down on the other side of the desk. Behind the tortoiseshell glasses Michael Harvey's eyes had started to age, but that had probably only happened in the last twenty-four hours.

'Shall I get you some coffee, Daddy?'

Harvey raised his eyebrows at me. I shook my head. 'No, thank you, darling.'

As soon as his daughter was gone, Harvey's face crumpled up. I watched it implode, as if someone had suddenly let the air out of it. He put his hands over his eyes to conceal whatever was happening to them. 'I'm so glad you've come. You can't imagine . . .' His voice was agonized. 'The strain.'

I gave him time to deal with the strain, and looked around the room. It was fitted out like a parody of a study, with an old-fashioned telephone and books lining the walls. The photographs were all of Michael Harvey: Harvey making a speech; Harvey in a big rosette; Harvey with his arms around his daughter and a faded, attractive woman in a dowdy skirt. Through the window drifted the sounds of children playing in the communal gardens that ran behind the houses.

'I know what you're thinking.' When Harvey took his hands away from his face he looked exhausted, as if whatever mask he'd been wearing for a day and a half had come away with them.

I shook my head.

'You're thinking, why didn't I do something?'

'You haven't told me what happened.'

He shook his head impatiently. 'I was only twenty yards away. I could have . . .' He stopped, his mind full of what he could have done.

'Tell me what you saw.'

Harvey took a deep breath. 'Don't you want to know why I was there?'

'Afterwards.'

'All right.' He took another breath, fighting for calm. I saw his knuckles clench white. 'I'd arranged to meet June at eleven o'clock. I was late. I had a speech in the city. That was why we arranged to

meet there. I was coming down the steps from Blackfriars Bridge
. . . by that pub . . .' His eyes had left the parody of a study. He
was seeing black water with city lights reflected in it, two figures
struggling by the parapet of the river walk. 'I don't think June ever
saw me. He came towards her from behind. I knew something was
wrong . . .' His face was twisting from inside, as if someone had
hold of it and wouldn't stop twisting. 'I didn't even call out. Or
maybe I called out. It was as if . . .' His eyes snapped back to me,
and to a present in which June Donaghy was no longer alive. 'As if
it wasn't happening. As if I was watching a film. He had hold of
her by the neck. He started dragging her towards the river . . .'
Michael Harvey stopped, his face frozen. He was seeing a figure
lying on the mud, no longer aware of him, or of what he might
have done to help her.

In a different voice he went on. 'I ran after him. That was when
I saw the car. I must have been thinking clearly then, mustn't I? To
take the number down. And to telephone . . . There was a box in
the alley. Then I started . . .' He finished with a deep breath that
was halfway to a sob. He buried his face in his hands, pushing the
glasses up on his forehead.

I waited until he was ready to go on. 'Will I get in trouble – for
not coming forward? It makes it worse, doesn't it? If it does get
into the press.'

'It might.'

He grimaced. 'I deserve it. It was stupid of me. I can't believe
I've been such a fool.'

I said, 'Did you see the man who killed her?'

'It was dark.' He frowned, trying to isolate the figure in his
memory. 'I wasn't that close.'

'How many of them were there?'

'Just one.'

'Try to describe him.'

'He was just a man. I don't know . . .' Harvey's hands flapped in
front of him.

I thought of the man Jimmy Bolan had described the day before.
'Was he black?'

Harvey shook his head. 'White. A skinhead, I suppose you'd call him. He had very short hair. A big man. Bigger than me.' His thin face twisted with self-contempt.

'What was he wearing?'

'A leather jacket. Trousers.' He shrugged. 'Nothing special.'

I said, 'Would you recognize him if you saw him again?'

Harvey put his head back and looked up at the ceiling. It took him time to answer, and when he did his voice was quiet and intense. 'Of course I would. How could I forget him?'

I watched him struggle with the idea that a killer's face would pursue him through the rest of his life; along with a face lying on cold mud, her eyes reflecting the red stars at the crown of Blackfriars Bridge.

I said, 'Why were you meeting June Donaghy?'

Harvey's gaze came back down from the ceiling. The memory of what he had seen had aged him further. 'It isn't what you think.'

I raised my eyebrows.

He flushed. 'I wasn't having an affair with her.'

'I didn't say you were.'

'It's what the papers will think. I was meeting June on business. You can ask my wife. She knew I was going to meet her. She was a constituent.'

I didn't point out that it wasn't the usual time or place to meet a constituent. 'Where's your constituency?'

'In the West Country.' His eyes registered the mistake. 'Not *literally* a constituent. She was *like* a constituent. She'd come to me with a problem. I was trying to help her.'

'Why did she come to you?'

'I'd known June in the past. I used to be a solicitor – before I went into politics. One of my clients was the company she worked for.' He looked at me. 'Some people called PTI.'

I could feel my mouth drying, promises made to Mary and to Mason shrinking slowly inside it as it dried out. 'What was the problem?'

Harvey shook his head. 'I don't want to go into that. Not into the details.'

I said, 'Was it something to do with Barney Thacker?'

Harvey frowned. 'How do you know that?'

'Her mother told me Barney Thacker had been harassing her. She said June was planning to go to the press.'

'That's right.' His face cleared. 'Except she didn't go straight to the press. She came to me. I was helping her with it.'

'Why didn't she tell her mother that?'

'I don't know.'

'What were you going to tell the papers about Barney Thacker?'

His thin face twisted with disgust. 'Some of the things Barney did to her were dreadful. Really dreadful. No one could have put up with him.'

'Why did you have to use the papers? She could have gone to the police.'

Harvey stood up suddenly and went over to the window. He was shorter than I would have expected, and more slightly built. His movements were athletic. He stood for a moment looking down into the gardens. He hesitated. 'I'm not sure I ought to tell you about it.'

'Why not?'

He turned round. 'June's dead now. It doesn't seem to matter any more.'

'What Barney Thacker did to her?'

'Anything.'

'It might do.'

He shook his head. 'It doesn't have anything to do with June's murder, if that's what you mean.'

I thought for a moment. I might have been breaking Mason's orders and my promise to Mary, but I didn't want to think about that. I said quietly, 'Yesterday I went to see the Thackers. They tried to bribe me to keep their name out of the papers. Later on Barney Thacker called a friend of his at Scotland Yard. Last night I was ordered not to investigate them any further. Why do you think they're doing that?'

Harvey's thin face twisted.

'They don't like publicity at PTI.'

'And they'll pull strings to avoid it?'

'You've seen them.'

'Did they try to stop you?'

'They would have done.'

For the first time Harvey looked bitter instead of scared. 'They carry a lot of weight.'

'And you thought going to the papers was the only way around that?'

'They've published stories about Barney Thacker before.'

'You could have gone to the police.'

Harvey's face twisted ironically. 'They've got friends in the police. You've seen that yourself. And in my party, too. I've only been an MP a few years. I don't carry a lot of clout.'

'Did the Thackers know what you and June were doing?'

'No. We were discreet about it. We needed to be.'

'What are you going to do now?'

'Nothing. June's dead. Like I said . . . it doesn't seem to matter any more. The important thing is to find who killed June.'

'Do you know who killed her?'

'Of course not.' The thought of June's killer crumpled his face suddenly. I saw his shoulders shiver. When he looked up his face had red blotches where his fingers had pressed it.

There were other questions I could have asked him – about the Thackers and about June Donaghy – but Michael Harvey didn't want to give me any answers and I couldn't get my promise to Mary out of my head. He repeated everything he had told me carefully, ticking points off on his fingers like a lawyer running through a brief. His signature on the bottom of the statement was a well-practised scrawl which filled half the sheet.

Michael Harvey said, 'What happens next?'

'We put out a description.'

'Is there anything else to go on?'

'Not much.'

'Do you think you'll find him, Chief Inspector?' It was almost the same question Mrs Donaghy had asked the day before. 'The man who killed . . . June.'

June's name drained the vigour from his face with a sudden rush, as if someone had kicked open a door. While he was telling me his story, Harvey had had something to keep his mind busy. Now reality was back, and reality, to Harvey, was a man struggling with a girl on the bank of the Thames, the office lights reflected in the black water. He'd spend the rest of his life wondering what would have happened if he'd tried to help: whether June Donaghy would still be alive, or whether he'd have ended up alongside her in the cold Thames mud. There was nothing I could say to save him from that.

He didn't get up from his desk to see me out. By the time I reached the door his mind was already on other things. I had an idea what the other things were.

The girl with blue eyes gave me a cursory smile before closing the door behind me.

8

I stopped off at Kennington to give Baring Michael Harvey's statement and to put out a description of the man he had seen, then crossed Lambeth to the jungle of estates behind the Walworth Road.

The flat Sarah Rider was minding for friends had an unlived-in feel, as if Sarah Rider wasn't the only one who hadn't bothered to put down roots there. The walls were bare; the oatmeal carpet was whatever the developer had given them; the books on an Ikea shelving unit were the ones no one would bother to take abroad with them. Through the windows I could see housing estates watching and wondering who was going to come and live there next.

Packing cases stood untidily in the corner of the living room. No one had bothered either to unpack them and stay there, or to finish packing and move out for good. The smell of new carpet hadn't yet been drowned out by the smell of people's lives: old coffee, and garbage, and the perfume hissing on to morning skin and fading slowly until, by nightfall, the whole place just smelled of tired clothes and saucepans no one had the energy to wash up.

I said, 'Where are they?'

Sarah looked up. 'George and Kate? They're abroad. Lucky bastards.' She put the coffee pot down and swore at it. 'Do you know how these things work? They left a note but I chucked it out.' I went and pressed the right buttons for her. Sarah stood watching, not moving away to give me space. Her hair had been dyed blonde again. She was wearing a knitted white top which looked good on her and black leggings which showed that her figure, at least, wasn't starting to age.

She picked up a dirty mug from the sink and began rinsing it under the tap. 'George is a photographer. Lucky bastard. I wouldn't mind a job like that.'

'When did you move out of your mother's?'

She looked up from the running tap. Her face was hard and amused. 'Yesterday morning. Makes you think, doesn't it? Even something like that. June gets killed. To start off we were all lovey-dovey.' She shook her fake blonde head. 'Twelve hours later she was already getting on my wick.'

'Have you always argued with her?'

'Not always. Didn't I tell you? I used to be her favourite.' She turned the tap off. 'I can't remember what I told you on Monday, to be honest. I wasn't all there.'

'What about now?'

She smiled briefly. 'I'm getting back. You do, don't you? You think nothing's ever going to be the same again. But it is. Like with Mum.'

She went and stood over the coffee machine, watching it drip black water into the pot. I looked around the room. Sarah hadn't bothered to keep the place tidy. Clothes were flung over the backs of chairs; a shoulder bag sprawled its contents messily over a glass coffee table.

I said, 'Are you staying here alone?'

She looked round and her eyes followed mine to a man's jumper hanging on the back of the door. Sarah laughed and shrugged. 'Why ask?'

'Your boyfriend?'

She took the pot out of the machine without waiting for it to finish and poured coffee into two undried mugs. The hotplate of the machine hissed as coffee continued to drip on to it. 'I suppose you could call him a boyfriend.'

'Long term?'

'We're not going out.' She sounded amused by something.

'I'm sorry.'

'What for?' Sarah put down the coffee pot. 'He was a bloke I picked up in the restaurant. Boyfriend for seven hours. Got him home about midnight, kicked him out as soon as I woke up. I told him I had to go to my day job.' She put her head on one side, remembering. 'He was sweet, asked me for my number. I told him the number of the chip shop, it was the only one came into my head. Stavros is going to start getting phone calls. Probably send him fucking flowers. I ought to warn him.' She shrugged. 'He won't give me away. He's a mate.'

She picked up the mugs and brought them round the counter to the coffee table. She sipped and made a face. 'What was it you wanted to ask me, then?'

I said, 'Does the name Michael Harvey mean anything to you?'

Sarah buried her face in the mug and watched me over the rim. She looked as if she was about to say something different, then she laughed. 'You've been busy, haven't you?'

'It does mean something to you?'

'Well done.'

'What?'

It took her a moment to answer that. 'He was someone June used to see.'

'Were they having an affair?'

'What makes you think they were?'

'I went to see Michael Harvey this morning. He kept telling me they weren't.'

Sarah snorted contemptuously. 'So you didn't believe him. Michael's scared of the press – that's all it is. He would be. New boy in politics.' She put her head on one side. 'I thought June wanted to, sometimes. She had a thing for him.'

'But it didn't lead anywhere?'

'Michael's too scared of his wife – even if he wanted to mess around with anyone.'

'So why did June see him?'

'Why shouldn't she? They were friends, I suppose.'

I said quietly, 'Michael Harvey was there when June was killed. He saw it happen.'

The hard amusement faded out of Sarah Rider's face completely. It left her looking older than I had seen her before. She moved restlessly on the sofa, folded her arms around herself.

She said, 'I know he was.'

'How?'

'I knew June was going to meet him.' I watched emotions wrestle for control of her face. 'I called Michael this morning. Why didn't he do something?'

'He was scared.'

'Even so.'

'Why didn't you tell me about this yesterday?'

'That she was meeting Michael? I didn't think it was any of your business, if you have to know.'

'Is there anything else you didn't tell me?'

'Only that.'

'Why were they meeting?'

'They were friends.'

I shook my head. 'It wasn't only that. It was something to do with Barney Thacker. Harvey wouldn't tell me what. He used to work for PTI when he was a solicitor – did you know that?'

'That was how he met June.' Sarah put her empty mug down on the floor.

'Why were they meeting last night?' I repeated.

'You don't give up, do you?' Her eyes appraised me. 'You were right the first time, if you really want to know.'

'What does that mean?'

'About June and Barney Thacker. Barney was fucking her about at work. June wanted to get her own back. Michael was going to help her.'

'What was in it for him?'

She shrugged. 'A favour. It does happen.'

'Was it only about Barney Thacker, or was June trying to get at PTI in other ways?'

'What do you mean?'

'Your mother told me June didn't like the way they did business.'

Sarah shrugged. 'There may have been something like that. Barney was the only thing she told me about. She was a bloody fool, if you ask me. Some people don't know when they're sitting pretty. Look at her . . . job like that, and . . . everything –' She'd been on the point of saying something else. 'I tell you, if it had been me, you wouldn't have heard me kicking up a fuss. Barney

57

Thacker wants me to go to bed with him? No problem. Some people don't know it when it's sitting on a plate.' She rubbed her eyes, smearing the make-up. 'June wasn't like that, I know. She wasn't like me.' She looked at me. 'I've heard that often enough in the last few days.'

There was a pause. I watched Sarah Rider ironing anger out of her face as if anger was something private, not to be shown in public. What was left was ironic and detached, the way her face looked in photographs.

'How well do you know Harvey?'

'Michael?' She made a face. 'He's not my type. I've met him a few times.'

'What did you think of him?'

She sat back and put one arm along the back of the sofa. 'He's a smooth one, isn't he? I suppose they all are. I met his wife. She wouldn't talk to me. She probably thought I was a tart. Michael only married her for her money . . . money and other stuff.'

'What other stuff?'

'Her dad's something grand. Michael's into that kind of thing. I suppose he would be, where he was brought up.'

'Where was he brought up?'

'Up in the North somewhere. Nowhere smart. You should see where he lives now.'

I said, 'You don't like him.'

'Well done.'

'Why not?'

Sarah smoothed blonde hair back from her forehead while she thought. I watched her face harden. Quietly she said, 'I thought he was using June, if you have to know.'

'Using her how?'

'He had some grudge against Peter Thacker — I don't know what. He was using June to get his own back. Making her do what he wanted.'

'She could always have refused.'

'No, she couldn't. Not Michael. June did whatever he fucking wanted.' The last part came out too angrily. Sarah picked up her empty mug and used it to hide behind.

After a moment I said, 'You used to protect her, didn't you?'

'I used to try.' She shook her head. 'I don't know if it was protecting her or just . . . not wanting her to listen to anyone else. She was my kid sister. Mine.' Her eyeliner was smeared into shapeless black rings. 'I'm not a very nice person, you know.'

'I've met worse.'

'Thanks.' Her voice was ironic.

'On Monday you told me you were jealous of her.'

'Did I?' She swept the hair back from her forehead. 'I didn't know what I was talking about. Should have kept my mouth shut, shouldn't I?'

'Were you?'

'Jealous?' She put the coffee mug down on the table too hard. 'Course I was. What do you expect? Little June gets the job. She gets the cash. She gets Michael Harvey bleating after her. What do I get? A junkie husband and a job in a Tex-Mex restaurant. I kept thinking, when do I get my share?'

I watched her face go through the same process of smoothing out emotions, arranging itself against the world. Each time she did that she ended up looking a little bit older, a little bit more tired.

I said, 'Tell me about your husband.'

'Jackie?' She snorted. 'There isn't anything to tell.'

'He's an addict?'

Her lips twisted. 'Did I say that? Can't keep my mouth shut, can I? Maybe that's why I never get my share.'

'Is that why it broke up?'

'Partly.'

'Did he treat you badly?'

'No.' She regarded me thoughtfully. 'I treated him badly. Still do, as a matter of fact.'

'How often do you see him?'

'Now and again. There's nothing wrong with Jackie. He's sweet. He's a musician.' She mimed someone playing a saxophone. 'It got on my wick not having any money and him saying yes to any of his friends who wanted anything. There's nothing wrong with Jackie except he's a dopehead and he doesn't have any brains

59

left. Jackie's a sweetie. I'm the one who couldn't handle it.' She looked away, then glanced fiercely back at me. 'You see? It still gets to me. You know the thing that hurt most when I divorced Jackie? It was knowing Mum had been right all along. It wasn't fair on Jackie, my marrying him. I still feel bad about that. Feel bad about leaving him as well.' Her mouth curled ironically. 'That's why I'm so horrible to him when I do see him.'

I drained my coffee mug and stood up. Sarah watched me from the sofa. Her legs were curled up under her. She was troubled about something. 'Don't go.'

'Is there anything else you want to tell me?'

'I'm sure I can think of something. Wait. I'll show you a picture of Jackie, if you like.'

She jumped up from the sofa and crossed over to one of the packing cases. She rummaged in it for a moment and pulled out a wooden picture frame. The picture showed a tall man with a weak chin and hair wet with sweat. The cord of a saxophone was hanging round his neck. He was grinning not at the camera but at someone to the right of the cameraman.

'Jackie's finest hour,' Sarah said. 'Gig at the Jazz Café. Don't remember who he was playing with. He was a stand-in. It was all downhill from there.'

She snatched the photograph away as if she was regretting showing it to me and threw it carelessly back towards the case. She hugged her arms across her chest, not sitting down, not moving away from me. Her eyes were appraising me again, the way they had in the kitchen at her mother's house when we first met. 'Why don't you answer some questions for a change?'

I started moving away.

'Girlfriend?'

I said, 'Two or three. And a wife as well.'

Sarah let her arms drop to her sides. Her smile was only there to mock herself. 'What is it about me? I must be losing it.'

She watched me open the front door, a hard, pretty woman whose only problem was that she wanted too much and was too honest to hide it from anyone; too honest to kid herself about her own mistakes.

When I left her she was sitting on the sofa again, composing her face for what was left of the day.

I hesitated outside. There was a phone box on the corner of the estate. Slowly I walked towards it.

I thought of the promise I had made to Mary. I thought of Mason's orders; I thought of June Donaghy's body spread-eagled on the black Thames mud. I thought of what Michael Harvey had told me – and of what he might have left unsaid.

It was a long time before I went into the phone box.

9

Neil Hudson worked from a tiny office on Victoria Street hidden behind narrow stairs, a one-man lift and a doorway with the names of travel agencies and small export businesses sellotaped to the Entryphone. The hallway smelled of trapped air and ageing carpet over which too many businesses had carried their furniture in and out too often. I took the lift and watched my own face reflected in tarnished mirror panelling. Neil was waiting for me in a door halfway along the corridor to the right.

When we'd started at college together Neil had been a sporting type: a big man, light on his feet, who spent most of the winter playing rugby and most of the summer staring out over a cricket pitch. He hid his brains from the people he played rugby with, and probably from himself as well. About halfway through college he found out he was gay, stopped playing rugby and started reading books instead. Everyone thought Neil would become a lawyer or something in the civil service; but when the jobs came through he turned them down and started writing articles for newspapers. The articles were about global warming, greenhouse gases and the other things newspapers buried next to the small ads. Neil had been writing them for ten years and the world still hadn't changed. These days there was something melancholy about him. Sporting muscle had melted into round lines about his chin and waist. He spent most of his time dieting because his actor boyfriend hated fat people. He had taken the office in Victoria Street because his boyfriend hated the noise of typing at night.

He ushered me into a tiny room heated to a fug by an electric bar over the door. Papers covered the only two chairs; a bookshelf on the wall was full of the sort of books that only Neil ever read. An outsize computer screen threw blue light over everything. Through a strip window on the far side I could see the top of a double-decker bus and crowds of shoppers staring into plate-glass windows on the far side of Victoria Street.

'Coffee?'

'If you're making it.'

'I'm not. Is this going to take long?'

'It might.'

'It better hadn't. I've got a piece to finish. How's Mary?'

'Fine,' I said.

'She's got a big concert soon, hasn't she?'

'Saturday.'

'I'll try to make it.'

I nodded. We both knew he wouldn't make it. 'Simon?'

Neil made a face. 'Moody. He's playing a walk-on in *The Bill* and he thinks they don't appreciate him.'

Neil pushed papers off both chairs and sat down next to the computer. He took his glasses off and laid them on the desk. Behind them his eyes were sensitive and hurt. 'What is it you wanted to ask me about? You said it was urgent.'

I said, 'How much do you know about a company called PTI?'

Neil raised his eyebrows. 'Have you got something to tell me?'

'No.'

'When you rang up I thought you were going to leak a story to me. I thought, that'll be the day. What do you want to know?'

'Anything you can tell me.'

Neil turned and touched buttons on the computer keyboard. The machine showed him some text. 'They're builders. Not houses . . . roads, stuff like that. Heavy engineering. Must be the biggest in the country by now.' He smiled ironically. 'An eighties success story. They even managed to sit out the recession.'

'What's so special about them?'

'They're well run. Peter Thacker's a good manager. They've grown fast. Ten years ago they weren't even getting a chance to tender for the big contracts. It used to be a family firm. They were quoted –' He glanced over his shoulder at the screen. '1987.'

'How did they grow so fast?'

'Good management. Taking chances.' He shrugged. 'The way anybody grows.'

'Are they in any trouble?'

'I should imagine they owe money. All the big construction firms do. It takes capital to run big contracts. PTI never had any. They must have borrowed it somewhere. I can't see them going bust, if that's what you mean.'

There was a pause. I looked at the computer screen over Neil's shoulder. I said slowly, 'Have they ever been in any trouble?'

'What kind of trouble?' Suddenly Neil was alert.

'Any kind. Are they honest?'

'None of these people are honest.' His laugh was bitter. He swivelled his chair suddenly and looked out at the offices on the far side of Victoria Street. 'Why are you interested, George?'

'A case.'

'Are you going to tell me what it's about?'

'Not yet.'

Neil looked back at me. His expression was serious. 'I wrote a series of articles about PTI two years ago. The editors wouldn't touch them. All you see in the papers about PTI is Barney Thacker playing golf and Peter going to parties.' He looked out of the window again. 'With politicians.'

'What were the articles about?'

Neil turned back into the room and leaned forward, his elbows on his knees. 'Do you remember the repair contract at Sizewell – the nuclear power station?' He snorted. 'Of course you wouldn't. You don't read newspapers. There were demonstrations and stuff. Summer 89. PTI did the job.' Neil was concentrating fully now. 'There were two things that were wrong about it.' He looked up at me. His clever eyes were troubled. 'The main problem was how come they got the job in the first place. PTI had never done anything like that before – nuclear power stations. They're road builders – bucket-and-spade stuff. The firms they were competing against all had a track record – they were specialists.'

'So how did they get it?'

'No one knows for sure. There were rumours.' Neil turned over his hand and looked at the nails. 'The minister at energy that year was a man called Philip Lord. He was a friend of Peter Thacker's.' He shrugged. 'It never got further than rumours. The papers wouldn't touch it.'

'Why not?'

'Because there was no evidence.' Neil sighed. 'With people like the Thackers you need something so strong they won't dare to take you to court over it. Otherwise you print, they sue, and before you know it the editor's got a libel bill to explain. With this there was no real evidence at all. PTI shouldn't have got the job; Peter Thacker's a crony of Lord.' He shrugged. 'Big deal. Doesn't prove a thing.'

'What else was wrong with it?'

Neil scratched one soft cheek. 'What you'd expect. What anyone could have told them was going to happen. I said PTI had never done work like that before. They're road-builders. You've got a bunch of guys with buckets and spades crawling all over a nuclear reactor. What the hell did they think was going to happen?'

'What did?'

Neil sighed. 'I'd give a lot to be able to tell you – in detail. My articles were put together from rumours. A guy at the *Guardian* printed one piece but they didn't go any further with it. There was some kind of an accident.'

'A meltdown?'

'Can't have been that big. They wouldn't have been able to cover it up. My guess is it was just a scare, but a bad scare. We know there was a report on it but no one's ever seen the report. *Guardian* tried to make them bring it out but we never heard anything else.'

'Was it PTI's fault?'

Neil spread his hands wide and shrugged. 'You tell me. It happened while they were working there.'

I nodded slowly. Neil's face was melancholy: it was another battle lost in a long war he had no chance of winning. I said, 'What happened after that?'

'Nothing. End of story.' He scratched his cheek, 'What have you found out about them, George?'

'Nothing.'

He looked at me shrewdly. 'What case are you working on at the moment?' When I didn't say anything he grinned ruefully. 'Worth a try.'

'You can tell me something else. What do you know about a politician called Michael Harvey?'

'He's a high flyer. New intake last time round. He took over a constituency in the West Country. Safe seat. His wife's family comes from round there. They're smart.'

'Isn't Harvey?'

He shook his head. 'Grammar school boy.' Neil pursed his lips and looked at me thoughtfully. 'Has Harvey got something to do with this?'

'Maybe. What else do you know about him?'

'Worked in the city – a lawyer's firm. Everyone was talking about him for a time but he left under a cloud. Didn't hear of him for a couple of years, then he cropped up again as an MP.'

'Is he honest?'

'Are any of them?' Neil frowned thoughtfully at the ceiling. 'I should think Harvey's better than most. I covered a speech he did last year. Methodist Central Hall. He was talking family values and stuff, but at least he's got brains.' He grinned suddenly. 'I don't suppose he'd have much time for me.'

'I don't suppose he would.' I stood up. 'What was the trouble Harvey had before he left the city?'

'I don't know that. Not my patch.'

Neil followed me to the one-man lift.

He fidgeted while we waited for it. 'We ought to see more of each other, George. You ought to come round sometime.'

'I'd like that.'

'When Simon's finished this part. He's a bitch at the moment.' He fidgeted some more. 'Are things going better – now you're back in the police? I hardly saw you for a couple of years.'

'They're fine.'

'And Mary? You two should never have broken up in the first

place. Best thing that ever happened to you, when you got back together.'

I didn't want to think about that. We both watched the lift sigh to a halt.

'Any time you do have a story to leak, you know who to come to.' I raised one hand and got into the lift. Neil grinned. 'I won't hold my breath,' he said.

10

It was late afternoon when I came out on Victoria Street. I called Baring from a phone box on the corner and learned that nothing had been found of a big white guy with short hair, or a bearded black guy in a purple leather coat. By the time I reached Brixton Road it was getting dark. Waiters were standing outside the Indian restaurants; outside a big pub, a group of black kids was sitting on the tables waiting for the pub to open, or for a friend to come past, or maybe just waiting because they had nothing better to do than wait. An old white woman was pushing a basket down the pavement in front of me, weaving a trail through forty years of change which she'd done her best to ignore; not looking up at the distant tower blocks or at the faces she passed. The shops of Brixton Road were a blur of light and colour beyond the railway bridge. The windows of Don's Jamaican café were misted with condensation.

I opened the street door of our flat. No music came from upstairs. I unlocked the door, switched on lights and went into the kitchen to put on some coffee. A red light was winking on the answering machine.

Mary's voice spoke to me. It wasn't her normal voice. Fear and tension had strung it higher and taken all the softness out of it. She was doing her best to sound calm, but I knew her too well to be fooled. 'I'm at Charlie's. Call me.'

The machine bleeped and clicked in for a second message. This time Mary's voice wouldn't have fooled anybody.

I picked up the receiver and pressed Charlie's number.

'Hello?'

'Is Mary there?'

'Sure.' Charlie sounded tense. 'I'll get her.'

Mary came to the phone too quickly, as if she had snatched the receiver from Charlie's hand. 'George?'

'What's happened?'

I heard her swallow. She didn't want me to think she was scared but I knew her too well. 'There was a man . . . following me. He followed me all the way from the studio.'

'Are you all right?'

'Of course I'm all right.' Tension snapped her voice. I heard her breathing too deeply. 'No. I'm not all right. I'm scared.'

'I'll come over.'

'Be quick.' Her voice broke again when she said that.

I ran out into Brixton Road. A taxi was dawdling along the opposite kerb, on its way back into town. From the window I watched traffic lights changing colour, women queuing at the check-out of a supermarket, streets to either side whose lights showed empty pavements and drawn curtains. The river opened up beneath me like a black tide flowing into the orange sky above London. At Hyde Park Corner we waited while the evening traffic circled the roundabout. Park Lane was two streams of tail lights burning a path under thickly massed trees. Against the shadows of the park I saw two figures struggling next to a deep black river.

It was Charlie who opened the door to me. From behind him Miles's horn floated downstairs, trying to set the world to rights. I followed him up to the living room. Mary was standing at the window with her coat on. Her lips were cold when I kissed them. For a moment she leaned against me, then pulled away.

'Tell me what happened.'

'I went shopping after we finished rehearsal.' She had her voice back under control. With one hand she reached up to brush a strand of dark hair from her cheek. 'Stage clothes. I noticed this man on the corner of Regent Street. He was looking at me . . .' The way he had looked at her made her shiver again. 'He *kept* looking. I didn't take any notice to start with. Then I realized he was following me . . .' She stopped with one hand crushed against her mouth.

After a moment I said, 'It's all right now.'

'No, George. It isn't all right.' She shook her head. There was anger in her voice along with the fear. 'I went along Oxford Street . . . The crowds – I thought I'd be safe. He *kept* following me. I called Charlie from John Lewis.' She shivered again.

I put my hands on her shoulders but she brushed them off. 'Did he see you coming here?'

Mary wriggled her shoulders free and turned away from me. She said, 'He must have done. He rang up.'

My mouth was dry. 'He rang here?'

'We found out how he got the number. He called the studio. He knows where I *work*.'

I swallowed. 'What did he say?'

'Oh . . .' Her face was disgusted. 'What you'd expect. I don't want to think about it.' Suddenly she looked up at me. 'That wasn't all, though.'

Her grey eyes were searching my face. I didn't say anything, but slowly I could feel myself growing cold.

'I said to him . . . When he rang up I said, "Why are you doing this?" He said . . .' She took a deep breath. 'He said to ask you.' Mary stopped. Her mouth was set in a firm line.

After a moment she said, 'Go on, George. I'm asking you.'

'I don't know what it's about.' My voice sounded false.

'He said you did. He said to ask you. That girl in the river – is that what it's about? Tell me, George. There's something you aren't telling me.'

I said, 'What did he look like?'

Mary frowned. 'What the hell does it matter what he looked like?'

'It might.'

'Is that what I am, now?' She couldn't keep the anger out of her voice any longer. 'A *witness*? Do you want me to make a *statement*?' She took a deep breath. 'I never saw his face properly. He was big. A skinhead . . . He looked . . .' She shook her head, trying to shake off the memory of how he had looked.

I said, 'Let's go home.' There was nothing in my mouth left to swallow.

Charlie watched nervously as we went downstairs. The road outside was dark, deserted. We found a taxi on the corner of Oxford Street. Mary squeezed herself into the far corner, as far away from me as she could get. The taxi driver pulled the glass screen shut. For a moment we drove in silence.

Mary said, 'George?' She was huddled against the cold glass. 'Those people you told me about last night . . . Barney Thacker . . .'

She stopped. I didn't say anything; I couldn't have said anything that would have sounded like the truth.

She took a deep breath before going on. 'You promised me you wouldn't make any trouble for them – didn't you?'

I said, 'Yes.'

'Do you think this might have anything to do with them?'

'I don't know.' Something was blocking my voice, twisting and raising it into the voice of somebody different, a liar.

After a moment Mary said, 'Is that what you've been doing today – investigating Barney Thacker?'

I watched a traffic light changing from green to red. Then I said, 'Yes.'

There was a long silence. From opposite sides of the cab we watched traffic going in different directions.

Mary said, 'You lied to me.' Her voice was hardly more than a whisper.

'It might not have anything to do with it – your being followed.'

'He said it did.' I saw her head move. 'Anyway, it isn't the point, is it? You lied to me.'

'Do you want me to arrange protection?'

In the darkness of the taxi I saw her face swing towards me. Her voice was incredulous. 'You don't understand, do you? It isn't the point – protection. Anyway –' She shook her head. 'I don't want protection. I want . . . I want it not to have happened. It didn't need to happen.' Her voice dropped. 'You don't understand, George.'

I did understand. But there was no way of telling her why I had broken my word. I wasn't sure I could explain it to myself.

'Who is he, this man?'

'I don't know.'

'Is he the one who killed –' She swallowed. 'That girl?'

'I don't know.'

'You don't seem to know a lot.' Her voice was bitter. 'Am I in danger?'

I reached out one hand to touch her but she wriggled her shoulder away. 'That means I am. I hate this, George. I hate it when you won't even talk to me.'

She looked out of the side window again, watching pavements and dark shops rather than look at me. I could see her face reflected in the black window of the cab: the wide cheekbones stretched wider by tiredness, the large grey eyes. I wanted to reach out towards her but the back seat of the taxi was too wide for that; and as soon as my finger touched her Mary tensed away from me.

'I could get you protection,' I repeated.

'I don't want that.' The fear was gone from Mary's voice now; anger had displaced it. 'I don't want to spend the whole time being trailed by some . . . *copper*.' She drew breath in through her teeth. 'Charlie said I could stay with him for a few days. I said there was no point. He knows where it is, doesn't he?' After a moment she said, 'I thought I could call Jack.'

Jack was the man she had left me for five years ago. I didn't say anything. I had already lost the right to say anything.

'George?'

'Yes?'

'You don't even mind, do you? Maybe you even want me to move out.'

'You know I don't.'

'You didn't say anything.'

I said, 'It might be safer.'

'Safer,' she repeated. After a moment she said, 'It's nice to know where you stand.'

In the orange glow inside the taxi I could see a tear scoring her cheek, but when I reached out my hand she took her own hand away.

We passed the rest of the journey in silence.

11

I reached Kennington Police Station early the next morning. There hadn't been any point in either of us pretending we were asleep any longer, and it hadn't taken long for Mary to pack and call a cab. After that it hadn't taken me long to realize I didn't want to stay in the flat by myself.

The incident room was empty except for one weary copper who'd been watching the phone all night. Baring came in just after me. For half an hour I took him through what Michael Harvey had told me the day before. Then I told him about the man who had followed Mary and watched his solid face register shock.

'Is she all right, sir?'

'She will be.'

'She ought to get some protection.'

'She doesn't want it. She's going to move out for a few days.'

He nodded. 'It might be better. Who do you think's behind it, sir?'

I told him I didn't know who was behind it. I didn't tell him why Michael Harvey had been planning to meet June Donaghy on Sunday night, or what Neil Hudson had told me about the Thackers.

I picked up the medical report. 'Did you find out what I asked you on Monday?'

'Whether she was a virgin, sir?' Baring's red face stiffened. 'She wasn't.' He sounded defensive. 'She wouldn't be, would she, sir? Not these days. The girls aren't any more. You wouldn't expect it.'

June Donaghy's mother had expected it. I said, 'Thanks.'

'Is it important, sir?'

I sighed. 'Her mother and sister both told me she'd never been interested in men.'

'They might not have known.'

I left him frowning at the doctor's report and took the stairs up to my office. Mason was waiting for me. He was holding a sheet of fax paper in his hand.

He didn't look me in the eye. 'Have you got a moment, George?'

He followed me into my office and stood nervously by the desk, still fidgeting with the piece of fax paper. 'I got this earlier this morning, George. From Scotland Yard – I didn't know they got to work so early.' He put the sheet of paper down on my desk. I didn't pick it up. 'From John Harlow . . . Someone thinks you're important. Go on. Read it. You might as well – it's about you.'

I went on not picking it up. Mason gave an exasperated sigh and reached for the letter. ' "Reference: Investigation into Ronald Whelan concluded 9.6.95 . . ." Remember Ronnie Whelan? "In view of continuing public concern about aspects of the investigation leading to Mr Whelan's recent conviction . . ." '

I said, 'There wasn't any public concern about Ronnie Whelan.'

Mason looked up at me. He said drily, 'Ronnie's wife didn't like him being banged up. Maybe she wrote to John Harlow about it.' He looked at the paper again. ' "I have decided to refer all aspects of the investigation for further internal enquiry. All officers involved in the investigation should be informed, and files submitted . . ." Blah blah blah.' Mason dropped the letter. 'I told you yesterday there were people who didn't like you. Didn't I tell you that?'

'Ronnie Whelan had half a kilo of heroin in his glove compartment.'

'I know that, George. I'm not saying you've got anything to worry about. As long as you keep your head down for the next month or so.'

'You mean, as long as I leave the Thackers alone.'

'Yes.' Mason folded the letter and put it away in his pocket. 'I told you that yesterday, George. There's no point fighting battles you can't win. You only harm yourself.'

I looked at him. Mason's grey eyes were flecked with brown,

like steel slowly giving way to rust. I said, 'Mary was followed home last night.' My eyes were on the picture of Miles behind his head. 'A man. He called up later. I think it's got something to do with this.'

Mason's forehead creased. 'Is she all right?'

'As all right as you could expect.'

'Do you know who he was?'

'She said it was a big man with short hair. A skinhead. That's the same description as the man Michael Harvey saw on Sunday night.'

'Michael Harvey.' Mason looked nervous. 'I've been hearing some things about Michael Harvey, George.'

I looked at him.

'Turns out Johnnie Harlow knows him. You know why he had to leave the city before he became an MP? Turns out he wasn't altogether . . . ' Mason grimaced. 'Wasn't the kind of man you could trust. Bit worrying he's the only witness we've got to rely on.' He sighed. 'Does Mary want protection?'

'Not yet. She's moving out for a few days.'

'Relatives?'

I said, 'A friend.'

'At least you'll be able to keep an eye on her.' Mason frowned down at the fax. 'You may be right there's a connection, George. Could be the bloke who killed June Donaghy found out who was in charge of the case. It's been known.'

I nodded at the fax. 'Why are they doing this?'

'What do you mean?'

'There was nothing wrong with the Ronnie Whelan case. Someone must have put Harlow up to this. Someone who knows him.'

'Come off it, George. Johnnie Harlow's a DAC. I went through training with him.' Mason shook his head. 'What are you saying?'

'On Monday Barney Thacker threatened to make trouble for me if I didn't leave him alone. Maybe this is the trouble.'

'No, George.' There was a hard edge of anger in his voice. 'Don't be a bloody fool. You don't get men like Johnnie Harlow . . . Anyway, it isn't worth Thacker's while. You're not that important, you know.' He blinked at me. 'Have you been stirring up trouble for them again?'

'I haven't seen them since Monday.' It was true as far as it went.

Mason nodded. 'Let's keep it that way. You need to be careful about this, George. I told you before there are people at Scotland Yard who don't like you. You've got a good lead with this car. I'd stick to that if I was you.' He tried a smile. 'I know what you think of people like the Thackers, George. It's like the people we let off at the end of the Mattie Hill business. I agree with you . . . part of me.' He shook his head. 'It's not the point. It doesn't matter what we think. We're not here to change the way anyone makes their money. We're here to catch lads in Cortinas. That's about our mark. A lad gets drunk, maybe has a difficult background, he attacks a girl walking home one night. We get him off the streets quick as we can and put him away somewhere he won't do anyone any harm. That's what we're here for. It's our job. You stick to that.' He shook the fax paper he was still holding. 'That way you don't have anything to worry about.'

12

Outside Kennington Police Station I took the road up towards
Lambeth Bridge. It was still early. The cars tailed back from the bridge
almost to the Imperial War Museum. As I approached the railway
bridge a Eurostar train rumbled heavily past on its way to Brussels or
Paris, or somewhere where different drivers were waiting in different
traffic jams to reach the same offices. I turned right just before the
railway, where the arches curved round towards Waterloo station.
Most of the arches were boarded up. A big sign halfway along advertised scrap metal. Outside the arch next to it, two bikers were staring
at a Harley-Davidson surrounded by pieces of machinery, like two
kids who couldn't figure out how to put a toy back together.

Just beyond them a car was jacked up on concrete blocks. The
arch behind it had no sign over the door. By the light of a single
fluorescent tube I could see the wrecks of cars which looked a long
way from going anywhere. Radio music blared from a glass kiosk
to the left of the door.

A man's legs were sprawled from under the car on blocks. They
were dressed in dirty trainers and jeans with smears of oil on the
knees.

I stopped by the legs. 'Tony?'

The legs twitched. Two dirty hands appeared, then a man's head
with smears of oil where the hair should have been and a pair of
round glasses covered in oil. The man was holding a spanner in
one hand. He looked at me impatiently.

'What the hell do you want?'

'I want to ask you something, Tony.'

'Don't waste my time.' He started wriggling back under the car.
'You don't have a motor.'

'I still need your advice.'

'Nobody needs my advice. Last person asked my advice, he wanted me to rebuild his gearbox for free. Told him to stuff it. I don't give advice any more.'

I said, 'Did you ever come across a guy called Jimmy Bolan?'

Tony sighed and worked his way out from under the car. He sat up and rubbed his bald head, leaving a few more oil stains. He jerked his head towards the car. 'Fucking waste of time this is. They've spent so much money on this, they could have bought themselves a Roller. Can't say I didn't warn them.'

'Do you know Jimmy Bolan?'

Tony took off his glasses and wiped some of the oil on to his jeans. 'How's Mary? Got a new car yet?'

'She doesn't want a car.'

'She ought to get a bike. That would suit her. Go with the image – know what I mean? I always meant to get a bike. Cost less to run than a car, too. Cars are fucking useless. I don't blame her.'

I said, 'Tell me about Jimmy Bolan.'

Tony stood up and stretched. 'He runs a shit-hole used-car dump down the Old Kent Road. Couldn't spot a decent motor if it ran him over. Used to see him at the go-kart track down there. Thinks he's a bit of a racer.' He looked at me. 'Ladies' man as well.'

'Is he straight?'

Tony put his glasses back on and looked scornfully at me. 'You must have been born fucking yesterday.'

'All right. How crooked is he?'

'He's flash. Too obvious – know what I mean? He'll take an old B reg and run the clock back to five thousand.' Tony shrugged. 'You've got to play a little bit clever, haven't you? Getting himself a bad name that way.'

'Does he work on the cars himself?'

'Jimmy Bolan? Wouldn't want to get oil on his face, might spoil his looks. No, he just drives 'em. Drives 'em and flogs 'em. Bloke called Charlie Wells rigs them up for him.'

'Where would I find his workshop?'

Tony frowned. 'Is he in trouble?'

'Jimmy might be.'

'I wouldn't want to mess Charlie about. He's a mate.'

'Where's the workshop?'

Tony thought for a moment. 'Battersea. You know the Dogs' Home? Industrial estate opposite there. Go to the end of the track. You can hear the dogs barking.'

'Thanks, Tony.'

He lowered himself to the ground and started working his way back under the car.

'Tell Mary to get a bike,' he said. 'Tell her I told you.'

The traffic was thick outside Battersea Dogs' Home. I waited for a gap, then crossed the road to a brick stairway let into the wall of the pavement opposite. Behind it a row of industrial sheds smelled of chemicals. Steam was rising from a vent in the wall nearest me. There were vans parked outside the sheds, boxes being loaded and unloaded; through wide loading bays I could see machinery.

I started walking down the side road past the sheds. A man was pushing a trolley across the road. He was whistling a tune that was lost under the sound of machinery.

'Is there a car workshop near here?'

'Up at the end.' He didn't stop pushing the trolley. 'Better watch out for the dogs.'

Beyond the last shed the road continued into a patch of waste ground alongside a railway embankment. Fifty yards away I could see the roofs of sheds. I heard the dogs long before I reached them. By the time I got there they were straining against the fence. There was a Rottweiler and a dog that might have called itself an Alsatian, and both of them wanted to see what I looked like from the inside. The fence that was stopping them from doing it was made of wire mesh with a thin strand of barbed wire wound along the top. The gate was fixed with a heavy padlock.

I stopped at the gate. The dogs snapped at air, just to let me know what would happen to me if I climbed over it. Inside the fence was a corrugated tin shed with the sliding door closed. The body of a Land Rover stood on bricks on a patch of concrete hard-standing outside it. To one side was a timber lean-to with the coupling of a trailer protruding from it. A small caravan stood to the right of the gate. The curtains of the caravan were drawn; a satellite dish hung crookedly from the roof; wires trailed away towards the tin shed. An orange gas bottle stood on concrete blocks by the door.

Nobody came out. I shouted, let the dogs bark some more and watched the caravan. Anybody who worked there would have a car, and there was no car parked on the hard standing.

I started walking around the perimeter of the fence. The dogs followed me. They were beginning to get annoyed now. I should have been running back up the path with a hole in the back of my leg. The Rottweiler was pressing its teeth against the wire, roaring at me with the sound that no other dog can make. There were flecks of white saliva on its muzzle.

I trod through patches of weeds. Where the fence butted against the metal shed it was held by steel brackets bolted to the corner. There was a window high up in the gable of the shed. It didn't seem to have any glass in it.

I looked around. I could have waited until Charlie Wells came back, but I didn't think Charlie Wells was going to tell me what I wanted to know. I could have gone back to the station for a warrant, and waited the hours it took to get that – waited and wondered what Mary was doing at Jack's place. Nothing was watching me except weeds, a pile of old tyres and tower blocks too far away to care.

I put a foot on the lowest bracket. The dogs didn't like that. I felt a grip on the sole of my shoe, kicked, and hoisted myself up higher. Below me I could see teeth. I tried not to think of the teeth. Rusty metal grazed my cheek. When I put my weight on the top of the fence it swayed and rocked. I gripped hard on the corner of the shed and tried not to think of teeth. My fingers scrabbled over ridges of metal towards the opening. They touched pieces of glass, the frame of a metal window. I felt for the sill with my left foot, paused, threw my weight towards it. Something jagged my hand. I lurched, closed my eyes and clutched the frame of the window. The barking sounded far away.

When I opened my eyes I was looking down into the interior of the shed. A dusty grey light covered the shapes of cars. The air smelled of rust. Along one wall was a wooden bench covered with tools and pieces of car engines. From somewhere in the roof I could hear pigeons cooing.

I worked my way along the window ledge. Jagged edges of glass stood up from the frame. From the far end of the window I should just be able to reach the bench. I didn't want to think about how I was going to get back up. I jumped, stumbled, fell heavily to the floor. The noise was like someone dropping a hammer on a tin tray. The cars looked disapprovingly at me. From outside the shed the noise of barking redoubled.

Slowly I stood up, ignoring a pain in my hand. I was standing next to the kind of truck I hadn't seen since I last watched an Ealing comedy. Thick dust covered the windscreen; the bonnet was open on to empty space. I moved slowly among the cars. Most of them looked as if they'd been there for years. Stuffing showed through holes in the seats; one looked as if it had been stripped down for stock car racing. An old Mercedes without doors or seats sat in the middle of the floor on a pile of bricks. I was starting to wonder what I was looking for.

I walked past more wrecks. At the back of the shed was a ghostly shape under a sheet. I lifted one corner of the sheet and looked under it. I didn't know what sort of car it was: I didn't know enough about cars. The bodywork was covered with thick anti-rust paint which looked new.

I took a key out my pocket and scored it down the red paint. The noise set my teeth on edge. I scratched some more, then squatted down to look at the scratch marks. In the grey light from the window the scratch marks were nothing but jagged black lines.

Suddenly there was a grinding of metal on metal. Light flooded into the shed, blinding me. The sound of barking echoed from the roof. Something hit me from the side. When I opened my eyes there were teeth inches away from me. The stench of dog's breath drove me back into the floor.

A man's voice was shouting. I felt something grip my leg and kicked. The barking was further from my face. I struggled back against the side of the car. The dogs were straining at me. A man stood between them, one hand on each collar. He was a short man with a pug face and a checked shirt rolled up over thick forearms. There seemed to be something wrong with one of his legs.

He shouted at the dogs again and the barking subsided to a low double growling like the drone of wasps.

The man said, 'Bet you thought that was pretty clever, chum, getting in through the window. Bet you thought no one ever tried that before.' He jerked his head at me. 'Get up.'

I got slowly to my feet and leaned against the car. My eyes were getting used to the light from the open door. I glanced quickly down at the scratches in the paint. The scratches weren't black any more. Blue and silver paint showed through the red oxide.

'What are you up to?' The little man's eyes squinted at me. He was having trouble holding the Rottweiler.

I didn't say anything. The man snapped something at the Rottweiler. The dog which might have been an Alsatian barked twice, then went back to growling at me.

'I could call the police.'

It was probably the wrong moment to tell him that I was the police, and had just happened to omit the formalities of waiting for him to come home or getting myself an arrest warrant. I could imagine myself explaining that to Mason.

I said, 'Go on, then.'

He didn't move. 'What are you doing here?'

'I'm waiting for you to call the police,' I said.

'You're funny now, are you? Think it's time to start making jokes, do you?' The Rottweiler lurched against its collar and growled something deep inside its throat. The little man said, 'He'd have your throat out if I let go.' He jerked the collar forward suddenly to show me how easy it would be for him to let go.

I said, 'Let him go.'

'What do you want here?' He nodded towards the open door. 'Knew there was something wrong when I saw the dogs. You're not the first one tried to get in like that. That's why I keep the dogs.'

I kept my eyes on the little man's face. Holding the dogs was starting to be an effort. I couldn't tell whether he'd noticed the scratch marks on the car or not. I pushed myself up off the car and started walking round him.

'Where are you going, chum?'

I said, 'You're not going to call the police.'

'I could let the dogs go.'

I shrugged and kept walking. I didn't think he was going to let the dogs go.

'What did you want here, chum? There isn't anything to nick, you know. Nothing that's worth anything.'

I said, 'I could see that.'

'You can tell your mates as well. There's nothing to nick here. You tell 'em.'

He was limping after me. His left leg trailed a little. The dogs were growling in a puzzled way.

'You know what I'd do with scum like you?'

An old Ford van was parked on the hard standing. Beyond it the gate was open. I kept my eyes on the gate.

'You'll know next time. Next time I'll let the dogs have you. Don't say I haven't warned you. You can tell your mates as well. Maybe they'll leave me alone.'

I was out of the gate now, walking fast towards the industrial estate. The man was no longer following me.

I wondered what would make a man live by himself in a caravan on a patch of waste ground with no one but dogs for company.

I could hear the dogs barking all the way to the main road.

13

Jimmy Bolan's garage was a forecourt with a row of coloured flags fluttering over half a dozen cars that were worth less than the flags were. Baring slammed the door of the police car shut and followed me towards them. Behind the cars a Portakabin was half hidden by timber struts which held up the wall of the funeral parlour next door. The cars smelled faintly of wax and more strongly of leaking oil. A faded green sign over the Portakabin had Puma Motors written on it next to a white shape that might have been meant as a cat.

Mesh over the windows hid whatever deals were being made inside. I pulled open the door of the cabin. Inside, a fluorescent tube threw a blue glare over a cheap metal desk, two filing cabinets and a television high up in one corner. The mesh on the windows kept out any real light. Behind the desk a kid in a green parka was dropping breadcrumbs on a mess of papers and invoice pads. He looked at us over the sandwich, his cheeks bulging. There was a rash of red spots around his nose.

He swallowed with difficulty. 'What do you want?'

Baring climbed up into the office after me and pulled the door shut.

'Is Jimmy Bolan here?'

'No.'

'Where is he?'

The kid's chin moved forward and upwards as he swallowed. 'Don't know.'

'Are you expecting him back?'

'Don't know.'

'When did you last see him?'

The kid didn't answer but his eyes strayed to a closed door in the partition halfway down the cabin. A girlie calendar on the back of it was stuck in February, with two models draped over the bonnet of an old Bentley. Either the next three months were ugly or Puma Motors hadn't made a sale in a long time. Next to the door two jackets hung off a wooden coat stand.

I walked towards the door.

'You can't go in there, mister.' His voice was full of panic.

From behind the door I could hear a sound like a car engine turning over without firing. The kid's voice bleated behind me. The door jammed, but gave when I kicked. Behind a cheap metal desk I could see the back of a woman's head and a shirt collar which had slipped halfway down her back. Her hair was the colour and style of a teddy bear's fur. I couldn't see past it to the face of the man whose lap she was sitting on. I could only see his hands kneading the girl's bare shoulders.

It took them a moment to realize they had company. I leaned against the door frame and waited for the girl to finish screaming and wrap her blouse across skinny breasts that looked too cold to be doing what she was doing. Jimmy Bolan swore at us until he saw who it was, then stopped swearing and started fumbling with his flies. In trying to do his flies up he knocked the phone off the desk and started swearing at that instead.

I said, 'I hope we weren't disturbing anything.'

The girl's face showed scarlet through face powder which clung to her like the skin of a different woman. Her fingers weren't making buttons go into holes, and her shoe was suddenly too big for her foot. Jimmy Bolan picked up the phone and swore at the girl.

'We've got some questions to ask your friend.'

She'd forgotten how to talk, or do anything except get out of the cabin. Baring stood aside to let her escape, dragging behind her a trail of sickly perfume. We heard the outer door slam, and the girl's voice outside screaming at the kid in the parka. Jimmy Bolan pulled his chair up to the desk and put his hands on top of it, palms down. His eyes had a shocked look. 'What do you want?'

'We want to ask you some questions, Jimmy.'

'I told you everything the other day.'

I perched on the edge of the desk. 'I don't think so.'

'What do you mean?' He did his best to look offended but the skin was stretched tight across his forehead.

'Who was the girl?' I asked.

'A friend.' His large brown eyes flickered towards Baring. 'Just a bird.'

'Don't you do enough trade to keep you busy?'

'It's been a quiet week.'

I leaned towards him. Jimmy Bolan leaned back by the same amount, as if there was a magnetic field holding us apart. 'You told us you sold Mark Mitchell's car the same day you bought it.'

'That's right.'

'Who did you sell it to?'

'A black guy. I told you. Guy with a beard. Purple . . .'

I said, 'You told us that.'

Jimmy Bolan blinked. His fingers fluttered on the edge of the desk.

'What colour was the car, Jimmy?'

'Silver and blue.' He was doing his best to sound bored. Behind me Baring cleared his throat noisily.

'You're sure about that?'

The neon light over the desk seemed to be bothering him. It had bleached Jimmy Bolan's dark face to the colour of old bones; the lover's forelock had become a hank of greasy hair which kept getting in his eyes.

Jimmy Bolan brushed the back of his hand over his forehead and said, 'Look, I bought the car. I flogged it. I don't know who bought it. End of story, all right?' He turned his troubled eyes towards Baring to see if the story was going down any better on that side of the room. 'All right?' When neither of us said anything Jimmy Bolan added, 'It's what I told you the other day. Yesterday.' His voice made it sound as if he had proved his point. A tongue appeared at the corner of his lips, trying to put moisture into them. If Jimmy Bolan really thought he had proved his point he wouldn't have had to keep on talking. 'We have a lot of blokes in. You don't remember all of them, do you? He was just . . .' One hand pumped the air, looking for more conviction. 'A bloke.'

'Who do you get to make over your cars?'

'What do you mean?' The light seemed to be getting in his eyes again. Ten minutes ago he'd been enjoying himself with a skinny girl with teddy bear hair; now he had two policemen in his office refusing to believe lies.

'Fix the engines. Touch up paint.' I kept my eyes on his face. 'Make them look like they're worth five hundred quid.'

'I use loads of blokes.'

'Who in particular?'

'I don't know.' He looked around the room for inspiration. Grey paint and old lino didn't seem to provide it. 'There's a bloke in Camberwell.'

'What about Charlie Wells?' I sat back and folded my arms. 'You ever use him?'

'Sometimes.' He nodded and jerked his head, as if he was trying to escape from an insect. 'I suppose.'

'What about this car?'

'It didn't need fixing. I told you. Got it in and sold it the same day.'

'What about afterwards?'

'After what?'

I leaned forward. 'After you took it back again.'

Jimmy Bolan shook his head too vigorously, as if he was trying to lose a headache. His grin showed the two rows of teeth you see in a skull. 'You lost me.'

'Were you supposed to get rid of it as well? Was that part of the deal – or did you just get greedy?'

Baring moved ponderously in his chair. 'I think he got greedy.' He sighed sorrowfully. 'He's a greedy boy, our Jimmy.'

Jimmy Bolan's mouth opened but didn't manage to come up with any words. He tried turning it into a smile, then a yawn, then gave up trying anything and just left his jaw hanging.

'I was up at Charlie Wells's today,' I said. 'Guess what I found in the shed? Old Ford Cortina covered in anti-rust paint. Used to be silver and blue.' Jimmy Bolan's left cheek was starting to contract. I went on, 'Is that your car, Jimmy?'

His face went on shrinking as if someone had left it too close to the heat. After a moment he looked down at the table to stop us watching it. 'I don't know. I don't know anything about a car.'

'Still have the chassis number on it,' Baring said conversationally. 'Even if you got rid of the plates. Mark Mitchell be back from Spain next week. Shouldn't be too hard to put the pieces together.'

I kept my eyes on Jimmy Bolan. Quietly I said, 'Why would anyone pay five hundred for a heap of junk like that, anyway? Unless someone wanted it for something special.' The lock of hair hung vertically down from Jimmy Bolan's forehead. His face was something private between himself and the table. 'Who wanted it, Jimmy?'

He rocked forward maybe an inch, then back again. It might have been an answer, or maybe he just couldn't keep his body still.

'We know what they wanted it for. Someone saw it down by the river on Sunday night. Saw someone killing a girl then driving away in your car.' Again Jimmy Bolan rocked forward in his chair. The creak of the chair was the only sound in the room. 'Did he tell you he was going to kill someone, Jimmy?'

Baring said, 'Better for you if he hadn't told you. You're an accessory otherwise. Ten years.' His voice was flat, matter-of-fact. 'Fifteen if the judge doesn't like your face. Better for you if he didn't tell you anything at all.' He sighed. 'We'd have to know his name, though – if we were going to believe that.'

Faintly we heard Jimmy Bolan gasp. His hands were fisted into two white balls on his lap, like the stumps of arms.

'What was the deal?' I asked. 'You provided the car, had to get rid of it afterwards. Have you done that before?' I put my head close to his. His head smelled of sweat and breath that was soured by fear. 'Maybe it wouldn't matter if you'd done it before, so long as you told us who bought the car.'

From behind me Baring's voice said, 'We can do it another way if you like. Pick up the car. Ask Charlie Wells who sent it to him.' He paused. 'Trouble is, that makes you an accessory. Could find yourself on a murder charge if you don't play your cards right.'

The gasp this time was almost a word – either a name or a plea for mercy. Either way, Jimmy Bolan didn't want to find himself on a murder charge.

'Who bought the car off you, Jimmy?'

His shoulders moved up too far, as if he couldn't get enough breath into his lungs to speak. The top of his head was trembling.

I said, 'I can't hear you.'

Jimmy Bolan said, 'Medd.'

I looked at Baring. Jimmy Bolan wasn't focusing on us. His face was all eyes and teeth; the colour had gone from it as if a child had scrubbed it out with an eraser. 'Medd,' he said. 'A bloke called Medd.'

'Is he a friend of yours?'

'I met him in the pub.' The forelock swung sideways. 'He didn't say what he wanted it for. He just said he wanted a car.'

'Of course he didn't.' Baring's voice was soothing.

'He told me . . .' The thin line of Jimmy Bolan's voice was blown away by a sigh.

'What's his first name?'

'I don't know. The blokes just call him Medd.' Again the end of the sentence died.

I looked at Baring. He nodded. 'Hard man, sir. Came across him on a B and E case two years ago. We'll have a picture of him on file.'

I turned back to Jimmy Bolan. 'What else do you know about him?'

Jimmy Bolan looked up again. His eyes were still scared, but no longer of us. 'He's a bastard. He'd kill me if . . .'

'A hard man.' Baring's voice was weary. 'World's full of blokes who think they're hard men.'

'He is. Medd . . .'

'What does he look like?'

'He's big. Shaved head.' Jimmy Bolan looked up suddenly. 'You won't tell him who told you?'

I didn't answer that. 'What were you going to do with the car?'

'Change the plates. Respray. I could have sold it by now. After you came round I told Charlie to hang on to it.' He looked up at me. 'What's going to happen to me?'

'Maybe nothing. It depends whether we find Medd.'

'You won't find him.'

'Why not?'

'Haven't seen him for days. I was in the pub last night. He owed me for the car.'

'Do you know where he lives?'

He shook his head. 'I only saw him in the pub.'

I nodded at Baring. Baring went round behind the desk and put his hand under Jimmy Bolan's elbow. Jimmy Bolan came out of the chair too quickly, as if he had suddenly become lighter. He sagged against Baring's arm.

'Take him through it back at the station. Make sure he gives you a full statement. We don't want him forgetting what he said.'

'What about you, sir?'

I said, 'I'm going to see Michael Harvey.'

14

The woman who opened Harvey's door had a beautiful, faded face with no make-up on it, as if she didn't want anyone to realize it was beautiful. Her spring dress was the kind rich English women pay money for so as not to stand out in a crowd. Washed-out brown eyes didn't stay on me for long but dropped to the steps behind me as if they didn't have the energy to look me in the eye.

'I'll get Michael.'

Her heels tapped on a woodstrip floor and disappeared up carpeted stairs. I waited in a big living room full of faded antique furniture and photographs of Michael Harvey. A bad oil painting over the fireplace showed Michael Harvey and the woman sitting on either side of the girl I had met the day before.

While I waited I looked at the photograph I had taken from Kennington Police Station. It was an ordinary police mugshot, taken in the hard white glare that turns everyone into a villain. The face was hard and hairless, with eyes too close together and a fleshy nose over a wide, cruel mouth. It looked as if it had been moulded out of clay, then squeezed out of shape a little before being baked hard. The eyes were two black holes where a kid had stuck his fingers into the clay. There was no expression in them at all.

I kept on staring at it. I didn't manage to make it blink. I pictured it standing in a telephone box, the wide mouth snarling threats into the receiver, Mary's eyes closed as she listened to him speak. It wasn't a picture I enjoyed.

I didn't have to wait long. Michael Harvey came in through a side door wearing a pale blue jumper and casual trousers. Without his politician's suit on he looked younger and more athletic: the school hero who won races on sports day as well as coming top in his exams. The tortoiseshell glasses looked faintly out of place, as if he should have had a different pair of glasses to wear over the jumper.

'Chief Inspector.' I shook the hand he stretched out towards me. 'I should have gone in to work today. I couldn't face it, I suppose. It's a reaction.'

He sat down in an over-stuffed sofa and pointed me towards an armchair. 'What is it you want to show me?'

I handed him the photograph of Medd. It looked wrong in that setting, as if an antique sideboard and an over-stuffed sofa couldn't possibly live in the same world as Medd.

Harvey looked at it with his head on one side. 'How did you find him?'

'We traced the car. Is that the man you saw?'

Harvey nodded once. 'I think so.' He looked apologetically up at me. 'It was dark.' Again he bent his thin face to examine the photograph. 'Yes. I'm sure.'

'Do you think you'd be able to identify him if we picked him up?'

'Haven't you found him yet?'

'Not yet.'

'I think so,' he repeated. He waved the photograph by one corner. 'Who is he?'

'His name's Medd.'

Harvey frowned. 'Did he know June? Was there any reason for him to kill her?'

'I don't know.'

'I suppose you couldn't. Not until you find him.' Harvey looked at the photograph again. One finger stroked the side of his mouth.

I said quietly, 'What happened between you and PTI?' The face Harvey turned up to me was shocked, the face of a schoolboy about to deny something, then realizing it was too late to deny it. 'You worked for them when you were in the city. Someone told me you left under a cloud. June's sister said you had a grudge against the Thackers. What was that about?'

Harvey sat slowly back in the sofa. He moved cautiously, as if he was worried about his own health. 'Left under a cloud?' There was a trace of bitterness in his voice. 'Who told you that?'

'It's what I heard.'

'What you heard,' he repeated. 'It's what a lot of people have heard.'

'You mean it isn't true?'

'I mean it's easy to put the word around against somebody. If they don't back it up with any details, then you don't get a chance to defend yourself, do you?'

'Who's putting the word round against you?'

'Peter Thacker.' He said it without malice, simply stating a fact.

'Why?'

Michael Harvey sighed. 'It's true I used to work for them when I was in the city. They were the firm's biggest client and I was the youngest partner.' He blushed. 'You can imagine how pleased with myself I was. More fool me.' He looked young again as he said it: too young to have the job he had, or a grown-up daughter; too young to be sitting in that kind of drawing-room. I could imagine the enthusiasm and confidence that had pushed him to the top. He was the kind of man people wanted to help.

'What went wrong?'

'Everything.' He turned his face away. 'I don't want to go into the details.'

I said, 'Did it have anything to do with PTI's work at Sizewell?'

I saw Harvey's shoulders stiffen. 'Where did you hear about that?'

I shrugged. 'I heard it.'

Harvey's face was tense. He was holding his hands near his face as if at any moment he might have to hide from me. 'What else did you hear?'

'That the way they got the contract wasn't straight.'

'Do you know why?'

'It was something to do with a man called Philip Lord.'

'Philip.' Harvey shook his head ruefully. 'He's an important man, you know. In my party.'

'I don't follow politics.'

'I don't blame you, sometimes.'

93

He dropped his head and pressed folded hands to his lips for a moment, as if he was praying. 'It was true,' he said at last.

'What was true?'

'The rumour about Philip and PTI. That was what I found out.' He looked up at me. 'I couldn't believe it at first. I suppose that was stupid of me. I thought all politicians were . . .' His smile was self-mocking. 'Honourable.'

'What happened?'

'Peter Thacker bribed Philip to get the contract. They shouldn't have got anywhere near it. They were the wrong kind of firm.'

'Have you got any proof of it?'

He didn't answer that. He stood up and walked over to the painting of his family. For a moment he stared at it as if it was a painting of strangers. 'PTI were in a hole. They had loans coming up and needed something to show the banks. Peter asked me to rush the Sizewell contract through – the one between them and the government.' His eyes narrowed. 'I started to ask questions. I suppose I shouldn't have. I should have done what I was told.'

'What kind of things?'

'There was a collateral contract – a contract with another party – that shouldn't have been there. Peter Thacker wanted me to do something . . .' He swung round. 'Something any lawyer should have refused. That was when I said I wanted a meeting with him.'

'What happened at the meeting?'

Harvey's thin face was twisted with the memory of humiliation. 'He told me I was naïve. The next day he rang the firm where I worked and told them he was going to take his business elsewhere. He found someone less . . .' I watched Harvey struggling to put the lid back on things he still resented. His face wasn't good at hiding emotion. In a quieter voice he went on, 'I'd never thought of myself as naïve before. Maybe I am. I'd never met anyone like Peter Thacker.'

I said, 'When did June get involved with it?'

Harvey lowered his face into his hands. 'She already was involved. She knew what was going on. She didn't like it any more than I did.'

'Is this what you were going to leak to the press?'

Slowly Michael Harvey nodded. 'It wasn't just the way Barney Thacker had treated her. That was important as well. We both knew this was bigger.'

'She wanted revenge.'

Harvey frowned. His voice was self-righteous. 'You can call it that if you like, I suppose. I'd say she didn't want to see people getting away with things.'

I sighed. It didn't matter to me how Harvey justified what he did. 'I talked to a journalist about this. He told me no one would print a story like this unless there was proof to back it up. Did you have proof?'

'Some. June had brought me a copy of the collateral contract they'd drawn up before the Sizewell job.'

'Do you have it here?'

His eyes moved towards one corner of the room. 'In the safe.'

'Was that enough?'

'Not by itself. It's in complicated legal language. It would take a lawyer to know what it implied. There was something else as well.' He frowned and made a church out of his fingers. When he was talking business I could hear the lawyer in his voice. It was slower and more measured than the frightened witness I had interviewed the day before. With law he could use the brain which had never failed him, rather than the instincts which had. He must have been a good lawyer. 'Did you hear anything else about Sizewell?'

'Something about an accident.'

Harvey nodded. 'There was a report which showed PTI's mistakes had almost caused a disaster. It was never published at the time. June found a copy of the conclusions in Barney Thacker's file. Just one page.' His hands dropped slowly to his lap. 'She never brought me that. I thought she might have had it when she rang me up that Sunday.'

I looked at him. Michael Harvey took off his spectacles and polished them on a white handkerchief he took from his pocket. He did it methodically, not missing anything. When he put them back on again he had to blink them into position. With one hand he pushed the wave of brown hair back from his forehead.

I said quietly, 'Why wouldn't you tell me about this yesterday?'

'There was no point. June was dead. There didn't seem any point in going on. And in that case it was better . . . if people didn't know. I had to get on with my life.'

On the mantelpiece photographs showed Harvey standing in sunshine by a war memorial, Harvey handing a silver cup to a schoolboy in a red blazer. A photograph of his wife showed her outside the portico of a big stone mansion. That was Harvey's life.

'What would the Thackers have done if they'd found out what June was up to?'

He didn't answer that.

'Do you still think her murder didn't have anything to do with it?'

'I don't know.' Harvey sounded reluctant. 'I've thought about it, of course. I told you that. I've thought about nothing else. I can't believe even . . . even someone like Barney Thacker . . . *Would* he?' His voice wanted me to reassure him.

'It depends. How much damage would it have done – the leak you and June were planning?'

'A lot. The thing is . . .' He sighed and rubbed his fingers into his eyes. 'If we could have exposed the story now it really would have hurt them. Now more than any other time.'

'Why?'

Harvey fiddled with the sleeves of his jumper. 'Have you heard about the privatization of the nuclear power stations? You might not have. It's politics. The first part of the sell-off is being announced next Monday. Sealed bids – they're not selling it on the open market and they don't have to give reasons for who they sell it to. National security.' His voice lifted ironically. 'Covers everything. June found out PTI were putting in a bid.'

'They're a construction company.'

'Doesn't matter what they are. After Sizewell they can claim to be experts in nuclear power stations. Maybe that was why they went into it in the first place. June found that out six months ago. From my end I found out which minister would be responsible for making the decision.'

His voice told me who the minister was. 'Philip Lord?'

He nodded. 'I don't know anything for certain. Maybe someone else will get it. Maybe Philip isn't as close to Peter as he used to be . . .' He spread his hands.

'But you were going to leak your story now anyway? Just in case?'

'People had a right to know.' Harvey sounded indignant. 'If it was true they were hand-in-glove with a politician. If it was true they weren't capable of doing the job safely. It was the only way.'

'Did you try approaching Lord?'

'Me? I'm a new boy. There's a pecking order in that place. If I want to get anywhere . . .' He didn't finish the sentence. His hand plucked at the edge of the sofa.

I said, 'So what about June? Could the Thackers have had her killed?'

'I still don't believe anyone would do that.' He hadn't believed Peter Thacker would break the law for the sake of profit either. Something was troubling him. 'There's something else you ought to know.' He looked up at me. There was an angry flush on his face. 'Sam got a telephone call last night. My daughter. A threat. That was when I suddenly thought . . .' He shook his head. 'Maybe these people *are* capable . . .'

He wasn't looking at me. There was a pause.

I said, 'My girlfriend was followed home last night.'

'Is she all right?' Harvey's face was shocked.

'She's moved out.'

Harvey sighed. 'Sam and Joanna are much braver about this than I am. I don't feel very brave at all. I just think, how's it all going to end?'

'Have you told the police?'

'I didn't want to. You know why.' He was still uncomfortable with that.

I said, 'What would happen if you got hold of the other document you needed? Would you still go to the press?'

'Of course. It's what we planned all along – June and I.'

'Even with the threats?'

'Of course,' he repeated. 'It's a duty.' I wondered which narrow church he'd been taught about duty in. He used the word with a

97

priggish tightening of the lips, as if duty was something no one except Harvey understood. 'If someone doesn't make these things public – where does it end?'

I nodded and stood up. Harvey followed me with his eyes. 'What are you going to do next?'

'Try to find Medd.'

'Is that his name?' Harvey nodded towards the pocket where I had put the photograph. He followed me towards the door. 'I'm glad I've told somebody. It's been weighing on me. I'm not good at secrets.' His face flushed. 'Why can't people just be . . . honest?'

I looked at him: a clever man who'd come far from where he'd started out but who hadn't grown much older along the way. Maybe the journey had been too easy, or maybe where he'd started out from was too narrow. He had charm and brains, and he knew what he wanted: a good job, a wife, a career. Peter Thacker was the first rock he'd stumbled on and he still hadn't recovered his balance.

I said, 'Sarah Rider told me you were using June. She thought June was only doing it because of you.'

'That's unfair.' He blushed easily, like a schoolboy who hated to be teased. 'I know Sarah didn't like me.' After a moment he added, 'June was as serious about this as I was. Am.'

Outside the drawing-room door there were voices: the woman I had met earlier and his daughter's voice.

Harvey called, 'Sam!'

The door opened. Sam Harvey was wearing a demure tweed suit with a long blue coat over it. The coat went well with her eyes. Behind her shoulder I could see Harvey's wife.

'I was just going home.'

'Will you be all right?'

'Of course I will, Daddy.' Her voice carried equal parts of affection and something left over from adolescence. 'Don't fuss.'

'You could spend the night here if you like.'

She rolled her eyes. 'I'll be fine.'

Michael Harvey's hands flapped. 'How will you get home?'

'I'll drive. How do you think?'

'You'll be careful, won't you?'

'Of course I will.'

Harvey said to his wife, 'Perhaps I ought to go with her.'

'I'll be all right.' Sam Harvey didn't look at me. Childhood was too recent for her to let anyone talk about her in the third person.

He looked at me. 'You're not going back to Kennington, are you?' I nodded. 'Sam lives in Battersea. She could give you a lift.'

Sam Harvey's foot tapped angrily on the woodstrip floor.

'It would set my mind at rest, love.'

Sam glanced at me. It was the sort of look her mother would have used to get rid of a tradesman. 'I'll wait for you by the car.'

I heard her footsteps on the hall floor and the sound of her kissing her mother good-bye.

Michael Harvey's face was rueful. 'Anxious father,' he said. 'I'm grateful.'

'Is she scared?' She hadn't looked scared.

'Not as much as I am. She doesn't take it seriously.'

'Have you told her about June?'

He nodded. His handshake was warmer than it had been when I came in. Joanna Harvey said good-bye with a tired smile that made it look as if the visit had exhausted her.

Sam Harvey was waiting for me on the pavement.

15

Her car was a new navy blue Golf that flashed orange lights at us as we approached.

Sam paused irresolutely by the driver's side door. 'You don't have to do this, you know.'

'I know.'

She scowled. 'It's embarrassing. I can look after myself.' She hadn't reached the age where she'd start to realize there were things she couldn't do for herself.

'I'm sure you can.'

'Anyway, don't you have work to go to?'

I said, 'This is work.'

Sam grimaced. She squeezed the car out of the parking space and set off down the road faster than a girl in that kind of tweed suit ought to drive.

I said, 'You can put on your glasses if you like. I won't look.' I pointed at the pair of glasses sitting on the front shelf.

'They're for reading.' Sam was blushing. She stopped too abruptly at some traffic lights. 'Do policemen always notice things like that?'

'Sometimes.'

Sam pulled out into oncoming traffic and accelerated past an old man in a Rover. A taxi driver coming the other way lifted one hand off his wheel in a gesture of protest. We paused at the turn into High Street Kensington.

'Daddy worries too much. He thinks I'm a child still.'

'It's not surprising he's worried.'

'It's not as if I'm in any danger.' Danger was something that happened to people older than herself, or poorer.

'You could be.'

'Anyone can make phone calls, can't they? They're hardly going to do anything here in the middle of the afternoon.' Sam scowled. She had a very long neck and neat white ears. Her black hair was cut just above the ears. 'What are you looking at?'

I said, 'You're indicating.'

She frowned and touched a lever. The indicator stopped winking. We were driving past Kensington Gardens. Children were playing on the grass with bored nannies watching them.

'What did your father tell you about June Donaghy?'

'He said someone killed her.'

'Did he say why?'

'He said nobody knew. That's right isn't it?'

'Nobody's sure,' I said. 'What happened when you got the phone call last night?'

'Oh . . .' She lifted one hand off the wheel. 'It was just a man. Making threats.' Her mouth was set in a determined line.

'You didn't let it bother you?'

'Why should I? Why should they stop me . . . ?' She'd been about to say enjoying herself.

The end of the rush hour was jamming the junction by the Conran Shop. Sam Harvey stuck her head out of the window to see red lights, then leaned on the horn anyway. It was probably for my benefit. At the King's Road she turned right among young bloods showing off their cars in the last of the daylight.

I said, 'Did you ever meet June?'

'No. Why should I?'

'I thought she might have come to the house.'

'She might have done. I'm not there often.'

'Too busy?'

She tilted her head in a gesture that might have meant yes, or no, or just that she didn't want to tell me what she did with her days.

'Has your father told you what this is about?'

'Some of it. I didn't really understand.' She rolled her eyes. 'Politics.'

The river flashed silver on either side. We turned left at the end of Battersea Park.

'Where shall I drop you?'

'I'll see you home first.'

She nearly bit my head off for that, but managed to restrain herself. She looked over her shoulder to park, her lower lip caught between small white teeth. 'I think Daddy'd be happier if I went into solitary confinement for a week.' She switched off the engine and looked at me. There were small flecks of hazel around the pupils of her blue eyes. 'You'd better see me up. There might be monsters on the stairs.'

The front door Sam Harvey led me to was the kind of door you'd expect a rich man's daughter to live behind. The hallway smelled of furniture polish; the carpet was thick enough to lose your shoes in. Someone had put an antique table on each landing, as if it was a private house. The brass numbers on the doors were polished.

'I'm on the top floor. I hope you're fit.' Through the stair windows I could see the trees of Battersea Park. 'You look fit.'

Sam fumbled with a key. When she opened the door an alarm shrilled; she pressed buttons. 'Come on, then.'

I followed her into a long, light room with windows down one side and white muslin curtains floating over the windows. The floor was made of some pale wood. On it floated newspapers, a low table, some coloured beanbags. There was no other furniture. The effect was partly Japanese and partly modern chic. Low shelves down the side walls carried books and a miniature hi-fi.

I said, 'It's a nice place.'

'I know.'

'When did you move out of home?'

'Daddy bought me the flat last year.'

'Did Daddy buy you the car as well?'

She glanced at me. 'Why shouldn't he? He's rich. He wants to make me happy.'

'I thought it was Mummy who was rich.'

'I don't think that's any of your business, is it?'

She disappeared into a door at the end of the room. From beyond it her voice floated back to me. 'Make yourself at home.'

I put down my coat and looked around the room, wondering

whether I was really thinking about security, or just didn't want to go back to an empty flat without Mary in it. At the back of the living room was an open-plan kitchen full of white tiles and stainless steel gadgets which didn't look as if they got much use. A cappuccino machine stood on the counter. The whole place was tidy except for an ashtray sitting next to one of the beanbags.

Sam Harvey came back into the room. There was no sign of the blue coat or the sensible tweed suit dress. She was wearing black leggings and a big white shirt open at the neck. Her feet were bare.

She said, 'No monsters.'

She went over to the shelves and touched buttons on the hi-fi. She seemed to be expecting me to stay. I didn't mind that, if it meant that she was more frightened than she looked – and if it meant that I didn't have to go home.

The room filled with jazz music, something cool from the fifties which I couldn't put a name to.

'Do you listen to a lot of this?'

She adjusted the volume. 'Why?'

'I was expecting something else.'

'Like?

'Mozart.'

'I didn't say you could tease me.'

'I didn't ask.' I nodded at the ashtray. 'Does Daddy know about this?'

Sam frowned irritably. 'If I'd known you were going to be like this, I wouldn't have asked you to come.'

'You didn't.'

'All right, Daddy did. But I could have stopped you if I'd wanted.'

'Does Daddy do everything you want?'

'Most things.'

'What does he think of this?' I meant the music and the ashtray.

'He thinks I'm old enough to make up my own mind.'

I said, 'Whatever gave him that idea?'

Sam scowled. Scowling didn't make her look any worse. 'I need a drink.'

She went into the kitchen; I heard the clink of glasses. When she came back she was carrying two small tumblers frosted with ice. She held one out to me.

'I'm on duty,' I said.

Sam threw her head back and laughed. It was the sort of laugh I hadn't heard for a long time. Suddenly I felt old: too old to be standing in a room with beanbags in it and muslin curtains floating over the windows.

'I didn't think policemen really said things like that.'

'They try not to. Sometimes it just slips out.'

'Go on.' She held out the glass. Her blue eyes were challenging.

I took the glass and tasted vodka.

Sam went on, 'Do you ever say, "I was proceeding in a westerly direction?" '

'Point taken.'

Sam sprawled in the beanbag next to the ashtray. I lowered myself into another, trying my best to keep looking like I was a policeman and she was the daughter of a witness, and to do all that without spilling iced vodka on myself. I didn't do it well; it wasn't something I'd ever practised.

'What time did you get the phone call last night?'

'Oh . . .' She made a face. 'That thing of Daddy's.'

'You don't believe in the thing of Daddy's?'

'I don't want to talk about it.' She shrugged. 'People don't do things like that. Not in real life.'

'So why did you let me take you home?'

'You didn't take me home.'

'See you home.'

She sipped from the iced glass. A small pink tongue like a cat's showed for a moment between her lips. 'To keep Daddy happy.' She said it seriously.

'What else do you do to keep him happy?'

'Anything he wants, within reason. I owe him a lot.' Something was troubling her. The trouble drew a small blue crease between her eyebrows. 'Is Daddy going to be all right?'

'I hope so.'

She looked at me frankly. 'Thank you.'

'What for?'

'For not saying, "Of course he will." Every time I try to ask Daddy about it he says, "Of course I will." Mummy's the same. I can tell they're both worried. Daddy in particular. He won't tell me what it's about.'

'I don't know anything about the politics.'

'Politics.' She made the same face she had used in the car.

'Aren't you interested?'

'It's so dirty. I wish Daddy hadn't gone into it. It was fun to start with.'

'When was he elected?'

'Three years ago. He fought another seat before that. Somewhere in Scotland. I had to go up and talk to lots of fishermen. And wear a short skirt. It didn't do him any good.'

'What did you mean when you said it was dirty?'

'Oh . . .' The small crease had appeared again on her forehead. 'Just the way they all behave. Do you know what they did? Daddy was going to be made a whip, or something – after Christmas. That man stopped him. The one he hates – Philip Lord. Don't you think that's dirty?' She asked the question as if she wanted my opinion on it, but didn't give me time to say anything. 'And all the people he has to have to dinner. There was one last week who got drunk and kept trying to touch me. Daddy was furious.' She put down her glass so she could laugh properly. 'He was going to write a letter. Daddy's very stern about things like that. It was his upbringing.'

'What was his upbringing?'

'He was brought up a Methodist.' She leaned forward, stretching out her legs. 'He's still very religious, although he doesn't talk about it much. He wasn't born rich, you know. He had to make his own way . . .' She broke off suddenly. 'Of course, you know all about our family already.'

'What about your mother?'

'Stop it. I don't want to talk about them any more.'

'What do you want to talk about?'

'I don't know.' She yawned.

I said, 'Do you have a boyfriend?'

'That's a bit nosey.'

'I was thinking about safety. Are you going to be alone here tonight?'

'Because of the monsters?' She looked away. I thought she might have been blushing. 'Not at the moment. They come and go, don't they?'

'Do they?'

She said, 'Does that shock you?'

'Was it meant to?'

Sam scrambled to her feet. 'You're quite rude, aren't you?'

She came towards me holding the bottle. The ice was melting from its neck. When she leaned over, her shirt hung open and for a moment I saw something soft and white inside. That was probably what I was supposed to see.

I put my hand over the glass. 'I'm on duty.'

'You could have fooled me.'

Close to, her skin was finely freckled. The hand holding the bottle wore a single silver ring on the little finger.

She went back to her beanbag and pulled the shirt down over her knees. For a moment there was silence. I'd remembered what the music was now: a Charlie Mingus track cut in 1958. We had the same album at home. I remembered buying it with Mary in Pie's record shop in the Portobello Road. It had played over and over while we moved into our flat together – the first time we moved in together, when all that mattered seemed to be records and afternoons in the Portobello Road.

Sam was listening to the music as well. 'Do you like this?' She wrinkled up her nose. 'I don't suppose policeman like jazz. They probably like . . .' She was teasing me again. 'Brass bands.'

'Where did you find it?

'Mike. An old boyfriend. At least he was good for something. He was a DJ.'

'I like it,' I said.

'Eddie Mingus. Mike thought he was a genius.'

'Mike wasn't the only one,' I said. 'Only most people called him Charlie.'

Sam flushed. 'I'm not sure I do like you after all. I thought I was going to.'

'You don't have to.'

'Have you got a girlfriend?' She was sitting up, her neck very straight.

I drained my glass and put it down. 'Bad subject.' I started to stand up.

'That means you have. I can tell. You're probably married.'

I said, 'Are you going out this evening?'

'No.' She made a face. 'I was stood up. You don't have to go yet, you know. Have you been a policeman for long? You don't look like a policeman. You're too young.'

'Ten years. I haven't been a policeman for all of it.'

'What did you do instead?'

I didn't want to talk about the instead. It was waiting for me at home, in a silent flat without Mary in it.

'Have it your own way.' She scrambled to her feet and followed me to the door.

'Will you be all right?'

'Of course I will. I would have stayed with Daddy if I'd been frightened.'

'Make sure you lock the door.'

'I can look after myself.' She scowled at me.

'Thanks for the vodka,' I said.

It was late by the time I got back to the flat. I'd been drinking too much vodka and listening to too many jazz records and talking about them to someone who was too young, and who wasn't Mary.

The flat seemed empty. There was a heavy stillness in the air, as if no one had lived there for years. I wandered into the kitchen, put on the kettle, watched it boil, then watched it cool down again. I wandered back into the living room. The flat didn't know me any more. I felt as if I was an intruder there, as if I'd broken in through the front door and was treading on someone else's carpet, breathing someone else's air. Now I knew what it felt like to be a burglar. This was Mary's flat but Mary didn't live here any more.

I sat down on the sofa gingerly, the way you'd sit on somebody else's sofa. I put on music but couldn't concentrate on it. Miles's horn jeered at me from the speakers. I tried to listen to it and found myself hearing only noise. The melodies were jumbles of notes; the harmonies shrilled painfully against each other. I might as well have been listening to a road drill. I kept trying for five minutes then went across the room and turned the music off. Silence was a relief for five minutes, then I started hating the silence.

I found myself thinking of the photograph Jimmy Bolan had picked out for us. A hard face without any pity in it: a face that wanted the camera to be scared. I pictured that face holding a telephone, eyes narrowed, spitting threats into it. I wandered over to the window. Outside Don was scanning the pavement for late trade. I watched him reluctantly fold up his sandwich board and carry it back inside.

I went back to the hi-fi and put on the Mingus track Sam Harvey had been playing. The opening notes took me back to our old flat – the way it was when we'd just found it and were proud of it, before things went wrong and Mary moved out. I remembered the house-warming party we'd had, with friends spilling out into the garden and Mingus blaring from speakers Pie had lent us. I remembered it the way it was at the end, too, with Mary's suitcases in the hall and a darker patch on the carpet where her table had stood. The same table was sitting under the hi-fi now. I shivered. It had taken weeks to divide up our possessions – longer than it should have done because neither of us knew how to speak to each other any more. Two stacks of records had grown on the carpet, two piles of books, a litter of odd glasses in the no-man's land between them.

I made myself stand up. I didn't want to start thinking about that – or about what happened later, after I left the police. I went over to the phone and dialled Ralph's number.

'Hello?' My brother's voice was formal – the voice he used for patients. 'Oh, it's you.' I could hear him relax. 'How are things?'

I told him part of what had happened. Ralph listened, said the right things but no more than the right things. The phone made him sound a long way away.

'Take care of yourself.' It was easy for him to say. After I had hung up I wandered into the bedroom and looked at the empty side of the bed where Mary wasn't going to sleep that night. When we were children I'd been able to tell Ralph everything. We'd divided troubles and halved them that way, but troubles in those days had seemed easier to divide. When our father was killed we'd locked ourselves away from the world for almost a year, hardly speaking to anyone except each other. The closeness of that time had stayed with us for years. It had bound us together as we grew up, discovered jazz records together, talked about the future together. For years I'd been able to think of Ralph when I was alone, and no longer feel alone. It didn't feel like that tonight.

I went back to the living room and changed the record. Louis Armstrong told me that it was a wonderful world. I didn't believe him. I thought of June Donaghy's body lying white on black mud churned up by policemen's feet. I thought of Sarah Rider, and of Mrs Donaghy sitting alone in a house full of photographs.

I wondered how many more evenings there were going to be like this one.

It was half past midnight when the phone rang.

'I hope you weren't asleep, sir.' Baring's voice.

I let out my breath. I had been expecting something else. 'No.'

'Can you get down here, sir?' There was something tense in the way he said it.

'Where are you?' Suddenly I was gripping the telephone too hard.

'I'm in Pimlico.' He said an address.

'What's happened?'

'It's the sister, sir.' Baring's voice was oddly soft. 'Sarah Rider. She's been murdered.'

16

The address Baring had given me was a row of unpainted houses
backing on to the tracks near Victoria Station. Under revolving
blue light I could see stucco peeling from the walls. On the
porches down the street small knots of people had gathered. They
stared at us, not asking any questions but not going away either.
Most of the faces looked foreign: recent migrants clinging to the
ragged edge of Britain only a hundred yards from where the train
had dropped them. The doorway a policeman pointed to had too
many bells screwed to the wall next to it. Inside, the hall had been
narrowed down to a corridor by a plasterboard partition. Someone
had started painting the walls red from one end and given up
halfway along.

I followed a trail of policemen up to the second floor. The scene
of crime was the doorway with unnatural white light flooding back
down the stairs – the sort of glare most people don't choose to
shine on their own lives. From the floor above I could hear hushed
foreign voices. Stale gas clung to the air, along with the smell of
too many people living in too small a space with the doors and
windows shut to keep out cold, fear and the visits of policemen.

Baring's red, square face was staring impassively into the room
the lights were in. In thirty years he'd seen a lot of rooms like this.
Maybe they didn't do anything to him any more, or maybe he was
just pretending, like the rest of us.

He nodded to me and made space for me at the door. Sarah
Rider lay on a shabby rug staring up at the ceiling. She was giving
the ceiling a cool, appraising look, as if death had finally managed
to cover her unruly emotions for good. A cheap wooden armchair
had skittered back from where she lay, turning back one corner of

the rug. There wasn't much else in the room: a music centre with wires trailing to speakers on the carpet, a bookshelf with records on it instead of books. Blood seemed to cover most of it; but when I looked away after a moment blood seemed to be covering everything else as well: the policeman on the door, the stair window through which I could see railway tracks. I looked back again. The blood came from Sarah Rider's head. It had dyed the blonde hair red on one side only, as if to prove that at least one of the colours was fake. From there it had soaked into the rug, darkened the floor, painted a crimson rainbow over the lower part of the wall. The shoulder of her white knitted top was ruined; Sarah didn't look as if that bothered her. She didn't look as if anything bothered her any more.

I said, 'Whose place is this?'

'Her husband's, sir. Jackie Rider. The neighbours told us.'

Jackie Rider, the junkie Sarah had married to annoy her mother. She had worried that she was too hard on him. She had watched him go downhill and hadn't wanted to go downhill with him. Now she was lying dead on his carpet. It hadn't been much of a marriage. I could hear Sarah's hard, self-mocking voice again: 'When do I get my share?'

'Is he here?'

Baring shook his head. 'No one's seen him, sir.'

I had seen him – in a photograph taken before things started to go downhill, when the future seemed to hold more than drugs and the contempt of his wife. I wondered what he looked like now.

'Who found the body?'

'Neighbours called us. They heard a fight.'

'Was that unusual?'

'Must have been. They wouldn't have called otherwise.' Baring sounded apologetic. 'They don't speak much English, sir. Asian officer with them now. We got him from Victoria.'

'Do they know who she was fighting with?'

Baring looked surprised. 'Must have been the husband.'

'Did they see anyone?'

'Stayed indoors. They called from the pay phone on the top landing.'

I looked at Sarah's amused face. Since I'd been there the amusement had started to fade from it, as if she was beginning to wonder how long this joke was going to go on.

'What time was this?'

'Half past nine? We can check with Victoria. They sent the Asian chap along to sort it out.' Baring shrugged. 'Knocked on the door. No answer. Time they found the body, figured out it was June Donaghy's sister and called us, it was as good as midnight.'

'How was she killed?'

'Back of her head stove in. Doctor had been and gone by the time I got here. He thinks it might have been an accident. I mean . . .' Baring shrugged. 'If you kill someone in a fight you don't hit the back of their head, do you? They're looking at you. Unless she turned away, he hit her. Must have taken the weapon away with him, though. There's nothing in the flat would do that.' His head indicated Sarah Rider's body.

'Is anyone searching the tracks?' It was the obvious place to get rid of a murder weapon.

'Blokes down there now.'

I went closer to Sarah Rider's body. From close to, the corners of her mouth were turned down, as if she was tired of holding the face and wanted a chance to rest. The police lights brought out the wrinkles around her eyes and mouth. She looked ten years older. I was sorry about that. If she'd known she was going to have policemen staring at her and photographers pointing cameras into her face, she would have made up more carefully – made her eyes bolder and her cheeks smooth. Given a bit of warning, she would have carried it off well. I saw she had used pencil to make her eyes look larger than they were. I had noticed that when I talked to her the day before.

There were footsteps outside and a slim Indian policeman came into the room. He tried hard to keep his eyes off what was lying on the rug. His voice was soft, more London than India. 'Sir?'

'Have you finished with the neighbours?'

'They couldn't tell me much, sir. They heard an argument.' He shrugged. 'That was all.'

'It must have been quite an argument to make them call the police.'

He nodded, his face serious.

'Did arguments happen often?'

'They said the flat wasn't used much. They knew Mr Rider a little. They only knew . . .' His head moved towards on the woman on the carpet. 'They only knew his wife by sight.'

'His ex-wife. Did she come here often?'

'Hardly at all.'

'Did they see Jackie Rider today?'

'They didn't see anybody. They just heard shouting.'

I nodded. 'What time?'

'Just before they called us. It went on for a long time. That was why they called up.'

I could picture them standing on the upstairs landing, listening to the angry foreign voices downstairs, then hearing blows, trying to calculate which would get them into less trouble: to call the police, or to go back indoors and turn the television up loud.

'Have you taken statements?'

'Yes, sir.'

'What about the other occupants? Did anyone downstairs see anything?'

Baring answered. 'Flat below's empty. Empty this evening, at any rate. Below that there are some Spanish students. Didn't notice anything; they had the telly on. Man next door says he thinks he saw a man with a knife running away down the street.' Baring's mouth was curled. 'He'd just been watching *Inspector Morse*. Said, he thinks it was a knife but it might have been a gun. He wants us to take him to the station and record his evidence. He says on *Cracker* they always record witnesses.'

I left Sarah Rider's body to the photographers and the men with tape measures and finger-print powder. It was probably a long time since she'd had so many people fussing over her but she didn't seem to be enjoying it. The flat only had two rooms: the living room where Sarah Rider had died, and a room at the back with a single bed in it and a window looking out over railway tracks.

113

From the window I could see passengers waiting on the ends of platforms. They looked cold, and wherever they were going looked a long way away. The tracks curved emptily out of sight to my left.

An instrument case under the bed had a saxophone case in it, a rag to polish the saxophone and a small black box without any reeds in it. Jackie Rider didn't seem to have any other possessions that mattered. A pair of jeans lay crumpled on the floor in the corner; some dirty underwear were the only clothes in a chest of drawers that had come with the flat. In the bathroom a constant drip from the shower had stained the tiles a rusty brown. The shower kept dripping behind me as I searched a medicine cabinet with aspirin in it, a half-used roll of Elastoplast and some mouthwash. It didn't look as if there was anywhere for Jackie Rider to cook. As I went back into the living room a train made the windows rattle.

Baring was running his hands along the shelves of records. I watched him pull out the sleeves and lay them aside. Some of them were familiar from my own shelves at home: John Coltrane, Hank Mobley, Wynton Marsalis. He picked up a small yellow business card.

'This might mean something, sir.'

He handed the card to me. It had the name of a recording studio on it and a bad drawing of a keyboard. I slipped the card into my pocket.

'Has anyone told her mother yet?'

Baring sat back on his haunches. 'Sent a man round as soon as I got here, sir.' His face was even redder than usual. 'I spoke to him half an hour ago. Old lady said she wasn't surprised. Said this one deserved to be where she is.' His eyebrows flicked up. 'Two daughters in a week. It must have done something to her.'

I joined him searching the empty rooms where Jackie Rider lived whatever life heroin had left him. We didn't find anything else. By the time the ambulance men came, Sarah Rider's face had stiffened and no longer looked detached, as if she had suddenly understood what had happened to her. The trains began to rumble past the block more frequently. The first commuters were coming in to Victoria, spreading out to offices all over the city. We moved carefully around one corner of the rug, as if Sarah Rider was still lying there. By the time we left the flat, it was dawn.

17

The address on the yellow card matched an unmarked door in the middle of a row of shops around the corner from Jackie Rider's place. I stopped on the way for a coffee, and telephoned Michael Harvey to tell him what had happened. Joanna Harvey told me he had left for work early. His office machine invited me to leave a message after the beep so I called Joanna back and told her the news instead. It wasn't the sort of message the machine wanted to hear.

I leaned on a doorbell which had another of the recording studio's cards taped next to it and stared back at the drivers waiting outside the minicab company next door. The name above the badly-drawn keyboard was Jerry Morris. The bell sounded as if it was tired of ringing so I took my thumb off it and knocked on the door instead. The minicab drivers looked at each other as if they had bets on whether anyone would answer.

After five minutes of knocking I heard a crash inside the house. It sounded as if an animal had got loose on the staircase. Chains rattled, then the door banged open and a man peered out at me. He was a big black man wearing a skull cap, a dressing-gown that didn't meet around the middle and nothing else. That didn't seem to bother him. He was more worried by the daylight. It didn't look as if he was used to daylight. He screwed up his eyes at it, then put up one hand and squinted at me under the hand. His eyes were still heavy with sleep.

'What do you want?'

I said, 'Are you Jerry Morris?'

'Uh-huh.'

'I want to ask you some questions.'

I showed him a badge. It took time for its meaning to fight its way through the layers of sleep. He couldn't think of a reason why I shouldn't ask him questions. He grunted something and backed off down the corridor. He seemed happier away from the daylight. For a moment he stood swaying in the corridor and blinked. I shut the door behind me to save his eyes from the light.

The corridor was a mess of instrument cases, mike stands and something that might once have been a drum kit. On the right a staircase climbed a wall covered with posters of jazz singers.

'You better come through.' Jerry Morris spoke through a thick layer of gravel. I knew the voice. It was the way people spoke after smoking too many cigarettes, and sitting in too many jazz clubs, and talking to too many other people who already sounded like that. At Ronnie Scott's you could find whole tables of old men growling at each other like mangy yard dogs. It was the way you started to sound when your vocal chords throbbed with nicotine and half-forgotten rhythms and whatever it was old jazzmen drank. One day most of Mary's friends would sound like that.

Jerry Morris turned and lumbered down the corridor. I followed him through a sound-proofed door into a big room with a dismantled piano that had mike stands pecking at its entrails like hungry birds. The rest of the room had chairs in no order, more microphones and a double bass lying on its side. The walls were roughly tacked with yellow insulation board. Across the far end was a home-made glass partition screening a recording console.

Jerry led me through a door in the glass partition. Behind it, shelves and worktop had been knocked up in chipboard by somebody who wasn't a carpenter. Wires trailed from the back of the console. In the corner an old fridge was trying to cool down Pimlico through a gap in the door.

Jerry slumped into the chair behind the desk and looked at me. He was as ready for questions as he was ever going to be.

I said, 'Do you know a man called Jackie Rider?'

Suspicion started to fight its way through the layers of sleep on Jerry Morris's face. 'Why?'

'We found one of your cards in his place.'

His head moved, acknowledging that. 'I know him.'

'How well?'

He scratched his ear before answering. Scratching his ear seemed to help him think. 'I know him OK. Why?'

'How do you know him?'

Jerry Morris's eyes narrowed. 'He works here sometimes. When I need help. He used to play.'

'What does he do?'

'He just helps out.' He shrugged. 'Whatever there is to do.'

'Does he play sessions?'

'Nah.' Jerry Morris made a face. 'He don't play no more.' His eyes searched my face. 'Is Jackie in trouble?'

I didn't want him to know what sort of trouble Jackie might be in. 'Why doesn't he play any more?'

'He gave up.'

'Because of the drugs?'

Jerry Morris's face hardened. 'He gave up,' he repeated. He put his fingers down on the edge of the console and looked at them. The nails of the left hand were bitten off short, half buried in leathery pads of flesh, a guitarist's fingers.

I said, 'When did you last see Jackie?'

'Don't know.' He didn't know anything that might help a policeman cause trouble to a friend.

'You want time to think about it?'

Jerry Morris looked at me. 'I want to know what this is about.'

'Will that make a difference to when you last saw him?'

Jerry moved in his chair and twitched the dressing-gown across his thighs. He said again, 'I don't know.'

I perched on the edge of the recording desk. Through the glass screen the ghosts of musicians played ghost tunes to the yellow insulation board.

'How bad was Jackie's habit?' I asked.

Jerry Morris looked at me and thought. 'Pretty bad,' he said at last.

'Heroin?'

'And stuff.'

'Did he touch crack?'

'I don't know what he touched. He just worked here.'

'How often?'

'When I needed him.'

'When was the last time he worked here?'

Jerry peered at his fingernails. 'I want to know what this is about.'

I sighed. 'Last night his wife was killed in Jackie's flat. Murdered. Did you ever meet her?'

Jerry didn't answer. His head was still too thick with sleep for anything to startle him, but I watched his eyes fill up with shock, then spread it slowly across his face.

'You're saying Jackie did that?'

'What do you think?'

'No way.' Jerry banged his palm down on the recording desk. 'No *way*.'

'Why not?'

'Jackie wouldn't do . . .' He shook his head. 'Nothing like that. He wasn't like that.'

'What was he like when he was on drugs?'

'Uh-uh.' Jerry shook his head. 'Stuff makes some people mean. Not Jackie. It just made him go sad.' Jackie Rider had had plenty to be sad about.

'When did you last see him?'

Jerry's eyes narrowed. It didn't hide the shock in them. 'Last night,' he said.

'Where?'

'Here. He was working.'

I looked at him. 'Are you saying that to protect him?'

'I'm saying it 'cause it's true.'

'Was he here all night?'

His jaw shifted. 'Most of it.'

'What kind of state was he in?'

Jerry shrugged. 'He was OK.' He didn't look me in the eye.

'Who did you have in here last night?'

'French guy. He was pretty good.'

I said quietly, 'I can find out from him what state Jackie was in. Why don't you tell me yourself?'

Jerry spread his fingers on the recording console. He looked at them. He said, 'OK.' That was all he said. It was a moment before he looked up at me.

'Was he bad?'

Jerry's head moved; his forehead wrinkled. 'He wouldn't have hurt Sarah. He loved that girl. He was scared of her.'

'Why scared?'

'Wanted her to take him back.' Again he frowned, maybe realizing that he wasn't doing his friend any good. 'Doesn't mean he'd have killed her. He loved her. Kept saying, any time he shook off the habit, she'd take him back. That's what he dreamed about.'

People had killed people despite their dreams before now. Jackie Rider wouldn't have been the first.

'What time did he leave here?' I asked.

'I don't want to talk any more.' Jerry pushed the console away from him. I watched him walk over to the fridge and stoop for a carton of milk. He drank straight from the carton, dribbling white liquid down his chin. He breathed deep and looked at me. 'Can't make me.'

'I don't need to. I can find out from the other people who were here.' He put the milk back in the fridge. I said, 'Maybe it would help him if you talked. Depends what you say.'

'Maybe it would put him in jail.'

'Only if he killed Sarah.'

Jerry looked over his shoulder at me. 'Sure.'

'How bad was Jackie last night?'

Jerry stood up and punched air, as if it was the empty air that was troubling him. 'He was pretty bad.' His voice was angry.

'So bad that you had to send him away?'

He stopped punching and nodded unhappily. 'French guy made me.'

'What time was that?'

'I don't know. Listen . . .'

'How soon after the session started?'

'I don't know . . . maybe . . . Might have laid down one track.'

'An hour?'

'Maybe.'

'What time did you start?'

Jerry punched the air again, more viciously. 'Eight, not long after. French guy was on time.' He turned his back on the air he'd just been punching. 'Jackie didn't do this, man. If you knew him . . .'

'I don't know him.'

'So listen to me . . .' Jerry came towards me fast. There was still a sheen of milk on his chin. 'I know the guy. I *know* him.' He shook his head. 'He wouldn't hurt anyone.'

I looked into his dark, troubled eyes. His fingers were playing angry chords on the rough chipboard. 'Do you know where Jackie is now?'

'No way.' He had retreated into the sullen silence from which he had started out.

'Where does he hang out? Does he have friends?'

'Don't know.' His bottom lip jutted out. He didn't know anything any more, at least not for a policeman to whom he'd already told too much.

I nodded at the console. 'What kind of stuff do you record here?'

'Jazz. Mostly.'

Jerry reached forward and hit a button on the console. Speakers hummed then filled the room with the sound of a trumpet. It started from low and climbed up to a pure, high note which dissolved in vibrato. A piano came in; a bass tramped steadily up the fingerboard. Jerry touched more knobs and drums whispered in the background. The trumpet climbed the same scale, dropped, feathered off into silence.

Jerry said, 'French guy. He was pretty good.'

'"Stardust",' I said.

Jerry acknowledged it with a movement of his head. He touched more switches, bringing in saxes, more bass on the piano.

I left him playing with the mix.

18

A phone call to the station put a call out on Jackie Rider. His photograph had been picked up from the flat where Sarah Rider had been staying. Nothing had yet been found of Medd. Baring told me that Mason had been half an hour in the incident room and spent most of it wondering out loud why I wasn't there myself. I was surprised it had taken him that long to realize I was avoiding him.

I looked through the dirty glass of the call box. Nothing in Pimlico told me who had killed Sarah Rider, or why. An old lady was pushing her zimmer frame slowly towards me, taking one paving stone at a time the way sensible people did all through their lives. Behind her a man was hanging over the railings of the Churchill Gardens flats. He looked as if he was searching for answers as well. Unlike me, he had all the time in the world to find them.

A Victoria line tube took me across town and dropped me in Bloomsbury. At the reception desk of PTI Holdings I asked for Barney Thacker and watched the same receptionist talk into the phone. She didn't seem to recognize me, but maybe she wasn't programmed to recognize people. Her smile stopped six inches short of my face, so as not to get dirty for the next visitor.

'He's in a meeting at the moment.'

'I'll wait.'

She told the phone that I'd wait, then told me that his secretary would be along in a minute. I spent the minute looking at the charts of PTI's profits and wondering whether they started again when the black line hit the picture frame, or whether they just bought a bigger frame. I tried not to think about what Mason would say if he knew where I was now.

'Chief Inspector Havilland?'

I turned round. The male secretary I had seen two days before was smiling at me from behind the desk. He had the corner of a white handkerchief protruding from the breast pocket of an old-fashioned suit. His tie-pin was an exact copy of the one Peter Thacker wore.

I said, 'I want to talk to Barney Thacker.'

'He's in a meeting with his brother. Would you like to come this way?'

He led me up the same stairs as before and along the gallery to the same conference room. Through the glass roof I could see grey clouds hanging over Bloomsbury. The two brothers didn't seem to have moved since I first met them. Barney Thacker didn't even look up as I came through the door; Peter Thacker stood up with a smile and a little formal bow that came out of another century.

I wondered if Barney Thacker was ever allowed to go into meetings by himself.

'Chief Inspector.' I shook Peter Thacker's soft hand. The secretary retreated to the far corner of the room. 'Have you made any progress in the murder investigation?' He sounded as if he was asking after a distant cousin.

I reached into my pocket and took out the photograph I had shown Harvey the day before. Peter Thacker's brows contracted as he looked at Medd's hard face. 'Someone I'm supposed to know?'

'His name's Medd. He killed June Donaghy on Sunday night. Do you recognize him?'

Peter Thacker's frown deepened. '*Should* I recognize him?'

'I don't know.'

Peter Thacker handed the photograph to his brother. 'Barney?'

Barney Thacker didn't take the picture. He leaned forward in his chair and glanced at it from two feet away. 'Don't know him from Adam.'

'We don't seem to be able to help you, Chief Inspector. Did you expect either of us to recognize this man?' He shrugged. 'I suppose you're only doing your job.'

Barney Thacker shifted in his chair, thrusting his hips forward.

He said, 'Doing his fucking job.' He gave a short bark of laughter.

'Is this man suspected of the murder?'

'Two murders,' I said. 'June Donaghy's sister was killed last night.'

It took a moment for Peter Thacker to react to that. He reached up long brown fingers and massaged his forehead into a frown. 'That's terrible news, Chief Inspector. *Terrible.* Is it thought to be connected?'

'What do you think?'

'I never met Miss Donaghy's sister.'

'Her husband was a drug addict. Sarah Rider's body was found in his flat. Some people think he must have killed her. Other people think that's too much of a coincidence.'

'It is shocking . . .' He stopped. He'd been about to say something about luck. Instead he said, 'How do you know it was this man who killed Miss Donaghy?'

'He was seen killing her. We've got a witness.'

'The man who telephoned?'

I nodded. 'Maybe it's someone you know. His name's Michael Harvey.'

If Peter Thacker was surprised he made a good job of hiding it. He pursed his lips and nodded slowly. From beside him I heard a chair scraping. Barney Thacker's red fist hit the table. 'Harvey's a fucking liar,' he said. His voice was thick.

'You know him?'

'Know Michael Harvey?' Barney Thacker's voice jeered at me. 'I could write a fucking book about Michael Harvey.'

I said, 'What would the book say about Sizewell?'

The silence lasted long enough for me to hear traffic in the street outside, a faint murmur of voices from the office next door. Peter Thacker's face changed slowly; the ghosts of dimples appeared in his cheeks; it took me time to realize he was smiling.

He sat back in his chair. 'Michael is a very charming man.' He leaned towards me. 'A very *plausible* man. You wouldn't be the first person to be taken in by him. We were taken in ourselves.' He raised one hand. 'I suppose it *was* Michael who told you about Sizewell?'

'He isn't the only one.'

'He may not be.' Peter Thacker turned his hand over and looked at his brown wrist. 'But you'd probably find that most stories could be traced back to Michael in the end. What exactly did he tell you?'

'He told me how you got the contract and what happened when things started to go wrong. June Donaghy knew about that as well. That's why they were meeting on Sunday night.'

Peter Thacker nodded. 'There could have been other reasons why they were meeting.' He glanced at his brother. 'I assume Michael told you the usual story. We bribed Philip Lord . . . and so on. None of these rumours are new.'

I said quietly, 'What's new is they had evidence to prove them.'

Again the ghosts of dimples appeared in Peter Thacker's cheeks. 'Have you *seen* this evidence, Chief Inspector?'

'I know where it is.'

'You mean Michael Harvey told you where it is.'

'Harvey's a fucking liar.' Barney Thacker's voice had dropped to a low rumble like the growling of a dog.

'Michael probably gave you a reason why he left the City as well. Did he tell you about that? The usual story is that he was too honest to do our dirty work. That it was a *moral* decision.' He made moral sound like a disease. 'There are two sides to everything, you know. You might be interested to learn what really happened.'

'What did happen?'

Peter Thacker sighed. 'Michael worked for Robarts Meade. He was the brightest lawyer I'd ever met. Very smart, very ambitious. When they made him a partner we asked if some of our work could be given to him. We believe in giving people opportunities – I think I told you that before. When Michael took over our work we'd just won the Sizewell contract.' His brows contracted. 'Won it in open competition, incidentally. There was nothing unusual about it. Michael was in charge of putting together all the contracts. It was complicated. There were a lot of people involved.' He spread his fingers on the polished surface of the table. 'What happened is simple. Michael made a mistake. A bad one. It nearly cost us a lot of money – it could easily have ruined us. Fortunately Barney spotted it in time.' He shrugged. 'You could say it was our fault for trusting such an inexperienced man. All the same, a lawyer has responsibilities. We didn't make a big fuss about it. We informed Robarts Meade, and we took our business away from them. What happened after that is between Michael and his employers – his *ex*-employers.'

'What did happen?'

'They asked him to leave. You can hardly blame them. Michael had lost them their biggest client. They kept it as quiet as they could – no firm likes to broadcast its own mistakes. That may be why Michael has been so successful in spreading these rumours.' He looked across at me, his face serious, his eyes no longer smiling at some private joke. 'Mistakes like that don't get forgotten. No other firm was going to employ him. It was lucky for Michael he had his wife's family to fall back on. He'd always planned to go into politics. His wife's uncle retired a year after he left Robarts. He inherited the seat at the last election.'

There was a long silence. Barney Thacker looked bored. The young secretary had his head bowed as if he was at a funeral.

'Unfortunately for us,' Peter Thacker went on, 'Michael seems to have developed something of an obsession about it. He's been spreading rumours ever since it happened. The sort of things you've heard – that we were dishonest . . . all kinds of things. It's been awkward for us.'

'How awkward?'

'We work in a sensitive area. It doesn't help to have someone trying to blacken your reputation. Particularly an MP. We tried to persuade Michael to stop several times . . .'

'You mean you tried to bribe him?'

Peter Thacker nodded frankly. 'It may not seem pleasant. It seemed to us the best thing to do at the time. Michael refused. He can be very . . .' He paused, choosing his words with care. 'Self-*righteous*. When he chooses.'

I said, 'Do you know why he was meeting June Donaghy on Sunday night?'

'I suppose you think she was involved in it as well.' Peter Thacker sighed. 'Is that what he told you?'

'Why else would they be meeting?'

126

An expression of sudden amusement crossed Peter Thacker's face. For a moment I thought he was going to laugh out loud.

Abruptly Barney Thacker got up from his chair. He leaned both fists belligerently on the table. He said, 'Michael was fucking the Donaghy, wasn't he? Had been for fucking years.' His voice jarred angrily off the ceiling.

I stared at his red, angry face. From far away Peter Thacker's voice was talking at me again. I didn't listen to him. I thought of the painting over Michael Harvey's fireplace: a family man in the middle of his happy family.

'They were having an affair?'

Barney Thacker gave his short bark of laughter. 'Look at him. Looks like a fucking pigeon shat on him.'

'They became close when Michael was working for us. I don't think many people knew about it. It was important to Michael that his wife shouldn't find out. Have you met Joanna Harvey, Chief Inspector?'

I thought of the tired-looking woman who had opened the door to me the day before.

'She's a lovely woman.' Peter Thacker said it as if he was praising fine porcelain or a bouquet of flowers. 'Michael owes her everything, of course. There was rather a scandal when she married someone . . . from his background. No one knew then how far Michael was going to go. Her family have been very supportive to him. If they ever found out he had been unfaithful . . .' His voice tailed off.

Barney Thacker said, 'He'd be fucked, wouldn't he? Jo would tear him into little pieces.' He seemed to relish the idea of Michael Harvey being torn into little pieces.

'Perhaps now you can see why Michael is so keen to provide . . .' Peter Thacker frowned. 'Other reasons why he might have been there on Sunday night. It would be awkward for him if the truth ever came out. More than awkward. People might start to wonder about . . .' His brown eyes strayed to the picture of Medd lying between us. 'What really happened.'

I stood up. Peter Thacker's smooth face expressed concern. 'It looks as if this has come as rather a shock to you, Chief Inspector.

If you don't believe what I've told you, we can produce evidence to back it up. We found some of Michael's letters in Miss Donaghy's desk.'

Both of the brothers followed me out on to the gallery. From above we looked down on the bent backs of office workers.

Peter Thacker gestured towards the roof. He seemed to be in the mood for conversation. 'We built this place three years ago. Norman Foster designed it for us.'

Barney Thacker grunted behind us. 'Stand up here, you can smell the sweat.' He grinned. 'Know you're getting your money's worth.'

Peter Thacker's face wrinkled with distaste. We reached the top of the stairs. 'You will keep us informed about the investigation, won't you, Chief Inspector? The sooner Miss Donaghy's murderer is arrested, the better. Whoever he is.'

I didn't say anything to that. I wouldn't have known what to say. I pictured Michael Harvey's thin, intense face. He was a liar and maybe even a killer. Suddenly the ground had shifted under me. I wasn't sure of anything any more.

At the entrance desk the receptionist was waiting for me. 'Chief Inspector Havilland?'

I didn't bother to deny that. It was about the only thing I was certain of.

'A message from your station. A Sergeant Baring. Could you telephone him?'

Her hand pushed the phone towards me. I picked up the receiver and dialled.

19

Baring's figure at the corner of the street was a bulky outline in a shapeless coat. The two policemen beside me were doing their best not to fidget, but they weren't doing it well.

Baring looked over his shoulder. 'You can see it from here, sir. Third door along. Before the green awning.'

I looked around the corner of the street. The road was empty except for a man unloading cans of Coke from the back of a car parked outside a row of half-derelict shops. Only two of the shops seemed to be in operation: a video store and the shop which sold Coke and newspapers. The green awning hung crookedly from a boarded-up shop front which had once been a butcher's. On our side of it the shops turned into ordinary houses, two-up, two-downs with rubbish in the front yards and yellowing net curtains obscuring the windows. Between the houses and the green awning was a black door.

A man stood outside the door. He didn't seem to be doing anything except standing, and watching the day get a little older. He was a big man in a bomber jacket with puffed up sleeves that had badges sewn to them. His gaze up and down the street was lazy, as if all he was interested in was cars and someone unloading groceries.

I pulled back from the corner.

Baring said, 'Medd went in about half two. We've got an undercover lined up for four o'clock, give or take, make sure he hasn't slipped out.'

'How did you find him?'

'Informer. Bloke in New Cross with a grudge. Medd beat up his brother once. You know what they're like.'

'Did you get a look at him before he went in?'

Baring nodded. 'He's a big boy.'

'Do you know what they're doing in there?'

'Checked with drugs, they hadn't heard of it.' He shrugged. 'Doesn't mean anything. These places open and close every week. Find any crack in there, we really will be in someone's good books.'

I nodded and tried not to notice the way Baring was looking at me. His big red face was creased with concern. 'Are you all right, sir?'

'I'm fine,' I lied. 'Is there a way out the back?'

'Not that we know of. Didn't have time to make a full recce. Looks like it's all gardens. I've got a car in each of the streets on the other side.' He put a hand on my sleeve. 'There's the undercover bloke now.' For some reason his voice had dropped to a whisper. 'Hasn't worked round here before. They won't know him.'

From the opposite direction a man had come into view. He walked with a loose slouch, hands in pockets, rising up and down on his toes as he walked. About twenty yards from the doorway he stopped and looked over his shoulder, as if he thought someone might be following him. The man on the door was watching him now. He wasn't interested in cars any more. We could see his arms folded, his head rising massively from the shoulders of the bomber jacket.

The walker turned reluctantly and moved on towards the doorway. He stopped. The doorman was asking him questions – a lot of questions. The plainclothes man's arms moved jerkily as he answered. He moved around the bouncer, unable to keep still. He knew his part. He ended up standing alongside the bouncer, with one hand on the black door. Dreadlocks hid his face. The bouncer still hadn't unfolded his arms. He nodded. We could hear distant laughter. The dishevelled figure clapped a hand on the bouncer's shoulder, then the door opened and he disappeared inside.

Beside me Baring let out breath as if he hadn't breathed for five minutes. 'Rather him than me. Don't know how they have the guts.'

'How long do we give him?'

'Ten minutes. He hasn't got any money on him.'

Behind us a car engine coughed gently. I turned. The back doors were standing open. Inside, the car smelled of cigarettes and chips. Baring got in beside me. The two coppers in the front seats didn't look round. I watched the back of a thick neck. Beside me Baring was fidgeting with the radio.

He muttered, 'Come on.'

Minutes passed. The man in the passenger seat flicked his elastic band at the windscreen and let it lie. The driver was beating time on the steering wheel to some tune only he could hear.

Suddenly the radio hissed and shouted something through static. The driver put the car in gear and eased forwards.

'Wait for him to get clear.' Baring's hand was clenched on the driver's shoulder. He talked into the radio. Through the entrance to our sidestreet we watched the plainclothes man come into sight. He was walking with the same loose slouch he had used on his way in. He didn't glance towards us. More minutes passed.

'All right.'

The car eased up to the corner.

The bouncer saw us straight away. His eyes registered the nose of the car, flicked lazily to the windscreen, widened. Suddenly we were moving, gathering speed. In slow motion we watched the bouncer's hand fumbling with the catch of the door, then the U-turn threw me against the side window. Tyres squealed; there was a judder as we hit the kerb. The seat beside me was empty. In the doorway two figures were rolling on the ground. I jumped over them and found myself looking down a narrow staircase into darkness. Outside it was mid-afternoon, but the stairs led down into black night.

Steps jarred up my legs. It felt like jumping into a wall. Suddenly thick noise was hammering at my ears, a mangled din of bass feedback and a voice that didn't sound like anything human. The darkness was full of faces. One of them came up close to me, teeth opened, eyes staring. I kicked somewhere below the face and the face disappeared. The noise cut out with the anguished screech of metal on metal. In the silence I could hear sirens. Baring was standing in front of me. He seemed taller than anybody else there.

With both hands he was holding a tiny figure who writhed under his hands, trying to kick out at his legs. The darkness was turning into walls, a low ceiling, a row of old car seats along one wall. Beside me a face was grinning at me. It was a white face, too thin, the scalp shaved bare. He was holding something out to me.

He said earnestly, 'It's a wonderful world.'

I started running towards a door at the back of the room. I still hadn't seen Medd. The door was hanging open; behind it was grey twilight. I hesitated, then launched myself into the twilight. I touched something soft and dug my nails into it. A voice screamed. There were wooden steps underfoot; I felt something soft touch my head and my head bang against cold brick. I tore at the soft thing in front of me and felt it lurch to one side. Somebody swore, foully and repeatedly. I could smell earth. Above me was a grey rectangle which swayed gently, as if it was behind a curtain of water. I clawed my way towards it. Baring's voice was shouting behind me. Cold air touched my cheeks, hurt the back of my head; buildings rose above me; at last I could see the sky.

I didn't have long to look at the sky. A weight took me over backwards. I felt my head jar against concrete. I couldn't move my legs. A face was snarling down at me; a red face whose lips were drawn furiously back over sharp teeth; the face I'd already seen in a police photograph. I clawed at thick wrists which were pressing up into my chin. The concrete came up and met the back of my head; clouds reeled; the concrete hit my head again. Everything dimmed except for the face above me. There was no feeling in my legs. Suddenly I felt as if I was floating. I was in the chapel at my father's funeral, floating somewhere above the pews of bowed heads. I could see my mother's head, a child kneeling beside her. The rumble of an organ deafened me.

Above me the face loomed closer. Its lips worked.

The lips said, 'I'm going to get you, copper.'

Suddenly the face was gone. I could hear Medd's voice shouting. Three dark shapes were struggling at the corners of my vision but I couldn't move. The weight was still on my chest, pressing down on it, forcing all the air out of my lungs. From a swirling orange sky hands tugged at me, pulling me upwards. I could taste blood. Baring was sitting over me, rocking backwards and for-wards. His face was the face of my father.

He said, 'Are you all right, sir? He almost had you there.'

Cotton wool filled my throat. My tongue had swelled into something huge, an animal trying to force its way inside me.

A voice shouted, 'Give him some fucking air.'

I gasped. The air flowing into my lungs burned, making me cough. It was as if I'd never breathed air before.

'Give him some fucking *air.*'

A light was swinging towards me across the garden. It looked as if it came from the end of a torch but as I watched it widened like the lens of a kaleidoscope, bringing in brickwork, nettles, the sleeve of a uniform.

Baring's voice said, 'It's all right, sir. We've got him. He's in the van.'

I struggled to speak. 'Medd?'

'He's in the van, sir. Take it easy, now.'

After a while I felt a hand under my elbow. I shook it free and tried to stand up by myself. My legs were as weak as if I'd never used them before. I took a few steps and groped for the stair handrail.

'Take it easy, sir.'

'I'm fine.'

At the foot of the stairs a figure was lying sprawled on the floor. He was thin, with his scalp shaved bare and deep pits around his eyes. For some reason he was familiar. A policeman was kneeling beside him.

Somebody said, 'Knife in his guts. God knows why. Someone settling scores.'

A crowd had appeared from nowhere to fill the road outside. They stood in the front gardens watching as we filed out of the black door.

Baring's face was grim.

I said, 'Did we find anything else in there?'

He shook his head. 'Clean as a whistle. We were too slow. We've got Medd, though.'

The car door was hanging open for me. In the front seats were the two men who had gone in with us. Baring got in beside me. He twisted round to watch the van through the back window.

'Shame he wasn't carrying. Bloke in New Cross said he normally has a knife on him. Still.' Baring shrugged. 'We can get him for worse than that.'

Over our heads the siren began to wail.

20

Medd sat with his elbows on the table and his hands clenched together. His hard, hairless face hadn't changed expression since the moment they brought him in. He'd been sitting like that for a long time now. It didn't look as if he was getting tired of it.

Behind me Baring's footsteps paced wearily up and down the room. I wanted to ask him to stop, but that would be another point to Medd and Medd had already won enough points. Between us the tape recorder listened to the sound of three people not saying anything.

Baring's footsteps stopped. I heard the squeak of his shoes on the lino floor.

I said, 'How come you were in such a hurry? Take a little more time, you could have thrown her further out. The tide might have caught her.'

Medd sat back and folded his arms. His face looked like a piece of rock cut from a mountainside.

I tried to keep my voice hard. 'Did you know she was going to pass that way?'

I felt Baring's weight on the back of my chair. 'You might as well help. Someone was watching. Saw you hit her and saw you drive off. Next best thing to a bleeding movie.'

Medd might not have been looking at us at all. His eyes were hard and flat, as if they weren't there to take anything in, but to stop any expression from getting out. He was a locked house, hermetically sealed, with the doors barred and windows closed.

I said, 'If you don't want to talk about June Donaghy, how about the phone calls you've been making?' After another moment I said, 'All right, so we'll talk about June Donaghy.'

Baring sighed and pushed his weight up off the back of my chair.

I gritted my teeth. 'Who told you to kill her?' It would have helped if I could have asked the questions without any doubt in my own mind: doubt about what Michael Harvey had seen, or whether he had seen anything at all.

The doubt didn't make any difference to Medd. He wasn't going to say anything anyway.

Baring said wearily, 'Loads of them start off like this, mate. You think you're the first hard man we ever saw?' His flat tread approached the table again. 'Soon as they get anywhere near court they start thinking what life looks like. How old are you?'

Medd wasn't interested in talking about his age. He put a finger up to scratch his cheek, but the itch on his cheek was the only thing bothering him.

I said, 'You bought the car from Jimmy Bolan on Thursday. Jimmy told us that and he told us you were going to sell it back to him afterwards. Sunday night someone watches you kill a girl and drive away in the same car. We're not trying to build a case here, we're just trying to save time.'

The slight movement of his mouth might have been because he thought that was funny, or because his mouth was tired of holding the same position for so long.

I got up from the table and nodded at Baring, who reached forward and switched off the tape recorder. Medd's eyes didn't even flicker. Sweat glistened through the quarter inch fuzz of hair over his scalp.

I went over to the door and opened it. A uniformed policeman was waiting outside.

'Is Michael Harvey here yet?'

'He's on the way, sir. We sent a car.'

'Have you got a line-up ready?'

'Downstairs, sir.'

I nodded. 'Tell me when Harvey gets here.'

I closed the door. Neither Medd nor Baring had moved. The neon light glared down on them as if they were statues in a museum.

136

I said, 'Does the name Barney Thacker mean anything to you?'

It didn't, nor would any other name. I was throwing questions pointlessly, the way a kid kicks a football against a blank wall.

'Did you kill Sarah Rider as well? Who told you to do that?'

Silence.

'Did you know June Donaghy before?'

I might have been putting questions to a corpse. Baring cleared his throat noisily. Outside we could hear footsteps in the corridor. I looked at Medd's hands. Two hours before they had been around my throat; two nights before they had been gripping a telephone receiver while he mouthed threats at Mary. Medd's hands could have done a lot of talking, but he had them locked up in fists with his elbows clamped over them.

There was a knock on the door. I went to it and opened it.

'Mr Harvey's here, sir. He's downstairs.'

'I'll come.' I nodded at the motionless figure at the table. 'Take him down, will you?'

Michael Harvey was waiting in an interview room in the basement. He was slumped in a chair and had a cup of tea in front of him. His face was exhausted, far more than the twenty-four hours since I had seen him last could explain. He greeted me only with a nod of the head; his eyes shrunk away towards the cup of tea. He picked the cup up and buried his face in it.

'I understand you've arrested someone.'

I made my voice cold and professional. 'It's the man we were looking for. The one in the photograph.'

Harvey nodded. 'I didn't get a very good look at him, you know.' One hand was scratching his belly as if he had a stomach ache.

'Are you ready?'

He gulped at the tea and made a face. 'I'm sorry. I'm tired. I was working most of last night. Trying to catch up.'

I gave him time to drink more tea. It didn't seem to be doing him any good.

'Thank you for taking Sam home last night.'

'That's all right.'

'She needs looking after.'

'Everybody does.'

'Yes.'

He looked down into the empty cup and grimaced.

I glanced over my shoulder. The other policeman had gone out into the corridor.

I said quietly, 'Were you having an affair with June Donaghy?'

Harvey's face swung towards me. 'Who told you that?'

'Barney Thacker.'

'They won't stop at anything, will they? They . . .'

I interrupted him. 'He said they had letters to prove it. June left some letters in her desk.'

Harvey's mouth was open, either with surprise, or to deny it. He didn't say anything, though. His face dropped forward. The cup hung from one finger.

'Barney Thacker,' he repeated.

'Does it make any difference who told me?'

'I . . .' Harvey passed a hand over his face. 'I suppose not.'

'Is it true?'

For a long time he didn't answer. Then his head moved slowly up and down. 'I didn't think anyone else knew. We did everything we could to keep it quiet.' When he looked up at me there was something defiant in his eyes. 'I . . . I love my wife, you know. It doesn't . . . Me and Jo, it never made any difference to that.'

I didn't say anything. It wasn't any of my business what happened between him and his wife.

'Does she know?'

He shook his head. 'God, no. If she knew . . .' He shivered at the thought of her knowing.

'How long had it been going on?'

He thought for a moment before answering, then shrugged as if it no longer made any difference. 'For a long time. It started when I was still working for PTI. I was in touch with her the whole time, you see, passing documents, going to meetings . . .' He stopped, remembering some of the meetings. 'June was very special. She understood . . .' Harvey hunched over on himself, both hands pressed against his stomach. The light seemed to be bothering his eyes.

'What did she understand?'

'Oh . . .' He pressed the knuckles of one hand against his forehead. 'I suppose I mean . . .' He looked up at me. His intelligence was turned against himself and it wasn't giving him any breaks. 'June understood things about me . . . I didn't feel as if I was on best behaviour with her. You'd probably be surprised if you saw the house I was brought up in.'

I didn't think I would have been surprised. It was the one thing that everybody had told me about Michael Harvey, and it didn't sound much different from the house I was brought up in myself.

'My father left us when I was a child. My mother had to bring us up. She always wanted us to do well. My sister died when I was ten. After that it was just me.' He looked down at his hands. 'It was so like June's childhood in some ways. It meant I could relax with her. I could never talk about that to Jo. She just knows me the way I am now.' He shrugged. 'She doesn't know anything else.' His eyes searched around the room as if they were having trouble finding me. When they did find me they fastened on my face as if I was the one who had to judge what he'd done. 'Do you see?' He used one finger to blot up tears from the corners of his eyes. 'I suppose June was the kind of girl I would have married if . . . if . . . maybe, the kind of girl I *should* have married.'

The kind of girl he would have married if he'd never left the small town in the North he'd been brought up in. The kind of girl he would have married – quite pretty, quite happy, quiet – if he hadn't needed to push himself higher: to university, and the House of Commons; to an accent, clothes and friends he hadn't started out with; to the bleak and faded drawing rooms of his wife's family. June must have been a relief from all that.

Harvey was talking again. I didn't think he wanted to talk about it, but talking was better than silence. 'You mustn't think I didn't care about what I did. I hated it. I was brought up . . . not to tell lies, to be faithful. In my church . . . I still go to church. I had an affair before, once. The same sort of thing. She was a secretary in my firm.' The confession was soothing to him, as if he was draining a poisoned wound. 'It was seven years ago. Sam was ill – she had anorexia nervosa. I suppose I couldn't cope with that.' He looked up at me. 'I broke that off but it made it easier when . . . when June came along.'

I watched the back of his head move. He had married well; he had a beautiful daughter, a rising reputation. A lot of people must have envied Michael Harvey. But the marriage wasn't as happy as it looked, and nor was the family. Michael Harvey had learned how to pass exams and make friends; but there hadn't been time to learn about bad marriages or families with problems. I could picture his childhood: the church on Sunday and the small joint after it; the rows of desks in the schoolroom and Harvey always the one putting his hand up with the right answer; and his mother indulging him, and teachers indulging him, because he kept working and kept passing exams. Those surroundings were a long way behind him now, but Harvey was still the smart kid with his hand up at the front of the class. He was still determined, and too narrow for the world he was living in. When problems did finally come along – not the sort of problems he could beat by brains or hard work – he hadn't known how to deal with them, and had chosen to run away instead. June was his way of running away.

There were footsteps in the corridor outside. Michael Harvey lifted his head slowly as if it weighed too heavy on his shoulders. A policeman appeared in the door.

His eyes flickered towards Harvey. 'Got the line-up ready, sir.' His voice was hushed and respectful.

Harvey walked by my side along the corridor. He looked better now that he had got the affair with June Donaghy off his chest. Baring was waiting outside the door of the basement interview room.

We filed in one by one. It was a big room, with rows of strip lights hung on chains from the ceiling. The strip lights were supposed to chase away shadows and doubts, to reveal the truth. All they showed at the moment was peeling green paint and four men standing in a row against the back wall. Medd stood second from the right. His arms hung by his sides as if he had left them there while he went away to do something else. His face was hard and blank; his eyes bored holes in the wall above our heads. Next to him a black guy frowned at the carpet. A kid at the far end was sticking out his chin at authority, police line-ups and breaches of his rights. On the end nearest Medd an untidy man in a jean jacket was shuffling his feet nervously and trying to keep his eyes away from the lights. There were the marks of bad acne on his face – maybe that explained why he hadn't shaved. Every few seconds he reached up to scratch the colourless fuzz on his chin.

Baring said, 'In your own time, sir.'

He spoke in a half-whisper, as if we were at the altar rail of a church and Michael Harvey was going forward to take communion. Harvey bowed his head for a few seconds, then crossed the room to the end of the line.

He took his time, spending the same time in front of each man. From the back of his head we couldn't tell what he was thinking, or if he was thinking anything. The man with acne was the only one who met his eye; the others looked over his head as if they didn't know they were being inspected at all. When he reached the kid at the end, the kid's chin rose an inch higher, daring him to make the wrong choice.

Harvey paused, turned and walked back to us. He didn't look any of us in the face.

He said, 'I'm sorry. I don't recognize any of them.'

'Are you sure?'

From somewhere he had managed to get back his composure. 'Quite sure.'

The three other men in the line were shuffling their feet and stretching arms. Only Medd didn't move; he was counting victories on the interview room wall.

I said to Baring, 'Where's Jimmy Bolan?'

'Out on parole, sir. We thought it was best to keep him on our side.'

'Get a car.'

Harvey followed me out of the room. He turned to face me at the end of the corridor.

I said, 'What happened on Sunday night?'

'I told you.'

'Did you see someone attacking June?'

'It happened just like I told you. The only thing . . .' Michael Harvey put a hand to his forehead. 'It was dark. I'm sorry.'

'You said you had a good look at him.'

'I wasn't close enough.' He grimaced. His mouth wavered then came to rest in a firm line. 'I didn't see enough to be certain.'

There was something self-righteous in the way he said it. I felt anger boiling up in me. Or maybe it wasn't anger – maybe it was fear.

'Do you think it was the same man?'

'I'm sorry. I'm not going to lie about it. I wasn't certain.'

A WPC was coming along the corridor towards us. I waited until she was past. She seemed to sense something was wrong. As she came closer her smile turned into business, as if she hadn't even seen we were there.

I said, 'Peter Thacker told me why you had to leave the City.'

'That isn't true.' He sounded hurt. 'I told you the other day their rumours weren't true.'

'What about your story about PTI? Was that true?'

'Yes.' He nodded. His eyes were troubled.

'Have you got any evidence for it?'

'I told you. In my safe.'

'Can I see it?'

Harvey breathed deeply for a few seconds. His fingers fidgeted with the sleeve of his coat. A line of worry ran down the middle of his forehead. It hadn't been there two days ago. He said, 'I can't take the risk. Sam had another threat.' He looked up at me. 'I'm sorry. It was horrible. The things they said . . .' His mouth set as if he had just reached a decision. 'I can't put my family through that sort of danger. What if they actually did something to her? I keep seeing June . . .' He kept seeing June falling from the river wall. He shook his head as if he was trying to shake the memory out of it. 'It wouldn't be responsible to take any more risks.'

'You mean you're backing out of your story?'

'No. I mean I'm not going to take it any further. I'm going to let it drop.' He sighed. 'I have to start looking to the future.'

From the corner of my eye I saw Baring appear at the end of the corridor.

I said, 'Where does that leave everyone else?'

'I'm sorry, George.' He hadn't used my name before. I didn't know why he used it now. His voice was firm and level, as if he'd never been crying half an hour earlier; as if he was never going to be persuaded.

He turned to Baring. 'Can I go now?'

'Yes, sir. Thank you for your time.' Baring's voice was subdued.

We both watched Harvey walk down the corrridor towards the stairs.

Baring said, 'Car's ready, sir.'

21

It was late afternoon outside. There was no sign of Michael Harvey on the pavement. He seemed to have disappeared: into backstreets, or into a taxi which would carry him safely back to his side of the river. Traffic nosed to one side as we approached. Above our heads the siren wailed and sobbed. In the rear-view mirror I could see Baring looking grimly out of the side window.

The traffic slowed as we reached the Elephant. The roundabout was jammed with cars heading south. Beyond it the driver gunned the engine past housing blocks and derelict Georgian terraces with boards over the windows. The Old Kent Road was just starting to come alive for the evening. A man was slowly unlocking padlocks from the steel grille over a pub door. On a garage forecourt a black guy in a red suit was spraying water at a blacked-out Mercedes the same colour as his suit.

Baring said, 'He'll be locking up.'

I glanced at the driver. He was leaning forward slightly over the wheel, willing the traffic to move out of his way. We passed a supermarket, a drive-in burger place, a big pub set back from the road.

We saw the coloured flags outside Jimmy Bolan's place from fifty yards away. The traffic was jammed solid. I pushed open the passenger side door and heard Baring's door open behind me. I was running down the pavement towards Puma Motors when I saw the child.

He was squatting on the pavement under the coloured flags. On his face was the earnest look that kids get when they've found something they don't understand. With a piece of stick he was slowly beating something that lay on the pavement in front of him. I couldn't see what it was until the sun caught it. Then I realized it lay all over the pavement. It looked as if the paving stones were made of silver. I slowed down and stopped in front of the kid. He saw my legs and frowned at them, then looked slowly up until he was staring into my face. He grinned suddenly, that nervous child's grin that wants you to stop being so serious. Then he lowered his head and went back to breaking the glass into smaller pieces.

I looked at Jimmy Bolan's forecourt. The half dozen worthless cars were still there but every window in them was broken. Glass covered the tarmac, the bonnets, the car roofs. Jagged edges of glass stuck out of frames in the car doors. Headlights had been smashed; windscreen wipers clutched at air. The car seats were littered with piles of glass as if a glass wave had broken over the cars and flooded them. The sunroofs were gaping holes in metal.

I made my way over to the Portakabin. The door was hanging open. Nobody was sitting in the outer office. The light switch clicked pointlessly; a grey twilight filtered through the steel mesh windows. When I took a step forward into the room thin shards of glass crunched underfoot.

I stopped at the desk. Behind me I could hear Baring's footsteps breaking glass on tarmac. The cabin swayed as he climbed up into it.

He said, 'Jesus.'

There wasn't anything else to say. The desk had been over-turned. Old invoices and papers were scattered everywhere as if someone had been plucking a paper bird. The coat rack had fallen sideways across the door to the inner office.

I wrestled it away from the door. For some reason it didn't want to move. When it came away the door swung open as if someone on the other side had turned the handle. I went cautiously forward into the inner office. I didn't need to be cautious. There was nothing in there except the ruins of Jimmy Bolan's desk, a rug scraped back against the wall, the thin grey light from the windows which was dying in front of our eyes.

I heard Baring draw a breath quickly inwards and looked the way he was looking. There wasn't much light left but it was enough to show dark stains on the wall behind the desk.

The cabin lurched suddenly. I swung round. A thin, lugubrious man was standing in the doorway with a raincoat wrapped around him.

He said, 'Coppers?'

'Yes.'

'Come to 'ave a look?' He nodded wisely.

'Who are you?'

'Run the shop over the road. I talked to the coppers who came before. The first ones.'

'When?'

''S afternoon.' He looked at his watch. 'Three o'clock?'

'What happened?'

'Didn't see.' He shook his head, mournful at having missed the show. 'Saw them take him away, though.'

'Jimmy Bolan?'

He nodded dimly, as if the name was new to him.

'Where did they take him?'

'Hospital.' His lower lip jutted out. 'Copper said he might not make it. One who came before.'

'Was it you who called the police?'

He shook his head.

'Do you know what happened?'

'Two boys jumped him. Smashed the place up.' He said it with relish.

'Do you know if anyone saw them?'

His thin face moved sideways. 'I was inside, wasn't I?'

He would probably have heard what was happening, but wouldn't have come out until it was all over. There would have been passers-by who saw two boys jumping out of a van and knew that they didn't want to see whatever was going to happen next. Jimmy Bolan might or might not make it. If he did make it he would probably choose to forget what happened next himself.

Baring said, 'Medd.'

'What time did you say this happened?'

'Three o'clock.'

At three o'clock Medd had been in the back of a police van, driving towards Kennington Police Station.

There were more footsteps outside the cabin. The thin man

146

looked over his shoulder, then turned and stepped down. Through the doorway I saw Mason's face.

'Are you in there, Havilland?'

Baring glanced at me. It was too dark for me to make anything of his expression. 'I'll have a look round outside, shall I, sir?'

I nodded. Mason was looking up at me from the doorway. He had to put both hands on the door frame to pull himself up. Inside he stopped and looked around the wreckage.

His face was grim. 'Bloody mess.' I hoped he was talking about Jimmy Bolan's Portakabin.

I said, 'Yes, sir.'

'Blokes at the Elephant picked it up this afternoon. Bob Munden gave me a call.' He looked at me. 'Do you know what happened?'

'Two men smashed the place up.'

'I can see that.' His voice was tight. 'Smashed Jimmy Bolan up as well. He's at Guy's.'

'Do you know what state he's in?'

'About the same as this place.' Mason's eyes flickered over the debris. 'What's happening, Havilland?'

I said, 'Jimmy Bolan identified a guy called Medd as the man who bought a car from him last Thursday – the car Michael Harvey saw . . .'

'Michael Harvey,' Mason said.

'He saw it driving away from where June Donaghy was killed.'

'Did Harvey see who was driving it?'

'He said he did.'

'What the hell does that mean?'

I drew in breath. 'We picked up Medd this afternoon. We put him in a line-up and had Harvey look at him . . .' I stopped.

'And he didn't pull him out.' Mason sounded as if he knew Harvey wasn't going to pull him out. 'What else did Bolan tell you about Medd?'

'He didn't.'

'Did he say what he wanted the car for?'

'He didn't say yesterday.'

'If he didn't say yesterday,' Mason said quietly, 'he isn't going to say any more tomorrow. You should see what he looks like.'

We both knew that it wasn't just a matter of looks.

Mason went on, 'Where's Medd now?'

'At the station.'

'You're still holding him?'

I said, 'We can hold him for this.'

'Why?' Mason snorted. The failing light had turned him into a silhouette. 'This didn't happen till this afternoon. Medd was with you by then.'

'He could have got someone else to do it.'

'Why?'

'Because Jimmy Bolan put the finger on him.'

'Could have been something else altogether. You know what kind of bloke Jimmy Bolan is. Might not have anything to do with Medd at all.'

He left a pause in case I wanted to agree with him. I didn't say anything.

'So you're still holding Medd. What else is there?'

'Sir?'

Mason said, 'What's the case, Havilland?'

I sighed. 'Jimmy Bolan . . .'

'Jimmy Bolan said Medd bought a car. End of story.'

'Michael Harvey saw him killing June Donaghy and driving away in the same car.'

There was a pause. 'Except he didn't,' Mason said quietly. 'You showed him Medd and he didn't know him. Where's the case?'

'He bought a car.'

'How do you know that?'

'Jimmy Bolan told us.'

And Jimmy Bolan was lying in a bed in Guy's Hospital with the ceiling a white blur in front of his eyes. And it wasn't Medd who put him there because Medd had the best alibi anyone can ever have: he was in a police station at the time.

Mason said grimly, 'I've been hearing some more stories about Michael Harvey.'

'What kind of stories?'

'Stories you don't want to hear about the witness that's supposed to be holding your case together. Turns out he's been spreading rumours about the Thackers. Turns out you can't believe a blasted word . . .'

I said, 'Where did you hear that?'

Mason's hand moved against the grey light of the door. 'Grapevine. Word gets around, doesn't it? The City's a small place.' His hand moved again, in towards his body. I heard him scratching his wrist. 'Didn't even pick Medd out, though, did he? Where's the case, Havilland?'

This time I didn't answer him.

'There isn't one.' Mason's voice was grim. 'Heard something else this morning, as well, Havilland. I heard you were back at PTI giving the Thackers trouble again.' His voice was angry, as angry as I had ever heard it. 'Didn't you understand what I said Tuesday morning?'

I said, 'Yes, sir.'

'Now I've got John Harlow on my back saying . . . saying, I told you so, basically. Saying George Havilland shouldn't have been trusted with a case like this one. Meaning a case where there are decent people involved, businessmen. You know what he told me? Said, he seriously questioned my judgement in recommending we take you back in. *My* judgement. Thirty-eight years and what have I got on my record? "Serious error of judgement." I'm going to spend the next five years keeping my own nose clean just because you wouldn't do what you blasted well . . .' He stopped. I heard his feet move and the broken glass move under them. 'That's what I've got,' he said grimly. 'What have you got to show me for it? One witness smashed up. Another who changes his story every time you look at him. This chap . . . Medd . . . sitting in the cells, no case against him. And the Thackers shouting at Scotland Yard because little George Havilland keeps running in to tweak their noses. Bloody marvellous.'

I didn't say anything; there wasn't anything to say.

'Remember that letter about Ronnie Whelan? John Harlow brought that up as well. Asked me what I was going to do about you. What do you bloody expect me to say? I could have made another serious error of judgement. I didn't, Havilland. I told him I was taking you off the case . . . taking you off the case as soon as I could get hold of you. He didn't understand that, either. He thought DCIs spent their time reporting back . . . letting their boss know what's going on. Not like you.' His sigh filled the wrecked cabin. 'I'm not suspending you. I'm taking you off this case. We'll find something else for you to do, something where you can't cause any trouble. That's until the Ronnie Whelan hearing. You'll need some time to get ready for that. I wouldn't take anything for granted, if I was you.'

He needn't have worried about that. I wasn't taking anything for granted.

Mason said, 'Where's Ted Baring? He can fill me in on everything else.'

'What about Medd?' My voice sounded dry even to myself.

Mason paused in the doorway. 'What about him? Have we got anything against him? Eyewitness who saw him? Forensic? Harvey told you he couldn't identify him, didn't he?' Mason sighed in exasperation. 'Maybe he's linked to what happened here. We'll have to see, won't we?'

Outside it was dark. I couldn't see Baring. The wreckage of Jimmy Bolan's cars looked like the skeletons of primeval monsters. Out on the pavement the child was still beating steadily at the shards of glass, smashing them into ever smaller fragments.

I started walking back down the Old Kent Road. Above London the sky was a dull orange.

22

It took me a long time to get back to Brixton. By the time I reached it the pavements were full and the night dark. Passers-by jostled me. A train rumbled over the railway bridge, making the earth shake.

Don was standing on the pavement outside his café. He was a tall man with a thin beard clinging to the end of his chin. He nodded as I reached my doorway. 'Someone looking for you.'

I tensed. But Medd was still safely inside a police cell.

'A girl.' He nodded to the café door behind him. 'Waitin' inside.'

Sam Harvey was sitting at a table at the back of the café. An empty coffee mug was in front of her. She looked small and lost in the long blue coat.

She waited until I went up to her before speaking. 'I lost my keys. I got scared.'

'Why didn't you go home?'

'I couldn't get hold of Mummy.'

'What about your father's office?'

'He wasn't there.' He'd been in the police station most of the afternoon. 'Mrs Cross will be back by now. My neighbour. She keeps a set for me.' Her blue eyes were troubled. 'I didn't like waiting by myself. There wasn't anyone else around.'

'I'll take you home.'

She left coins on the table to pay for her coffee. Don nodded at us as we went out.

'Can you give me a drink first? I feel . . .' She looked away from me, not telling me how she felt. Her voice was still small.

'All right.' I felt for my keys.

'I want to use your loo as well.'

'You could have used Don's.'

Her face wrinkled. 'It wasn't clean.'

She climbed the stairs to the flat behind me. I unlocked the door. The air inside smelled dead, as if it was a long time since anyone had lived there.

When she came out of the bathroom I had two glasses of whisky waiting on the side. She took the whisky and sat down on the sofa, curling her legs up under her. She was wearing a big blue jumper that would have looked stupid on anyone else over a cream skirt. It didn't take her long to look at home.

I sat down across the room from her.

Over the rim of her glass she said, 'One bedroom.'

'I'm sorry?'

'One bedroom. You live with someone. There were women's things in the bathroom.'

'Yes.' I tried to pull myself back into the sort of shape that could talk about women's things. 'I told you that.'

'No, you didn't. You wouldn't say.' She sipped whisky. 'I guessed.'

'All right.' I ran one hand over my face. 'You guessed.'

'Where is she?'

'She moved out yesterday evening.'

There was a pause. 'I'm sorry,' Sam said.

'That's all right.'

'Why did she move out?'

'Because of the threats and . . . other things.'

Sam hugged her legs. 'What other things?'

I said, 'Do you always ask this many questions?'

Sam flushed and buried her face in her glass. Cornflower blue eyes stared at me over the rim of the glass.

'Did your father tell you June's sister had been killed as well?'

'I don't want to think about that.' She shivered. 'That's what I was thinking about before, when I got scared.'

'What did he tell you?'

'Stop it.' She put her hands over her ears. Her eyes were closed. Slowly she relaxed. 'Put some music on, will you?'

'Why?'

'It would be nice.' She shrugged. 'It would stop us talking about that.'

I sighed. 'What else do you want to talk about?'

'You're not being so nice today.'

She skipped up from the sofa and went over to the hi-fi. I watched her back moving along the shelf of records. While she chose, she stood on one leg, her stockinged foot rubbing slowly up and down one calf.

'Who's Jay McShann?'

'He's a pianist.'

'Would I like him?'

'I don't know what else you like.'

She swung round and stood in front of me. Her face almost seemed amused. 'Something's made you cross.'

'It's been a long day.'

'It's over now.' She made a face. 'Or do I still count as work?'

After what Mason had said that afternoon I wasn't sure what counted as work and what counted as survival. I said, 'You count as work until you're tucked up in bed with the door locked.'

Sam's face went serious all of a sudden. 'I'm sure that could be arranged.'

I looked down into my glass. 'Finish your drink. I'll see you home.'

'I want to put some music on first.'

She pulled out a CD and fumbled with the machine. Sax music spilled out into the room.

'You've got lots of records.'

'Yes.'

'Yes,' she imitated my grumpy voice. 'Have you always listened to jazz?'

'For as long as it matters.'

'Anything else?'

'If I like it.'

'Why did you start?'

'My father had some records,' I said.

'I see.' She frowned. 'Mummy and Daddy don't listen to

anything except classical. Daddy's tone deaf.' She nodded towards the door. 'Are they her records as well?'

'Some of them.'

'What does she do?'

I said, 'She's a singer.'

'*Very* glamorous.' Sam made a face. 'Is she going to move them out?'

I stood up. 'You ought to be at home.'

'I was scared.' Her eyes were very large. 'Are you angry with me for coming here?'

'Not as long as you let me take you home.'

The blue Volkswagen Golf was parked around the corner, looking too smart for a Brixton street. She drove home in silence. The streets were empty. Far away we could hear the sound of a police siren. We parked fifty yards down the road from her front door.

'Will you see me upstairs?' Her voice was small. 'Maybe that's silly of me. This was the bit that made me frightened before.'

I sighed. 'That's why I came.'

I watched her ring her neighbour's bell and say something into the Entryphone. A door on the third landing was open as we approached. There was no one else on the staircase and no one waiting inside the flat. I went through rooms switching on lights. Sam followed me without saying anything.

'Will you have a drink? Now you're here?'

I turned round. She had kicked off her shoes and was standing with a bottle of white wine in her hand. Under the blue jumper she was wearing the same big cotton shirt I had seen the day before.

I thought of the flat we had just left: cold and empty, with nothing inside it but the ashes of an argument. I thought of Mason.

'All right.'

'Put some music on, will you?'

I went over to the shelf of CDs. The sound of Gerry Mulligan's sax filled the room. When I turned round Sam was holding out a glass. I took it and sat down in one of the beanbags.

'Tell me more about June's sister.' Sam was sitting with her head on one side. 'I want to know now. I'm not scared any more.'

'What did your father tell you?'

She shrugged and hugged her knees. 'He said she'd been killed.'

'We found her last night. In her husband's flat. Did you ever meet her?'

She shook her head. 'Was it her husband who killed her?'

'It might have been.'

'So it doesn't have anything to do with . . . with June? With our case?'

'I don't know.' I sipped at the wine. It was very cold. I said, 'It isn't my case any more.'

'Why not?'

'They took me off it.'

Sam was sitting up straight in her beanbag. 'But why?'

'It would take too long to explain.'

'But . . . Have you done something wrong?'

'I don't think so.'

'So why should they take you off it?' She folded her arms again. 'Daddy will hate that. You're the only one he trusts. He told me.'

'Am I?'

'He said you were the only one who . . . who really wants to get at the truth.'

I said drily, 'That's nice of him.'

'Did you know you're quite like him in some ways? You care about the same things.'

'I didn't think you knew me that well.'

'I don't.' She frowned. 'It's the way you look . . . when you care about something.'

'You've never seen me care about something,' I said.

'Yes, I have. You care about this.' Her smile was challenging.

I said, 'It's a job.'

'Why do men always say things like that?' She held out her empty glass to me. 'Pour me another, will you?'

I got up and poured wine into the glass. She held her forearm with the free hand. The glass was steady.

'Why did you break up with your girlfriend?' Her blue eyes were staring up at me.

'We haven't broken up.'

'So why did she move out?'

'I told you. She was worried about the threats.'

'You said it wasn't only that.'

I sighed. 'We've had arguments before. About what I do and the way I do it. That's why she's angry with me.'

There was a pause.

'Will it blow over?'

I shook my head. 'I don't want to talk about it.'

'That bad? It's horrid when things break up. When I broke up with Steve . . .' She stopped. 'Morbid.'

I went back to my beanbag. The music was getting through to me, or something was. I could feel the tension starting to drain away.

'Why did you become a policeman?' Sam asked.

'I don't remember.'

'Of course you do. How could you forget something like that?'

'It's as good as anything else, isn't it?'

'Don't be so touchy.' She laughed. 'You don't do something like that by accident.'

'I wanted to ever since I was a kid.'

'Why?'

I hesitated. 'My father was killed when I was thirteen. It started after that.'

'Killed?' One hand had gone to her mouth.

'It was a mugging which went wrong.'

'That's awful.' Her face was shocked. 'Did they ever catch them?'

I shook my head. 'They were just street robbers. No one saw it happen.'

'Where did it happen?'

'In the town where I grew up.' I wanted to change the subject now.

'I can't imagine that.' She buried her face in her knees. 'If something happened to Daddy . . .' She wiped her face on her knees and looked up. 'This is morbid. Put something else on. It's the music.'

I went over to the hi-fi and flicked through to a faster track.

Jimmy Witherspoon's voice growled out into the room, the sax weaving and rolling underneath it. Outside it was dark.

'Fill up your glass,' Sam commanded. 'It's nearly empty.'

'Are you trying to get me drunk?'

She laughed. 'I've never seen a policeman drunk. Yes I have . . . Daddy had the Chief Constable round for a drink last Christmas. In the constituency. He tried to put his hand on my knee.'

I didn't blame him for that. Her knees were very white and soft.

'I'll try not to get drunk,' I said.

Suddenly Sam's voice was solemn. 'Don't hold back for me.'

I pretended I hadn't heard that. I looked down at the wine in my glass. Gerry Mulligan was racing through a fast solo. The afternoon seemed a long time ago, a long way away from white wine and coloured beanbags, and Sam sitting across the room from me.

'I was scared earlier,' she said. 'I don't feel so bad now.'

'Will you be all right tonight?'

'I don't know.' Her voice was light. 'I wish . . .' There was a long silence. She didn't tell me what she wished. We both of us listened to the music, or to the space the music was filling.

'You could always go to stay with your parents.'

Sam laughed quietly. 'You keep talking about the wrong thing . . .'

I heard light footsteps. Suddenly the lights dimmed. The pattern of street lights relaxed over the ceiling. There was the sound of a beanbag dragging across the floor. Sam sat down near me.

'Better mood,' she explained.

I knew that I should have got up and left, but I didn't move.

'What about you?' she asked. 'Is your singer coming home tonight?'

'No.' That was true.

'Are you safe there?'

I didn't answer. I didn't know where I was safe.

'There's an alarm here,' Sam said. 'You could stay here. I've got a sofa-bed.'

I still didn't say anything. The tension was pouring out of me in a great flood, and along with it went fear, the memory of June Donaghy lying on the Thames mud, the thought of Mary.

Sam Harvey leaned forward. Her hand was small and cold on my forehead.

'Don't worry about it now,' she whispered. 'We're all right here.'

I didn't have the strength to argue about it. I felt her hand stroke its way across my temples until it lay against my cheek.

The music had finished. Something clicked on the hi-fi. I started to get up.

'Don't,' she whispered.

There was a movement in the half-darkness. All of a sudden she was lying against my side. I felt the slight weight of her head on my shoulder; her hand lay across my chest. Lips quickly touched my cheek.

'Don't go back,' she whispered. 'I want you here. It's not as if you've got anything to go back for.'

Her smell was light and uncomplicated. Under my cheek I felt soft hair. When I turned my head I saw her eyes shining in the darkness. We lay like that for a long time.

I knew I should have moved but something was stopping me from moving. It would have been an effort and I'd already had too much effort. For a moment I thought of Medd's face, then pushed him out of my mind. I listened to Sam's breath in the darkness. Her hip was digging into my side.

After a while I felt her lifting herself up. Her eyes looked down on me. The cool hand was back on my cheek. She kissed me. Her lips were warm and soft. I felt her tongue probing softly into my mouth. When we stopped kissing she was smiling.

'Don't move,' she whispered.

I didn't move. Her lips were kissing my neck; fingers were undoing the buttons on my shirt. I felt her leg move against me and a weight pressing down on my stomach. I twined my fingers into her hair and sighed. Sam's lips moved slowly down over my bare chest and stomach.

I didn't move.

23

I woke up in darkness. My mouth was dry. In my dreams I had been running down streets. I couldn't run properly because of a weight on one of my legs. A red light was winking ahead of me in the darkness.

Slowly the light through the windows filtered into my eyes. Sam's white body was lying alongside me. Her ribcage rose and fell. She was asleep with one arm over my chest. Three long windows took shape out of the darkness. The room smelled strange, felt strange around me. There was an odd emptiness between my legs.

I wriggled out from under Sam's arm. She frowned and murmured something in her sleep, then settled back against the beanbag. I stood up and looked down at her. It was a long time since I'd seen any woman's body other than Mary's.

A wine glass was lying on its side next to her. I picked it up and tiptoed over to the kitchen. The empty feeling was growing. It had reached my stomach, as if someone had put a block of ice there and the cold was spreading slowly through my body. At the kitchen sink I found the taps by feel and drank water out of the wine glass. It had a musty taste, spoiled by the wine.

Outside few cars were passing. I didn't know what time it was or what had happened to my watch. The numbness had spread down my arms and legs. I shivered. Suddenly I didn't want to be there any more. In darkness I fumbled for my clothes. Sam lay with her head pillowed on white arms. Her breath was almost imperceptible; she might have been dead.

I picked up my shoes and tiptoed towards the door. By the phone I found a pad and left a note propped up on the kitchen worktop. Outside the streets were empty. At the Prince's round-about a night bus sighed past, heading for Chelsea. I walked down the pavement alone. My feet seemed too heavy. Their echo came back out of the darkness, accusing me. I might have been trying to throw the sound of my own footsteps away, but it kept coming back to me, following me past blank walls and closed shops. A drunk was meandering slowly along the pavement with the help of parked cars. His open mouth sang a song that didn't have a tune or words. The dismal noise followed me round the corner. It took me an hour to reach home.

The staircase to our flat seemed narrower than it had before, and shabbier. I might have been seeing it for the first time. I couldn't remember which key fitted the lock: it was as if I was going to a stranger's flat, turning the key for the first time. I stood in the hallway without moving, smelling darkness that had once been familiar. Dimly I could see the shape of the living-room windows.

Suddenly I froze. When I'd left the flat the door to the living room had been closed; now it was open. Something else had changed as well. Mary's coat was hanging from the hook in the hall. I stood shocked for a moment. I couldn't breathe; the numbness had reached my throat. Why had she come home? That thought evaporated quickly. She had a right to be there. It was her home; I was the intruder.

There was something alien in the smell of the flat. Sam Harvey's perfume seeped from my hair and clothes, betraying me. Earlier that evening it had seemed almost imperceptible; now it was a thick musk, an animal smell fouling the air of the flat. I went into the bathroom, closed the door, pulled the light cord. My face stared out at me from the mirror. It was unshaven, wild: a traitor's face. For a long time I stared at it, trying to find myself in the eyes and nose. It was as if I'd never seen myself before.

From next door I heard a voice. Mary's voice. I turned on the taps to drown the voice out, then reached behind the curtain and switched on the shower. Slowly I peeled off my clothes. They reeked of deceit. I dropped them in the corner and looked at the mirror. A man looked back at me – a naked man with brown hair, a tired face that women liked, cold blue eyes. He was about my height, about my age, but I'd never seen him before. He had a powerful chest, a stomach that was still as flat as you could hope for, narrow hips. I shivered. In the shower I scrubbed at my back and legs. The skin reddened under my nails. It didn't do any good. My chest still bore the imprint of Sam Harvey's fingers. I closed my eyes. Sam's face cheated my eyelids, smiling at me, whispering words I couldn't hear.

Suddenly the water ran cold. I must have been standing there for half an hour or more. I let the cold water torture me, as if that would be enough to wipe out what I was feeling, or to numb me so that I didn't feel anything at all. After a moment I reached out my hand and switched the water off. Sam's smell rose up from my body instantly, as if it had become my own smell. As if no water would ever exhaust it.

The bedroom smelled warm. In the glow through the curtains I could see a shape in the bed. Mary was awake.

I lifted the covers and slid into bed, turning my back against her. Behind me I could feel her warmth but my own skin was still cold. I pulled the covers close about me.

'George?' Mary's voice.

I muttered something as if I was already asleep.

'Where have you been?'

The mattress moved. A shape was leaning over me in the darkness.

'I was scared.' There was a rasp in her voice. 'I was scared, so I came home. You weren't here.'

My voice said, 'I had to work late.' It sounded detached, as if it came from somewhere outside me. The lie hung in the darkness, refusing to fade away. Suddenly the darkness was full of lies: lies that I'd told and lies I would have to tell. They swarmed over us, plucking at our skin and hair. It was I who had let them in.

'I tried calling your work.'

I grunted. The tongue lay in my mouth like a heavy weight, a stone I wasn't strong enough to lift any more.

Mary sighed. Her arm enfolded me. I could feel her lips nuzzling my neck. 'I'm glad I came back. I shouldn't have gone. I'm sorry.'

I closed my eyes. How come she could kiss me without noticing the difference? How could she touch my skin without recoiling?

I said, 'I'm tired.'

'Me too.' She gave a long sigh. 'We were rehearsing all evening. I didn't get back till one.'

'How's Jack?' Getting used to my new voice was like getting used to a new house: one day it would be familiar; I would forget I had ever sounded different.

'He was a pain.'

She wriggled one hand over my stomach and started kissing my shoulders and back.

I said, 'Don't.'

'What's the matter?'

I didn't say anything.

'I missed you.' She started kissing my back again. I could feel her heavy breasts squeezing against my spine. I had a sudden image of Sam's breasts, small and white. I closed my eyes. 'Two nights away . . . it's too much. I can't sleep without you.' Her hand had reached between my legs, was stroking me. Despite myself I felt something stir. I rolled over on to my back.

Mary was leaning over me. She was propped up on both arms. Tears glistened on her cheek.

'I shouldn't have gone. I'm sorry, George. It wasn't your fault . . . none of this.'

I said, 'Please . . .'

'I should have been helping you. Instead of . . . I was just think-ing about my concert. About myself.' She pressed her forehead down into my chest. Cold tears made my skin contract. 'Forgive me?'

I couldn't speak. Mary moved her weight on to me. Her breath-ing was growing rhythmic.

'George . . .' She hadn't stopped crying. Something warm was engulfing me, forcing itself down on me. Mary put both hands on my shoulders and pushed herself up. She was sobbing openly, now, rocking herself back and forwards on me and crying in the darkness. The sobs turned into gasps; she collapsed on to my chest.

For a long time she lay there panting, then rolled suddenly off me and turned her back.

'Mary?'

She didn't answer. My mouth was too dry to speak again. After a while I couldn't tell if she was asleep or pretending to be asleep.

I watched the glow of the clock staring at me in the darkness.

24

Jerry Morris should have been getting used to mornings by now. He leaned on the door and peered past me at Lupus Street. He didn't look as if he liked this morning any better than yesterday. He didn't look as if he liked the sight of me any better than yesterday, either.

'Yes?' His eyes registered a face that hadn't slept and a chin that hadn't been shaved. They narrowed.

'I want to ask you some more questions about Jackie Rider.'

'Uh.' He didn't take his weight off the door. He didn't want to let me in.

'Can we go inside?'

He hesitated, then turned grudgingly and walked back down the hall, leaving the door open behind him. Once again he led me through to the studio, but this time he collapsed on the piano stool. The recording desk was too far away.

'You know what time this is?'

I'd spent most of the night watching a clock; I didn't need anyone to tell me what time it was. At half past seven I'd stopped pretending I had any chance of sleep, showered and dressed, and closed the door on lies I didn't want to hide and didn't know how to undo. Mary hadn't woken up. I was trying not to think about what I'd say when I saw her that evening.

Jerry tried to massage his face awake and ended up staring at the piano with a puzzled expression, as if it hadn't been there last time he looked.

'What else you want to know?'

'Where Jackie went after he left you on Wednesday night.'

'I don't know that.'

'Has Jackie been in touch with you? Called you up?'

He shook his head.

I said, 'Does that mean no, or can't you remember?'

Jerry gave me the meanest look he could find. It wasn't bad for that time in the morning. 'He ain't called.'

'Would you tell me if he had?'

Jerry shrugged. The shrug might have meant anything.

'Where does Jackie hang out? Is there a place he likes to go when he isn't at home?'

Jerry stood up. He said, 'Excuse me. I got business to do.'

He walked across the studio floor and went into the glass cubicle. Through the glass I watched him sit down and start to press buttons on the console. Jerry was only doing what jazz musicians had been doing for a long time: if anything might bring trouble then he didn't know anything about it. The studio speakers buzzed. I didn't know how I was going to get through to him. For the moment I felt too tired even to get up off the stool.

It took me a moment to recognize the tune. The arrangement was sparse, lighter than Louis Armstrong had made it. There was no vocal; the melody was taken by a reedy saxophone with a tone that sounded like someone's heart breaking. Words came back into my mind above the sound of the sax:

> I see skies of blue and clouds of white
> The bright blessed day, the dark sacred night
> And I think to myself
> What a wonderful world

I got up and went over to the door. Jerry didn't look up at me. His fingers were busy on the console.

'Who's playing?'

He turned his face towards me. His eyes were hostile. 'The guy you looking for.'

'Jackie Rider?'

He nodded. 'In the old days. 'Fore things went . . .' His voice dropped. 'Bad.'

We both listened to Jackie Rider play. It wasn't a strong sound; there was nothing flashy about it; just a sad, reedy tone picking its way over the notes and somehow making them cry with him. The song died away.

I said, 'He was good.'

'Sure he was good.'

I sighed. 'What did Jackie do for you here?'

Jerry was angrily pressing switches. 'Whatever needed doing.'

'Do you need an assistant?'

He didn't answer that. He jabbed his short, guitarist's finger at another button.

'What did you do when Jackie wasn't around?'

'Made do.'

'Did you pay him?'

'He wasn't going to get money anywhere else.'

I leaned my head against the side of the door. The sound of Jackie Rider's saxophone was still filling it.

'Why did he start using drugs?' I asked.

'Same reason everyone else does.' The anger was still there in his voice – either against me or against what had destroyed his friend.

'I need to find him,' I said.

'Sure you do.'

'If he didn't kill Sarah . . .'

'He didn't.' Jerry glanced up at me. 'I told you.'

'Is that what he's hiding from?'

'He's hiding from you.' And from a world where someone like Jackie Rider would not get the benefit of any doubt.

'So how does he clear himself?'

'He doesn't. You find him, you put him in jail. How can he clear himself?'

'Maybe he can tell us something. Maybe someone saw him after he left here. Until we find him, Jackie'll just be running. How long do you think he can run for?'

Jerry stopped playing with the console. His eyes were shrewd. 'You think he killed her?'

Slowly I shook my head.

Jerry gave a snort of disgust. 'So why don't you tell them?'

'It isn't up to me.'

'You're the one looking for him, aren't you?'

'Not any more.' Telling him that took away any reason I had for being there. Jerry swivelled slowly on his chair, moving around until he sat facing me.

'So why you here?'

'I want to find Jackie.'

'Why?'

I shook my head. 'I can't tell you that.'

'Still want me to tell you where he is, though.'

I nodded. 'Do you know where he is?'

'I might do.'

I kept my eyes on his face. 'What would Jackie do if he found out Sarah was dead?'

Jerry sucked air through his teeth. The idea troubled him. He put the backs of two fingers against his arm and injected air.

'He must know about it,' I said. 'Jackie hasn't been home since it happened and he hasn't been in touch with you. What do you think he's doing now?' We both knew what Jackie would be doing: seeking escape from his troubles in the way he had always escaped before.

The thought of it twisted Jerry's face into a frown. I could see him struggling with it. 'If I told you . . .' His finger stabbed out at me again. 'You going to arrest him?'

'I'm not working on the case any more.'

He thought some more. It took a long time for him to reach a decision.

'There was a place we used to go.' His voice was husky.

'A dealer?'

'Dealer. Friend of his.'

'Where?'

Jerry cocked his head at me. 'You're not gonna bring him trouble?'

'I just want to talk to him.'

His grimace showed me how hard it was for him to say it. 'Place in Camden Town. 'Bove a baker shop.' He said the name of a street.

I looked at him. Half of him was already regretting giving it away. His eyes flickered anxiously.

I said, 'You ever go there yourself?'

'Uh-uh.' His face screwed up in disgust. 'I got a little boy.'

'You used to.'

Jerry rocked from the waist again, looking down at his bare knees. He said, 'I'm getting old. You have to stop doing stupid things. I got a wife. Got a little boy.'

I said, 'Thanks.'

He nodded. 'You don't hurt Jackie. Tell him to call me.'

'You care about him.'

'No one else did.'

'What about his wife?'

'She didn't care.' His face screwed up. 'She didn't care about no one but herself.'

He showed me to the front door. I left him peering out at Pimlico in the morning. He looked puzzled by it and a little scared: a new horizon for a man who was getting older.

25

The baker's shop was a dirty window hiding two loaves and a meat pie from an old man who didn't look hungry anyway. The man and the dog next to him were the only living things in the street and neither of them looked as if they were going to stay that way for long. I waited for them to pass and looked at the windows above the bakery. The top floor windows were shrouded by the backs of curtains covered in gaudy flowers. Sun had bleached the orange petals to an autumn yellow. It had taken a lot of sunlight to do that, which meant the inside of the flat had been dark for a long time.

I crossed the road and rang the only button on an Entryphone next to a door which didn't have a letterbox or street number. Maybe whoever lived in the flat didn't want to receive any post. Maybe no one had ever sent them any.

A second ring made the Entryphone crackle as if it was picking up signals from a distant planet. I said, 'Can I come up?'

I didn't understand what the Entryphone said, but pushed the door anyway and felt the catch give. Inside the hall I could hear it buzzing behind me until the door closed. The hall was a narrow corridor with a bicycle standing guard over uncarpeted stairs which disappeared round a corner ahead of me.

A voice from upstairs called, 'Who is it?'

I didn't tell the voice who it was. I fought my way past the bicycle and started climbing stairs. From the half-landing I could see a face peering down at me from above. It was a white face with black rings under the eyes, and cheeks which were stretched tight between the eye sockets and a slack mouth. When it saw me the mouth closed and the face disappeared. I kept climbing. There were footsteps ahead of me. A man appeared on the next half-landing. He was wearing a black sleeveless T-shirt and black jeans that might have started out blue. He had the same face on but this time the mouth was set in a determined line.

'Who are you?'

I said, 'I'm looking for Jackie Rider.'

'That isn't . . . what I asked.' The words came out loose and disjointed, as if someone had undone the bolts which held them together. It was a surprise to find they still added up to a whole sentence.

I stopped two steps below him. He was taller than I had thought. That didn't bother me, but the unfocused look in his eyes did.

He squeezed his eyelids together as if he was trying to home in on me. 'Who's Jackie Rider?'

'You know who he is.'

The man in the T-shirt shook his head. He did it slowly and carefully as if he wasn't sure how well his head was fastened to his body.

'Is he here?'

'Why would he be?'

I said, 'To buy heroin.'

A white finger tried to point at my face but was throwing to the left. 'Who are you?'

'A friend of his.'

'What's your name?'

I told him my name and saw his lips repeating it like a child who can only read by saying the word aloud.

I said, 'That's right. Now will you get Jackie for me?'

'I don't know who you mean.'

Either the smell of the police station still clung to me or he just made a principle of not trusting anyone who could talk without slurring their words. I took a chance, turned and pushed open the landing door behind me. The room behind it was half dark, with a brown twilight that smelled of warm bodies and dirty sheets. It was as if the air had turned dark just by staying there too long, like water in a stagnant pond.

A voice behind me said, 'You can't go in there.'

On the other side of the pond I saw something moving. A woman's face appeared above the edge of a blanket. Her hair was wet grass that she tried to push aside with one hand. 'Davy?'

'What are you doing?' The man's voice came from behind me.

'I told you. I'm looking for Jackie.'

The woman gave a deep sigh and collapsed back into the bed as if talking to me was the biggest effort she'd faced for a week. 'He's upstairs.'

Davy's face was tinged brown by the half light. He didn't block the door but backed away from me across the landing. 'What do you want him for?'

'I want to ask him some questions.'

'Questions about what?' Panic made his voice lurch suddenly, as if he had lost his footing on ice. 'Are you a cop?'

I shook my head. I wasn't sure whether that counted as a lie or not. I said, 'I'm a friend of Jerry Morris.'

The woman's voice called from behind the bedroom door. 'Davy?'

Jerry's name seemed to do something for Davy's nerves. He hugged himself and scratched a thin white elbow while he thought. 'Jackie isn't so good,' he said at last.

'What kind of not so good?'

Davy made a movement with his jaw as if he'd seen too many kinds to start listing them.

'How long's he been here?'

'Two days?' Davy looked for a calendar on the wall over my head and didn't find one. His narrowed eyes tried to remember light and dark. He shook his head. 'You a friend of his?'

'Sort of.'

'You going to help him?'

I said, 'Maybe I will.'

There was enough space between Davy and the balustrade for me to start walking through it. He thought about stopping me but the woman's voice called him again and by the time he'd stopped hesitating I was already halfway up the stairs. I didn't look back. On the top landing two doors were shut, as if in a last line of defence against reality. I opened the one at the front and saw a dim shape sitting against the wall. Black hair outlined a face that looked too pale to belong to anyone living. He was the only thing in the room. It looked as if removal men had taken out the rest of the furniture and now Jackie was waiting for them to come back for him. His knees were huddled up against his chest and both hands folded on top of them. He looked like something dug out of the lava at Pompeii, as if a volcano had exploded inside his head, years ago, and what I saw now was just grey plaster poured into the space that Jackie Rider used to fill. All he had left from the photograph Sarah had shown me was a wide, open forehead, sunken eyes, a mouth that might have looked good smiling but seemed to have forgotten how.

I closed the door behind me, went towards Jackie Rider and sat down next to him with my back against the wall. Whatever he could see in his hands was taking up all of his attention. I let the silence settle around us again, like dust falling in an unused attic.

Gently I said, 'Jackie?'

He was too far away to hear me, too far from the shore to see me wave. I reached over and touched his shoulder. That made him shiver and contract, as if my finger was made of ice. He contracted slowly, like a flower crumpling under a late frost. Slowly he started to cry.

He didn't have anything to cry with. It was like watching a man trying to vomit from an empty stomach. I listened to the dry sobs racking him, scouring his body for tears. After a moment I reached over and put an arm round his shoulders. Jackie folded up beneath it like a kid looking for his mother's arms. His head weighed too little, like a blown egg; his skin had the dry unnatural touch of desiccated leather. Gradually the sobs grew lighter, and his breathing more normal. He might have been asleep.

I said, 'Jackie?'

'Yes?' His voice was as dry and light as his skin. Somehow he had come back from wherever he had been. I wondered how many more journeys he could stand.

My hand gripped his biceps. There seemed to be nothing inside it, as if something had sucked out all the flesh and left only bone in a tube of withered skin.

'When did you last see Sarah?' I asked.

Jackie Rider tensed. The tension moved his arms awkwardly. He pushed away from me and sat up. His eyes were empty. They fed on my face as if they hadn't had a meal for a long time. 'Who are you?' I didn't answer that. He pushed a hand through his hair. 'Are you a policeman?'

'Why would I be a policeman?'

He was too far gone to make links between one idea and another. His eyelids flickered like moths trying to get through glass towards light.

I said gently, 'You know she's dead, don't you?'

Jackie's mouth opened – not as if he was about to deny it; as if he needed to release some hidden pressure inside him. Crooked yellow teeth peered out at the half light.

'Did you kill her?'

The empty expression on his face was replaced by horror. It was the first normal expression I had yet seen on him. 'Do you think I did?'

I shook my head. 'I talked to Jerry.'

The expression of horror slowly faded. 'It was my fault, though.' His head fell slowly forward, as if he was exposing the nape of his neck for an executioner's axe.

'Why?' I asked.

'Because I wasn't there.' The whispered phrases were cold and remorseless, like the summing up of a prosecuting counsel. 'She wanted me to be there.'

'Why?'

His head rocked slowly from side to side. 'She didn't say.'

'Why did she come to your flat?'

'She wanted . . .' Jackie gave a swift intake of breath, as if in pain. 'She was meeting someone there.'

'Why there?'

'She didn't say. She wanted me to be there.' A hollow eye glanced at me. 'I wasn't there.'

I let him suffer by himself for a moment. I didn't have any painkillers that would do him any good.

'When did she ask you, Jackie? When did she ask if she could use your flat?'

'That morning.'

'The same morning?'

He nodded. 'She telephoned me.'

'What did she say?'

'She said . . .' Grief overwhelmed him suddenly, like water pouring into a wrecked ship. He sobbed twice, then stopped on the intake of breath, as if he was never going to breathe again. His frame relaxed with a kind of shudder, as if the effort of relaxing cost him energy that he knew he would never win back.

'What did she say?'

'She said she was doing some business. A deal. She needed somewhere to meet someone. She needed someone to be there. She asked me.'

His voice carried the ghost of the pride he must have felt when she asked him. The abandoned husband was being entrusted with a task; Sarah needed him for something. But Jackie had not been there. He – or the drugs inside him – had failed her as I guessed he had failed every time she had given him tasks before. And this time it had cost Sarah her life.

I said, 'When did you last shoot up?'

'I don't know.' His voice was unwilling.

'Do you feel all right now?'

His right shoulder moved once, as if he didn't want to start thinking about how he felt.

'Did Sarah tell you about June?'

'What about June?' His white face swung towards me like an animal staring into the headlights of a car. 'What's happened to her?' Panic was starting to scratch at his voice.

I said, 'June's fine.' I said it loud enough to force his own voice to silence.

He sat there nodding for a moment as if that reassured him. 'Sarah's dead,' he said at last.

'Did you see her?'

The nodding continued. 'I came back. I remembered she'd said . . . to be there. After I left Jerry's. She was *dead*.' The word hit an anguished pitch as if it was a nail he was trying to force deeper into his own flesh.

174

'How did she get in?'

'She had keys.'

'Why?'

'In case . . . I used to lose mine.'

'Did you still see her often?'

'When she wanted.'

'How often was that?'

The pace of the questions was too much for him. His voice was starting to fade. 'I don't know.'

I gave him time to recover. 'Sarah told me she was too hard on you. I saw her the day before she died.'

'Did she?' He looked eagerly up at me. 'What did she say?'

'Just that.'

'Tell me.'

I repeated what Sarah had told me, leaving out the bad bits, leaning on affection I thought I'd still heard in her voice. Jackie listened with his head on one side as if he was hearing a favourite tune. I'd been right that his mouth was good at smiling. For a moment I could see in the ruined face what Sarah Donaghy must once have seen: someone young, kind, full of life and music. That was before it turned out that Jackie was too kind, and that the high sound of his sax was about to be driven out by darker music.

When I finished he sighed and looked at his hands. It took time for the memory of Sarah's body to take over his face again. It ate away at the smile gradually, like acid burning through a picture. At the end he looked as ruined as before.

He said, 'I promised her. She made me promise.'

'What did you promise her?'

'To be there.'

'Why did she want you there?'

'She said . . .' He frowned. 'It was to do with money. She said there was a lot of money. Sarah always wanted money.' He sighed again, remembering the first of many failures. That memory was almost a comfort, now, compared to his last betrayal. It was in the past and it hadn't killed anybody.

I said, 'Why didn't you call the police, Jackie? When you found her?'

'I . . .' He shivered. 'I was scared.' He looked at me. 'Are you from the police?'

'In a way.'

'Have you come to arrest me?'

I shook my head.

'I thought . . .' He hugged himself. 'They'll all think I did it, won't they?'

I said, 'Yes.'

'Are they going to arrest me?' He frowned at the floor. 'It *was* my fault.' Maybe it would have been a relief to him if I'd put handcuffs on him and dragged him out into the light of courtrooms and police cells. At any rate it would have been kinder than the punishment he was inflicting on himself. 'I didn't kill her, though.'

'I know you didn't.'

'I'd never have hurt Sarah. I loved her.'

He'd hurt her badly enough along the way, but none of that mattered now. All along Jackie had clung to the dream that one day she might have him back – if he could only deserve her. She was his light at the end of the tunnel, and now that light was gone. That was the other reason he was sitting alone in an empty room with nothing but frenzied dreams to keep him company.

I stood up.

Jackie's eyes followed me beseechingly. 'Don't you want me to come with you?'

I shook my head.

'You're not really a copper, are you?'

'Not really.'

A pale tongue appeared on his lips. 'Do you have any money?'

I hesitated. Money would buy him more dreams to fill the gap Sarah had left, the gap Jackie Rider had left. But the monsters in his mind were too powerful already without giving them any more to feed on. I shook my head.

Jackie let his own head fall softly back on his knees.

I left him sitting alone in the empty room.

26

Outside it was mid-afternoon; I didn't know what time it was inside the flat. I started walking towards the tube and found a phone box on the corner of Camden High Street. I had to wait while someone looked for Baring. When his voice came on the line it sounded breathless, as if he had been running.

'Sir?'

I said, 'It's me. Have you spoken to Jimmy Bolan yet?'

'Saw him this morning, sir. He's in quite a mess.' He said it with the considered judgement of a man who'd seen a lot of messes.

'Can he talk?'

'He didn't want to, sir.'

'What did he say happened?'

'Said he got jumped by a group of blokes. Doesn't remember what they looked like. They went for the cash box. It's true the cash box is gone.'

'Did you ask him about Medd?'

'Yes, sir.' Baring sounded unhappy about something. 'I asked him if he could identify Medd as the man he sold the car to. He said . . .' Baring swallowed. 'Said he wasn't sure any more. He might have made a mistake.'

'Does Medd know anything about what happened to Bolan?'

'He says he doesn't . . . He would say that.'

'Did anyone see it happening?'

Baring sighed. 'No, sir.'

Suddenly I realized I was gripping the receiver so tight my fingers hurt. 'Does Mason know about this?'

'He's taken over the case himself, sir. I've just been with him now.'

'What's happened to Medd?'

'He said . . . Chief Superintendent Mason said there wasn't any reason to hold him. He said he hadn't committed an offence. His lawyer started making trouble, by all accounts . . .'

The walls of the phone booth seemed to be closing in on me. I said, 'Where's Medd now?'

Baring's voice sounded as if it came from a long way away. 'He was released half an hour ago.'

I put the phone down. For a moment I stared out through the windows of the booth. The world looked in: a roadsweeper leaning on his broom, a pair of traffic wardens, a man on the other side of the street. This was how paranoia started. Somewhere Medd was staring in at me as well. I was in a glass box in a city of six million people and there was nowhere I could hide from him.

A fist rapped on the glass. I looked round. A stranger's face was mouthing words at me, showing its teeth.

I picked up the phone again and dialled the number of Mary's rehearsal studio. Engaged tones droned in my ear. I tried again, repeatedly, getting more and more desperate. Somehow I had to warn Mary that Medd had been released. On the fifth attempt I heard the click of a machine and a metallic voice asked me for a message. I slammed the phone down and dialled Charlie's number.

'Hello?'

'It's George. Have you seen Mary?'

'She was trying to get hold of you.'

'Is she there?'

'She was.' His voice sounded cold. 'She left.'

'Where did she go?' I could hear my own voice tightening.

'Back home.'

'To Jack?'

'To you. She wanted to talk to you.' He made it sound as if no one could understand why Mary would want to talk to me.

Outside the box a man was waiting angrily to talk to me. His mouth said, '. . . Ten minutes . . .'

I pushed him aside and started to run. I wasn't sure whether I was running away from something or towards it. Suddenly the pavement seemed too narrow; passers-by turned angrily as I pushed against them. In Camden High Street I was fighting against a tide of people. Eyes jerked away from me; from the windows above shops I could see faces looking down. Medd lurked behind every corner, watched me from the wheels of passing vans. Outside the tube station a man was cutting up the road with a power drill, chewing tarmac into long black shavings. The noise of the drill pursued me down the tunnels of the subway. The tube platform was filled with the wail of distant trains; I watched the clock counting minutes towards four o'clock. Inside the carriage I caught sight of a face in the glass, white, scared and tense. It took a moment for me to realize it was my own. A woman standing next to me walked down the carriage to sit down, throwing anxious glances back at me over her shoulder. At Brixton tube I ran up the steps.

I saw Don from fifty yards up the pavement. He was standing in the doorway of his café. His face was troubled.

I came to a halt in front of him.

He said coldly, 'Your friend just left.'

'What friend?' I stopped.

His fingers touched his scalp, indicating no hair. 'Your *white* friend,' he said.

The cold look turned to shock when he saw my face. I fumbled with the lock; the stairs smelled of blood. The door to our flat was hanging open.

I stopped. The blood was pounding in my ears. Through the open door I could see a strip of carpet, the doorway into the living room. It all looked normal. I took a deep breath and pushed the door wider. Nothing happened. No one jumped out at me.

I took a step forward into the flat.

'Hello?' My voice sounded shaky.

The blind over the kitchen window lifted slightly in a draught, rattled into place again. I turned and went through into the living room.

Mary was lying by the sofa. Her arms were wrapped around her head. The carpet under her was stained red.

27

The ambulance driver was a fat Sikh in a turban. I watched him through the windscreen. He was talking into a radio microphone. There were folds of fat around his eyes and mouth. The din of the siren had been cut off and the blue light turned in silence, picking up the kids lining the opposite pavement, the steps they had carried Mary down, Don's horrified face. A woman in green overalls was talking to me. She had her hands on my sleeve: she wanted me to go somewhere. Mary's face was whiter than the sheet. Her eyelids were very dark. For a moment her face flickered and I saw Sam Harvey's face instead.

The woman pulled at my sleeve. 'All right, sir. Is there someone you'd rather call instead? A relative?'

I squinted down at her. She wasn't pretty. She had a snub nose and a face that would be remembered only by people in shock. The silver rack Mary was lying on was sliding slowly forward between the ambulance doors.

'You could get someone else to bring you, if you'd rather. I don't think you should drive.' She gave my arm a little shake.

Someone shouted, 'All right!' Doors were slamming. I found myself walking. Between the doors of the ambulance was a red cave. It looked like an open wound. A man was kneeling over Mary.

He said, 'Come *on*.'

I was sitting on a bench, rocking, staring up at a bright fluorescent light which rocked above me. Someone was wailing in the background. I wondered who was wailing. Surely it was too early for that. I tried to stagger forwards.

'Leave them alone, sir. They know what they're doing.'

I found myself sitting on the bench again. Mary's hand dangled from the edge of the stretcher. I stared at it. The fingers were long, the nails badly cut. There was a ring on her little finger I'd never looked at before. She couldn't sleep without my hand to hold on to. They ought to know that. I ought to explain . . .

'All right, sir. We'll be there in a minute.'

They were taking us up a mountain. The bright light rocked overhead. They were taking us up a mountain and women were wailing in the distance, a long procession of women winding up the mountain path behind us.

'The doctor knows we're coming.'

Her fingers tapped out a little rhythm on my sleeve. I wondered what the song was: I didn't recognize it. Maybe Mary would know. Mary's hand still dangled from the stretcher. It was a beautiful hand, so beautiful it made me want to cry. The fingers were poised, balanced as if she was about to pick up a glass and drink from it.

'All right, sir. There soon.'

The man beside Mary was turning. He had crooked brown teeth and tufts of hair straggling over his ears. I strained to understand what he was saying. I couldn't hear him. His lips moved but no sound seemed to be coming out. Instead, I could hear a voice somewhere else shouting, 'Oxygen.'

Oxygen. I thought of divers plunging into black water, capsules of oxygen strapped to their backs. The doors of the ambulance were opening. Somebody pushed me back against the wall. Mary's face drifted past me, white and peaceful as if she was floating down a river. Glass doors batted at me. Some force was steering me away from Mary. I tried to protest about that. She could only sleep with me next to her. The force was too strong for me. It made my knees buckle, pressed a chair against my back. A man's legs were standing in front of me. I looked upwards to a white coat, a mask dangling under the chin, a tired face in spectacles.

I heard, 'Bloody lucky . . . She was bloody lucky . . . Bloody lucky you got there when you did.'

I didn't understand. I wanted to ask questions, find out what he meant. The legs were gone, though, striding away from me across a marble field. There was someone in white standing over me, a hand on my shoulder. She was holding something in front of my face: a china cup with something brown in it. A hand squeezed my shoulder. I picked up the cup and tasted blood. It was Mary's blood. I couldn't swallow that.

'Never mind, sir. We'll get someone to mop it up. Never mind about the cup.'

She wasn't talking, she was singing: an odd sing-song with a rhythm like the galloping of a horse. My legs were burning. I was walking again. People in white robes and dressing gowns were hurrying to escape from me. I was in a psychiatric ward and they were all afraid of me. Jackie Rider was shuffling away from me dressed in a black T-shirt, holding his saxophone.

'This way, sir.'

I found myself in a lift. We were rising in silence with no sense of movement but the faint juddering of the walls and floor. The people around me had the pallid faces of undertakers. The lift doors opened on to a corridor which went on for ever. Doors lined it on both sides. Mary was in one of the rooms. I was sure of that, and I was sure Medd was hiding in another. I had to find Mary before he did, but there were so many doors to open. I didn't know where to start.

Suddenly I saw the tired doctor. He was standing in one of the doorways, watching me walk towards him.

His lips moved. His voice reached me a moment after they moved, as if he was shouting at me across a deep canyon. 'I'm sorry it's been such a wait. You can see her now, if you like. She seems to be coming round.'

It was a small room with a window on to lights outside which looked like stars. An iron bed stood in the middle of the floor. Around the wall were posters and racks of equipment. To start with I didn't think there was anyone in the bed. I shuffled forwards. Mary was lying flat on her back. Her eyes were still closed but on her face was an expression of pain. The eyebrows were drawn together with a faint knot of discomfort between them. Her hands were hidden under the sheet.

Plastic tubes ran from her nostrils to somewhere behind the pillow. A white bandage around her neck divided her head from her body, as if it had been severed and sewn back on. I looked wildly behind me. The room was empty, the door closed.

Slowly I sat down on the edge of the bed. The knot between Mary's eyebrows darkened and then relaxed. There was a faint hiss of air in the plastic tubes when she breathed.

Words were coming back to me. They rose up from turmoil, like flotsam rising to the surface from a sunken ship. 'She was bloody lucky.' Someone had spoken very seriously to me, using words I didn't understand. I remembered the rise and fall of his hand as he spoke. There were phrases that meant nothing without the phrases around them: 'Loss of blood' . . . 'Signs of damage.' Gently I reached forward and touched Mary's hair. The frown crossed her face again like a gust of wind ruffling grass. Even in repose her face was lined. She was thirty-two years old and lost her temper whenever I mentioned it. I pulled back the sheet and drew out one hand. It was cold between my fingers. The muscles were relaxed. I spread Mary's fingers out between my own. Her nails were stained yellow from cigarettes. She always hated her own hands, never allowed me to look at them. With my index finger I traced the bones across the back of her hand. The air kept hissing in the plastic tubes.

For ten years I had known Mary. We had lived together for half of that, on and off. Maybe we hadn't been happy in the way couples were supposed to be happy, but we'd found our own way instead. I could no longer imagine what it would be like without her. I thought of Sam Harvey: a neat white face with freckles under cornflower blue eyes. Something inside me contracted. The frown knotted itself again on Mary's forehead. I realized how hard I was gripping her hand and slowly released it. But the hollowness inside me remained. Sam Harvey. I saw a darkened room, pale shapes where the windows were, heard Sam's voice whispering in my ear. I closed my eyes.

After a while I let go of Mary's hand. There was a chair pushed back against the side wall. I went over and sat on that, watching the white sheet rise and fall over Mary's chest. Tomorrow she should be singing her concert: the date she'd wanted for ten years. Instead she was lying in a hospital bed; lying there because I had put her there, with plastic tubes coming out of her nostrils and pain buried deep in her face.

Time passed. I thought of Jimmy Bolan, of Jackie Rider hunched in an empty room; I thought of Mrs Donaghy with the cross swinging over her neck; I thought of June lying in Thames mud. I remembered the way Michael Harvey had looked at me as he walked out of the police station. I thought of Peter Thacker in his elegant suit, of the lines of power criss-crossing London, of the deep sewers of fear into which all its streets drained.

Mary stirred on the bed. I stood up. Her eyes were open, searching the white ceiling for something familiar. Quietly I walked over to the bed and looked down at her. The dark eyelids flickered. She was casting around for where she might be, why she might be there. Her grey eyes moved slowly across the ceiling and came to rest on me. Understanding came back into them. Gradually her forehead creased; the knot hardened between her eyebrows; she looked old.

I whispered, 'It's me.'

Mary didn't say anything; maybe she couldn't say anything. Slowly her head turned to one side, away from me. Her eyes closed.

28

Outside the hospital it was cold; the pavement was deserted. I walked fast across Westminster Bridge. A woman's face stared out at me from a late bus. The river was lit up in the orange glow of the clouds; from far away I could hear traffic.

I didn't know where I was walking. The pavement stamped up at my feet, carrying me past empty streets, darkened shops. Trees massed thickly about me. I saw grey buildings looming above streetlights, narrow side streets running away from me in both directions. A brick wall left me in empty space where my footsteps were the only sound.

I was a child walking down a street too big for me to comprehend. Ralph had run on ahead and I was alone; the sound of wailing filled my own ears but reached nobody else. When I looked ahead I could see my father. He was standing fifty yards away, wearing a blue raincoat with his hands in the pockets. His lips moved but he was too far away for me to hear what he said.

My footsteps carried me on to soft grass. I stumbled and looked up. The sky was an orange tent suspended between trees. Beneath the trees was dense shadow. I walked towards the shadow. Something was hammering in my head – a tune too indistinct for me to make out. It came to me in the tone of Jackie Rider's saxophone – 'Diane'. I could hear Mary singing it. She was standing on a stage too small to let her move. Sunlight came through windows behind her shoulder. Just for a moment the audience of old men and Sunday drinkers had stopped everything else and were craning their heads to look at her. Afterwards someone introduced her to me and we talked and then didn't stop talking. Her face was young, full of hope. She described dates she would play and places she would go. As I watched, her eyes closed and the lids darkened. Colour fled from her cheeks, leaving trails of lines around her eyes and mouth. A purple scar appeared on her neck.

I was walking on pavement again. A woman ahead of me was crossing the road to avoid me, her heels tapping quickly on the empty tarmac. I turned corners, passed silent doorways. The rhythm of my steps numbed my brain, driving out all other thoughts.

It was the feel of cold iron under my hands that woke me. My hands were gripping railings. I looked through them and saw stairs descending into a basement, a window covered by shabby curtains. I blinked. A cold wind pierced my coat, making me shiver. For the first time since leaving the hospital I was fully awake. Now I knew why I had walked this way.

For two years this was where I had lived; some instinct had brought me back to it. I stared at the curtains. This was what I had been avoiding whenever anyone asked me what I did after leaving the police – this staircase, these railings at which I had stared for too long. There was no secret; there had been no disaster; only the slow transformation of iron railings into bars, of a home into a prison. Outside the world had gone on. I had watched its footsteps passing me; children had peered down at me through the railings. I had refused to compromise with Mason; I had made my stand against the police; and this was where it had taken me: to the narrow cell of a hermit; to a prison of my own making.

I remembered long days when all tunes merged into each other; when I picked up a book to read, then turned my head and found that the whole afternoon had gone by. I remembered letters from Ralph worrying about me, and I remembered answers I had started but never managed to send. I had spent hours staring at cracks in the bedroom ceiling. In them I had found a map of the town where we grew up. It showed the Market Square and High Street, our house, the street where my father was killed. I walked along the High Street in my imagination: a child trailing behind a shopping trolley, a boy walking slowly behind a black hearse. In the church, far over in the corner of the ceiling, I heard prayers for a man who had never believed in church. Ralph shuffled uncomfortably next to me in the pew. The smell of flowers drove out the smell of grief.

It was Mary who rescued me from it. A friend had asked what had happened to me, or told her that he was worried. One day the doorbell rang and when I opened the door she was standing there. Her grey eyes were full of compassion. We had walked across the road to the park and the clean wind blowing across grass seemed to sweep away two wasted years. Six months later we were living together again. Afterwards we hardly talked about what had happened. I told her the bare bones; somehow she understood the rest. To Mary I owed everything that had happened since.

And now Mary was lying in hospital and somewhere in London the man who had put her there was still hunting me. There was no way back through the police; and yet I couldn't return to that lonely flat any more than Michael Harvey could go back to his mother's cramped house in the North. The only way to go was on. Somehow I must find Medd. Somehow I must discover what Michael Harvey and the Thackers were really doing.

I pushed myself off the railings and started walking again. In the Bayswater Road a solitary bus was waiting at the lights. On impulse I climbed on just before the lights changed. The passengers dozed with their heads leaning against the windows or against each other. I got off at the end of a long street of stuccoed houses with shabby hotel signs outside them. Handwritten cards in the windows advertised vacancies. I chose one at random and went into a lobby which smelled of drains. A woman with dyed blond hair was dozing behind the reception desk. On the walls were bleached posters of the Highlands and Stonehenge. A fluorescent light hung from the ceiling. The clock over the desk told me it was just past two.

'Do you have a room?'

The woman jerked herself out of dreams and back to the lobby which smelled of drains. The mascara had run under one eye. She looked past me into the night, then back at my face. 'Alone?'

I told her I was alone.

She wrote details on a yellow form and handed me a key tied to a plastic Big Ben.

'Top floor, end of the corridor. The light's on the wall.'

I turned away from the desk.

'Do you want company?' She sounded weary, not embarrassed or coy. She had seen too many men walk in out of the night in need of company.

I needed company, but not that sort. I climbed stairs past rows of sleeping doors. The room was a bleak cell: a bed covered in a dirty green counterpane, a cupboard with hangers swaying emptily inside it, a mirror which reflected a different face every night: tired faces, lonely faces, faces ashamed of the whores lying on the bed behind them. I was too tired to wash. I left my clothes on the lino floor and climbed between cold unfamiliar sheets. My last thought was of Mary's face lying on pillows at the hospital.

The sound of drilling woke me. It brought with it Medd's face hunched over a road drill, chiselling into the foundations of some building. Medd faded to the cupboard door hanging open. My left arm was numb with cold. I looked at my watch. It was half past seven. I got up, showered under a freezing trickle of water and dried myself on a piece of sandpaper with the hotel's initials printed on it. Down in the lobby the tired woman from the night before had been replaced by a man in a mustard yellow jacket whose face was still raw from shaving. The radio behind the desk was tuned to Jazz FM, playing happy songs to cheer up unhappy commuters on their way to work.

I crossed to the pay phone in the corner. It took a long time to get through to the hospital. I spoke to clerks and to nurses, and listened to silence echoing in long empty corridors.

'Mr Sullivan?' It was an Indian voice, a man.

'I'm not Mr Sullivan.'

'It was you who brought Miss Sullivan in yesterday afternoon?'

'That's right.' I paused. 'Can I speak to her?'

'She's sleeping now. She woke up at six. She's very confused.'

'Is she all right?'

'It depends what you mean by all right.' The doctor seemed to be thinking. 'She's concussed. These things take time to get over. And even if the physical injuries aren't bad . . .'

'Will you keep her in for long?'

'A couple of days. It should be longer, really. I'm sure you want her home. Will you be coming in to see her?'

I said, 'Tell her I called.'

I hung up and dialled again, hoping Baring's shift had kept him at the police station. I didn't recognize the voice that answered the phone and didn't introduce myself. It took him time to find Baring, and when Baring reached the phone his voice had the hollow sound of someone who'd been up for too long.

'Hello?'

I told him what had happened and didn't give him too long to tell me how sorry he was. 'There's something I need to know.'

'Yes, sir?'

'We found Medd through an informer. Do you still have his name?'

'Bloke in New Cross, sir. A feud. Family thing. Medd beat up his brother.'

'How did you find him?'

'Beat copper knew him. They grew up next door.'

'Do you have an address?'

Baring's voice was hushed. 'Do you think it was Medd who attacked Mary?'

'Don't tell Mason that. Just give me the name of the man who knows him.'

'Endell, sir. Tommy Endell. Runs an arcade – games and stuff. New Cross Road.'

He gave me directions and some warnings about being careful which I didn't need.

'There was something else, sir.' Baring's voice was gruff with embarrassment. 'Before you go. A phone call yesterday.'

'Who from?'

'A girl, sir. Wouldn't leave her name. She called twice. I think she was in a bit of a state, sir.'

I closed my eyes and thought of Sam Harvey. 'Thanks.'

The man in the mustard yellow jacket was waiting for me when I came out of the phone booth.

'Mr Havilland?'

I nodded.

He said, 'There was a message for you during the night.' His face was bright and shining, not yet spoiled by the troubles of the day.

'Nobody knows I'm here.'

He shrugged. 'That was the name. Someone knows you.'

'What was the message?'

I watched his raw red hands fumble under papers on the reception desk. He pulled out a desk pad with the hotel's logo on it.

'Wanted you to meet him. Said, twelve o'clock, 35 Elm Park Gardens, NW5?' He looked up at me to see if the address meant anything.

'What was his name?' I asked.

'Primrose Hill, isn't it? NW5?'

I said, 'What was his name?'

The receptionist squinted at the clumsy biro scrawl. His face cleared. 'Thacker,' he said. He looked up at me and smiled. 'Mr Peter Thacker.'

29

I drank coffee in a deserted sandwich bar near the river. A Saturday morning hush covered the pavement as if the whole city was recovering from something that had happened the night before. The Italian girl behind the counter leaned on her elbows, gazing out through the window at olive groves and sun-drenched towns she had probably never seen. From Kensington Gardens I caught a bus which took me south, past sleeping offices and abandoned tourist buses. The river was a silver thread running behind trees.

Mrs Donaghy wasn't expecting to see anybody. The curtains in the house in Renshaw Road were drawn over windows which had already seen too much, and which no longer expected any news to be good. Drawn curtains marked the house out from its neighbours. It was no longer afraid of the tower blocks at the end of the road, or of what the neighbours might see. All of its fears were on the inside.

Mrs Donaghy's face was grey, like the face of a stone mourner on a tomb. The soft wrinkles I had seen on Monday had turned into harsh lines too deep ever to fade back into the skin. I didn't think time would heal Mrs Donaghy's face. Resentment would continue to gnaw away at it until the day she died.

'Yes?' She held the door across her chest like a shield. I wondered if there was any more bad news she could possibly fear. She didn't have any more daughters to die.

I said, 'I'm Chief Inspector Havilland. I came on Monday.'

'I remember.' She said it with a kind of harsh finality. Remembering was all she had left to do.

'I'm sorry about Sarah.'

Her mouth rose and tightened. I couldn't tell whether that was grief, or what her mouth had always done when Sarah's name was mentioned.

'Yes.' Mrs Donaghy's fingers whitened on the edge of the door. 'Can I come in?'

'Is there any news? About June?'

'There might be.'

'They thought he was a random attacker. The man I spoke to yesterday.' She was used the words with contempt. Mrs Donaghy believed in killers, not attackers; in evil, not in random misfortune.

'Did someone come to see you?'

'On the telephone. A Chief Superintendent.'

She led me back down a hall which had already been changed by a week of silence. It wasn't just that the place sounded like a tomb; it had already become Mrs Donaghy's tomb. Nothing would change here – the wallpaper, the flowered carpet, the heavy brass lamp. Her resentment would keep them the same until she died herself, entombed in the house June had left to go to work one Sunday morning.

The living room was in semi-darkness. Any light filtering through the drawn curtains was the dim light of a crypt. The photographs of June Donaghy on the wall winked darkly like time-blackened icons above invisible side altars. The side lamp by the sofa threw a cone of light on the upturned bible Mrs Donaghy must have been reading when I rang the bell. Next to it on the side table was a little pile of change, a bunch of keys, a security pass with a photograph of June in it. June's face looked up at me, still squinting at the light of a flash gun which went off months ago. Her effects must have been returned to her mother; now Mrs Donaghy was treasuring them like relics of a martyred saint.

'I'm sorry to disturb you,' I said.

The shadows had clawed more lines down Mrs Donaghy's cheeks and forehead as if some giant bird had fastened its talons on her head. The big cross on her chest winked faintly in the darkness.

'I always want to hear news about June.' Her eyes followed mine to the pile of loose change and upturned bible. 'And about who killed her.' The bible wouldn't be turned to a chapter about forgiveness. I could hear the blood curdling in her throat when she spoke of June's killer. She had worshipped a stern and unyielding Lord all her life and now she expected him to repay. 'Have you found him, Chief Inspector?'

I sat down after her. She didn't sit back in the sofa but kept her back rigidly straight, her hands folded on her lap.

I said, 'We've got some ideas.'

She shook her head impatiently. 'I know who did it. That was why I telephoned yesterday, to tell the Chief Superintendent.' I could see her teeth glinting in the darkness. 'Have you found him yet?'

'Who?'

'It was that man, wasn't it? The man Sarah brought into the house. You bring evil into the house and you reap the results.'

'You mean Jackie Rider?'

She winced when I named him, and her hand flew to the bottom of the cross. 'He killed Sarah didn't he? He must have killed June as well. He hated everything that was good and clean and . . .'

Her voice was starting to rise. I said, 'I don't think Jackie Rider killed your daughters, Mrs Donaghy.'

Her pale eyes stared at me across the dark room like a saint watching unbelievers condemn themselves from their own lips. When she spoke again it was from further back and higher up: I'd become one of the enemy. 'You don't know what he was like. He took Sarah away and destroyed her. She used to be just a normal girl. She used to be like June. He turned her into . . . what she became.' Mrs Donaghy's voice was thick with resentment against both of them. 'He hated all of us,' she went on. 'He hated me because I wouldn't let him come into the house. I was *right* not to let him in. He was an *evil* man.'

'Jackie wasn't a killer,' I said. 'He was a drug addict. That doesn't make him a killer.'

'Maybe it was the drugs that made him kill them.'

Her voice was truculent. She knew who had killed her daughters and she wasn't going to give ground on that or anything else. I wasn't going to get anywhere by disagreeing with her.

I said, 'When I came here before you told me June had

been unhappy about her job. She wanted to go to the papers about it.'

Mrs Donaghy's eyes switched focus, looking further into the distance at enemies she was no longer fighting. Without interest she said, 'It wasn't that she was unhappy. She didn't like Mr Thacker. He said dreadful things to her.'

'You told me that wasn't all. You said June didn't like some of the things his company was doing.'

Mrs Donaghy's lips pursed. She didn't agree or deny it. She was waiting to see what I wanted.

'Did she ever tell you what it was she didn't like?'

'She told me everything.' Mrs Donaghy didn't want to have to think. Thinking exposed unhealed nerve ends in her mind. She preferred mantras she could repeat without raising her face to the light.

'What did she tell you about this?'

'She said . . .' I could hear Mrs Donaghy's voice groping. June's memory was already stiffening into scenes from the life of a saint: little girl at school; girl by the Eiffel tower; exhausted woman coming home late from work. It was hard for her to find anything which fell between those images. 'It doesn't matter now, anyway.'

'It might.'

'Why?' She turned her sombre face towards me. 'What good would it do?' She wasn't hiding anything from me; she was fighting for an excuse not to think about it.

I said, 'Barney Thacker didn't treat her properly, did he?'

She shook her head. Another line of resentment had opened up in front of her like a gunpowder trail. 'He wouldn't leave her alone. He kept on chasing her even after she told him to go away. At a conference in Scotland . . .' I didn't mind listening to it again if it made her think about Barney Thacker. 'My daughter wasn't like other girls. She wasn't interested in men.'

'I know that,' I said. I tried not to think of Michael Harvey, or of what the police doctor had told us.

'He didn't understand. How could he understand? That's not how I brought the girls up – either of them. Sarah was the same until that man . . .'

Whatever the subject she would always circle back to Jackie Rider. He was the private demon who had destroyed her house and left two daughters dead; by the hidden connections which forge easy paths through minds like hers, all evil would now be traced back to him.

I interrupted her, 'Barney Thacker did other things June didn't like as well, didn't he? Things she didn't think were honest.'

She nodded. She couldn't remember what I was talking about, but for the moment I was on her side.

I said, 'Last time I was here you let me see her room. There were some papers in it.'

She didn't nod. Her face was absolutely still.

'Are they still there?'

'I haven't touched anything. She wouldn't have wanted me to. I never pried.'

Her daughter had told her everything; she didn't need to pry.

I said, 'Would you let me look at them?'

Pain cut a mark in the side of Mrs Donaghy's face. She didn't want anyone going into June's room, and I hadn't given her a good enough reason to allow me in. It wasn't Barney Thacker who had killed her daughter, it was Jackie – Jackie who had stolen both of her daughters from her and who was still lurking outside, beyond the drawn curtains. I should have been searching for him and bringing him back in chains like the monster in a medieval painting.

Her fingers sought guidance in the cross at her neck. The cross told her to stall. 'We had her funeral yesterday.' She meant June's funeral. Sarah was still unforgiven. Mrs Donaghy's baleful pale eyes turned towards me. 'No one from the police was there.' To Mrs Donaghy, as to all victims of crime, June's murder was the only crime ever committed – the only one that mattered. There wasn't anything I could say that would be a substitute for policemen in mourning and voices hushed all across London. It wasn't just us. She couldn't forgive the whole world for carrying on after her daughter's death as if nothing had happened. That was why the curtains were drawn.

'I'm sorry.'

'Father Driscoll and me. No one else. Mr Thacker sent a lovely wreath.' She looked at her knees. 'The other Mr Thacker. He sent me some money as well.'

I hoped that flowers and money hadn't bought his brother forgiveness. 'Was Barney Thacker there?'

The top of her head moved. 'He wouldn't have dared.'

I said slowly, 'I met Barney Thacker on Monday. I told him what you'd said to me about June.'

Mrs Donaghy's head was absolutely still. 'What did he say?'

'He denied it.'

'How could he deny it?' Her voice was angry.

I said, 'He told me you were lying.'

Her head went up like a hound sniffing blood. In the dim light from the side table I could see her nostrils flare. 'He *couldn't*. How *dare* he?'

'It's what he said.'

Her knuckles tightened on the arm of the sofa. Anger made her small mouth cruel. Peter Thacker had tried to buy her off; he hadn't known that Mrs Donaghy's forgiveness was not for sale. 'He's a *wicked* man. June told me. She was always right about people, June.'

I said, 'Some of June's papers might be about him.'

'About Mr Thacker?'

I nodded. Mrs Donaghy hesitated. 'Why do you need to see them?'

'It's important to get a full picture.'

She knew that didn't mean anything, but now I was on her side. I followed her up stairs darkened by grief to a bedroom which already smelled of a week of neglect. To Mrs Donaghy it was still the room her daughter had left on the morning she went to work for the last time. Anyone else would have recognized it as a shrine: a tidy room which hadn't been cleaned so that a fine layer of dust had already started to settle on June Donaghy's chest of drawers and on the romantic novels piled up by the bed.

I went forward into the room. The desk was still closed, the bedspread folded neatly over the pillows. Glancing back at Mrs Donaghy's face, I saw that it was contorted with pain. On Monday she had still been in shock; now the grief was fully awake, and her body was no longer anaesthetized from it.

I didn't look at her for long. I went over to the desk. Inside, the envelopes were still as I remembered them. I opened the top one and saw the logo of PTI Holdings. It was a letter from Barney Thacker to someone in a firm I didn't recognize. There were more letters beneath it.

Mrs Donaghy shuffled her feet. 'Have you seen all you need to, Chief Inspector?' She was already regretting letting me in to June's room. The sight of a policeman in there – or of any man – only brought home to her that it wasn't June's room any more. With the door shut and the teddy bears tidied carefully away in the corner she could pretend that her daughter was going to come home to her.

'There's a lot here. It'll take me some time to look through them.' I glanced at her. 'Could I take them away?'

She shook her head dumbly. I might as well have asked to take away the teddy bears.

I started to go through the papers. It wasn't easy with Mrs Donaghy watching, and there was nowhere I could put papers down which wouldn't disturb memories of June. Nothing in the first envelope seemed to me to prove anything about the Thackers. It might just have been an ordinary day's work that June had decided to finish at home.

Mrs Donaghy coughed and moved against the door. 'It was only her job. She . . .'

The telephone rang. She hesitated, glanced at me. It rang again, a hollow, distant sound like the ringing of metal footsteps on stone. Without another word Mrs Donaghy turned and went out of the room. I dropped the first envelope on the desk and opened the second. I knew she wouldn't leave me alone for long. It was in the next that I found what I was looking for. I glanced over my shoulder. Mrs Donaghy's voice was a distant murmur from the front bedroom. Quickly I took out two sheets of paper and folded them into my pocket. Just as I finished replacing the envelopes I heard the phone go down. I turned as Mrs Donaghy appeared in the doorway.

'Father Driscoll. He calls every afternoon.'

'That must be a comfort.'

She hardly even noticed that the envelopes were back in place. She didn't ask me whether I had found anything. She was too eager to get me out of the house.

Mrs Donaghy hesitated by the front door. The coloured glass over the door turned her face a vivid crimson. 'You'll find that man, won't you, Chief Inspector?'

'We'll do our best.'

Her hand grip burned. If she called Mason again she would tell him that I had been there, and then she would find out that wasn't the only lie I had told her.

I walked quickly away from Renshaw Road. I didn't think she would open the curtains to look after me. They would stay drawn now, hiding grief, trying to stop time, until Mrs Donaghy died herself. People would move away; neighbours would change. Renshaw Road would forget, after five or ten years, why the woman in number 26 kept her curtains drawn. Rumours would grow up around her. Father Driscoll would be the only visitor climbing the steps to the front door. Neighbours might complain about smells from the drain or uncleared gutters. And inside Mrs Donaghy would slowly age while one daughter stayed as young as ever, on the photographs on the living-room walls, and the other burned for ever in hells of an old woman's imagination.

30

Peter Thacker's address was painted on two white gate posts north of Regent's Park, in streets of quiet villas which made London look suddenly like a part of Hollywood. A tongue of gravel between the gate posts led to parked cars and the front of a big white stuccoed house. Neatly-trimmed shrubs lined the drive. The street number was painted again on the columns which held up its porch. The number seemed wrong somehow. I couldn't believe there were thirty-four other houses like this in London, let alone in Elm Park Gardens.

A woman watched me approach the portico through one of the long windows at the front of the house. She was slim and blonde, dressed in black silk with a simple row of pearls around her neck. She watched me without interest, as if she was only watching me because she couldn't find anything better to do. Her face didn't change when I caught her eye.

The bell push didn't seem to do anything. Either it was broken or the bell was so far away I couldn't hear it. I never heard footsteps. The door was opened suddenly by a man in a tailcoat who looked over my head as if he was expecting to find somebody taller.

'I've come to see Peter Thacker.'

'Your name?'

Maybe a lot of people were coming to see Peter Thacker at twelve o'clock that day. The butler took my name through a door at the back of the hall and left me looking at antique furniture and a modern painting which had spotlights on it, as if it was something I was supposed to recognize.

A voice from behind me said, 'It's Derain.'

I swung round. The blonde woman was standing in a doorway on the left. She was leaning against the side of the door, holding her pearls in one hand. She was looking at the painting, not at me.

She yawned. 'Peter bought it. Peter buys everything. Do you like it?'

I didn't say anything.

'I hate it. I hate Derain.'

She took an attitude in front of the painting, as if that might help her suddenly to like it. Her face hadn't recovered from the shock of reaching thirty. She had tried to diet her way back into her twenties and only succeeded in stretching her skin to a glassy tautness. A deep tan looked good with the blonde hair but had left her eyes bored. She might have been a model once: she had a model's figure, unnaturally long and thin, and a model's consciousness of the shape her body was making.

Her shoulders dropped, 'He bought it for three-quarters of a million pounds. At Christie's. Do you like it?' She didn't seem to notice that she'd asked me the question before.

'I like it.'

'He bought me as well,' she said. Her voice slurred when she mentioned herself. I wondered if she'd been drinking, but any smell of liquor was buried deep under expensive perfume. She struck the attitude again, as if she was comparing herself with the painting and wondering which of them was worth more.

'I hate Derain.' Footsteps were approaching the door at the back of the hall. They were quicker than the butler's. 'Would you have spent . . ?'

I said, 'I don't have three-quarters of a million pounds.'

The door opened. The young male secretary from Peter Thacker's office came in. His face tightened with irritation when he saw Thacker's wife. She ignored him and kept looking at the painting she hated.

I wondered whether it was her husband's money she was jealous of, or something else.

The secretary gave me a smooth smile which didn't include the woman. He seemed sure of his ground. 'Will you come this way?'

The corridor led me to a long study with French windows at the far end. The windows looked out over lawn and, beyond the lawn, at a canal boat passing under a willow tree. We might not have been in London at all. Peter Thacker was waiting for me behind an antique desk in front of the windows. One leg was folded easily across the other; his smile had been prepared while I came down the corridor. He wasn't alone. In front of the fireplace in the side wall, a heavily-built man with silver hair was rocking himself up and down on his toes. He had his hands clasped behind him like a sergeant-major, and his chin thrust forwards at imaginary troops. He might have been trying to warm his back at the fire, except there was no fire in the grate.

He didn't look towards me when I came in. Peter Thacker got up from the desk and approached me with his hand out. He walked softly, as if he didn't want anyone to hear he was coming. His smile was charming, cultivated, as if I was a friend of his who'd come to admire the view or to make him an offer for the antique desk.

'Chief Inspector.' His smile told me that neither of us much cared for titles, or for what they said about anyone. It was a nice smile, gentle and self-mocking, and if anyone had told him the smile was fake, he would have been ready to laugh at that as well.

I didn't take his hand. Peter Thacker turned the handshake smoothly into a gesture towards the man in front of the fire. 'Have you *met* Philip Lord?' He made it sound as if I spent my life going to parties with people like Philip Lord, spending weekends in the country, doing the other things people like Philip Lord did.

I said, 'I never had the pleasure.'

Philip Lord didn't make it look much of a pleasure. He gave me a short ungracious nod and went back to haranguing the troops. He was taller than he looked on television, more vigorous, less of the old-fashioned gentleman. His cheeks were a bad-tempered red with broken veins splaying over his nose and forehead. His blue double-breasted suit would have looked better on someone younger, but Philip Lord didn't look ready to start admitting his age.

'We're both grateful to you for making the time to see us.' Peter Thacker had gone back behind the desk. There wasn't a chair for me to sit down on. That wasn't the kind of detail Peter Thacker left to chance.

I said, 'Did I have the choice?'

'We all have choices.'

'How did you know where I was staying?'

Peter Thacker gave me a rueful smile, like a favourite child who's been caught breaking the rules again but knows he's going to be forgiven. He looked at the male secretary. 'How about some coffee, Charles?'

The coffee was waiting in a silver thermos on the side table. It came in small china cups with handles designed for the fingers of children or elves. I didn't take the cup Charles offered me.

I kept my eyes on Peter Thacker. 'Was it you who sent Medd to attack Mary yesterday, or did he do that of his own accord?'

'I don't think I know either of those people.' The humour was gone from Thacker's eyes. He glanced at Philip Lord. 'We wanted to talk to you about something else. Shall I start, Philip?'

Lord shrugged as if he didn't care who started as long as they didn't go on for too long.

'You told us the other day that you'd been talking to Michael Harvey.' Thacker gave the name an ironic stress. 'That worried me. I thought it would be sensible to let Philip know what was going on. It was Philip who suggested this meeting today.'

I said, 'I'm surprised you've both got time.'

'Why?'

'Haven't you got an announcement to make on Monday?' I looked at Lord.

'What announcement would that be?' His voice was gruff and reluctant, as if he hated wasting it on someone like me.

'The sell-off of the nuclear power stations. PTI are bidding for them. Don't tell me you'd forgotten that.'

'Did Michael Harvey tell you about that?' Peter Thacker's voice was unruffled. 'That makes it all the more important that we talk to you now.' He took a pen out of his pocket and turned it over in his fingers. 'I told you two days ago what Michael is doing. I hope you've had time to think about it by now – you might have reached your own conclusions. Michael wants to cause us trouble.

Unfortunately this sell-off gives him the chance to do it. He doesn't have any evidence of wrongdoing on our part . . .' Thacker pointed the wrong end of his pen at me. 'There hasn't been any wrongdoing. But it wouldn't take real evidence to cause us a problem. The nuclear issue is sensitive.' His lips twitched as if it was his own skin which was sensitive. 'Michael could use it to get his revenge on us.' He made revenge sound like a game for children in the school playground. 'He could start a rumour. I don't know exactly what. He could use you to help him. And other people as well.'

By other people he meant June Donaghy. His face expressed condolences to the room. When I didn't say anything he went on, 'I rang Philip yesterday morning. I told him that if – *if* – we were fortunate enough to have our bid accepted, there was a chance someone would start a whispering campaign against us.' His hands moved judiciously in front of his waistcoat. 'Only a chance, of course. I don't know exactly how bitter Michael is.' Peter Thacker sighed. 'Philip was good enough to tell us that our bid had been successful.'

I kept my eyes on his face. 'That must have been a surprise to you both.'

Philip Lord grunted at the hearth rug. Peter Thacker appeared not to have heard what I said. 'He was sticking his neck out by telling me ahead of time, and we're both taking a risk by telling you.' He leaned over the desk towards me. 'It's important that we find out exactly what Michael has in mind. Do you see? You've been in touch with him. We want you to help us with this.'

The secretary was frowning in the corner.

I said, 'What kind of help did you have in mind?'

'Michael told you he has information about us. Now June Donaghy is dead you're the only one who knows what that information is. We need to find out how much mischief he can cause.'

I kept not saying anything. I was waiting for the punch line.

Peter Thacker sat back in his chair. 'You might not appreciate how sensitive the whole business is.' He sounded weary. 'For some reason you only have to say the word nuclear and the press loses whatever balance it normally has. Philip has examined all options and decided we're the best people to run the power stations. We can't allow one man's petty grudge to upset . . .' His fingers flexed over the blotting pad. 'A whole government policy. It doesn't matter whether you approve of that policy or not.' His eyes narrowed. 'It's a matter of your responsibility as a police officer.'

'Harvey hasn't broken any laws,' I said.

'He might have. We don't know how he obtained his information. We don't know what he's done with it. He might have passed commercial secrets to other people.' He gave me a bland smile. 'Including yourself.'

Outside, the roof of a canal boat was passing the end of the lawn. Two men in swimming trunks were larking on the cabin roof, trying to impress a girl who was trying to sunbathe.

Peter Thacker sighed. 'Philip rang up John Harlow at Scotland Yard this morning. He wanted to find out what kind of officer you are.' He looked at the man in front of the fireplace. 'You might tell him, Philip.'

'He said you were a bloody good man.' Lord's voice was too loud for the room, as if the three of us were an audience at a political speech. He delivered the speech to the air six inches above my head. 'One of the best officers they've got. Said you were in line for an early promotion, had a job carved out for you at Scotland Yard. Could go all the way to the top, he said.' His mouth snapped shut as if the autocue over my head had blinked off. He turned his brooding gaze back to the hearth rug.

'That's rather flattering,' Peter Thacker said. 'Don't you think?'

'It's not what John Harlow was saying about me yesterday.'

'What was he saying about you yesterday?'

'He had me taken off the Donaghy case. You know that already.'

From the fireplace, Philip Lord said, 'That was a misunderstanding.'

'You could be in line for a promotion.' Peter Thacker smiled at me like the headmaster handing out prizes at sports day.

I said quietly, 'So long as I do what you want.'

The smile faded. He looked at me bleakly. 'And what exactly to do you think we're asking you to do?'

'To bury anything I've found out about Sizewell or about how you've won the bid for the power stations. I don't think you need me to tell you anything about Michael Harvey. You've already turned him into a suspect for June Donaghy's murder.'

There was silence in the room. Philip Lord cleared his throat noisily but didn't say anything.

'I understand . . .' Peter Thacker was frowning at the ceiling, his fingers pressed together in front of him. 'I understand that you dislike our business. That may be *political* . . .' He made political sound like a kind of perversion. 'I don't know what your *politics* are.' His gaze dropped from the ceiling to me. 'I rather think it has something to do with my brother, though. You don't like the way he treated June Donaghy. I don't blame you for that. I didn't like it myself.' Peter Thacker got up suddenly and went over to the coffee tray in the corner. With his back to me he said, 'Do you know, when we inherited the business, it was Barney who made all the decisions. He's older than me. He'd been in the firm longer – our father assumed that he would naturally take the lead.' His voice lowered. He was frowning out at the lawn. 'Barney knew about building roads . . . engineering. He didn't know anything about business. He's very like our father.' Thacker turned the chair back towards me. He was holding a full cup of coffee. 'We've never argued. Even Barney would admit that I make most of the decisions these days. We've never fallen out about it.'

I said, 'That's nice.'

'I'm not telling you this because I think you're interested in our family history.' His face wore a faint, mocking smile. Suddenly he looked serious. 'Barney was stupid with a girl once before. I told you that. She threatened to prosecute him. We had a hell of a business talking her out of it.' One hand rose and fell on the arm of the chair. 'I don't know why he's like that. He's got a happy marriage – as happy as you could want. Angela's a saint.'

'She'd need to be.'

Peter Thacker smiled thinly. 'I'll be frank with you. Barney's behaviour is starting to embarrass us. He's always been . . .' His lips twitched fastidiously. 'Aggressive. It's becoming worse. One of the few reservations Philip had about us . . .' His eyes swivelled towards Philip Lord. 'Is Barney's behaviour. The thought of him dealing with issues as sensitive as these was worrying.' He sat down behind the desk again. 'I took a decision last night. The hardest I've ever had to. I wrote Barney a letter suggesting that he resign his position on the board. We can't risk a scandal . . . If what he said to June Donaghy came out in the future . . .' His hands rose and fluttered down on to the desk. He looked towards Lord. 'Philip has agreed that my brother's resignation will be the end of the matter. What about you, Chief Inspector? Do you think it's the end of the matter?'

Lord said, 'Harlow spoke very highly of you.' It was as if he'd lost the thread of the conversion and jerked back to the last subject he could remember. 'Said you were a bloody good man. Someone we could depend on.'

I looked at Thacker's charming, smooth face. He'd sacrifice his brother to get what he wanted. I wondered how much else he'd been prepared to do. I said, 'Who killed June Donaghy?'

'Muggers?' Peter Thacker's frown almost looked sincere. 'It's a dangerous city.'

It wasn't dangerous where he lived. It was dangerous on the other side of the plate glass windows and the security alarms: dangerous for anyone who had no power.

'How did you know where to call me this morning?'

Peter Thacker laughed nervously until there was no reason to go on laughing. He stopped when I started backing towards the door.

Philip Lord seemed to be lost in thought; the secretary was looking nervously at his boss. I turned abruptly and walked up the corridor and into the hallway. Nobody followed me; gravel crunched under my feet. I looked back just before reaching the road.

The woman in the black dress was staring out of the window again, one hand playing with her string of pearls. She looked tired of being rich, and pampered, and beautiful, tired of having nothing to complain of.

She was still staring out of the window when I reached the road.

31

Tommy Endell's arcade was tucked in between two warehouses for used office furniture. The filing cabinets and office chairs spilled out on to the pavement as if some bankrupt was trying to restart his business from the north pavement of the New Cross Road.

The arcade had a low opening with glass that glowed red and blue from flashing lights inside. A black guy in a leather jacket watched the pavement from a stool by the door. He was keeping a careful eye on it, knowing that real trouble only came from outside, not from the interstellar bandits behind him. When I approached the door his gaze switched from the pavement to me.

'Yes?' He had a smooth brown face and eyes as flat as video screens.

I said, 'Is Tommy in?'

He nodded without speaking, rose from the stool and cast a last suspicious glance at the pavement, as if he was warning it not to move while he was gone. He led me through darkness rent by the explosions of star wars and commando assaults. Most of the kids in there were under age. By the time anyone was old enough to play video violence they were old enough to be doing the real thing – or so scared of it they didn't want to pretend any more. From the corner of my eye I saw electric racing cars spinning through cartoon bends and video warriors kung-fu kicking their way into adolescent heaven. The kids' faces were tense and excited. Either they hadn't worked out that virtual reality only brought virtual kicks, or else any reality was better than living in New Cross.

The security man knocked softly on a black-painted door at the back of the arcade. Next to it obsolete machines were shrouded in dust jackets. From behind it I could hear the drone of a television. The security man opened the door and nodded at me to go in. Inside was a narrow office with a sofa on one wall and a desk ranged alongside the door. The television sat precariously on top of a dead gas heater. A fat man in a red T-shirt was watching the wrestling with his feet on a milk crate and his fat arms weighing down the back of the sofa. On the screen a man in a leotard was trying to open up the floor of the ring using his opponent's head as a drill.

The fat guy on the sofa chuckled. He looked round at me to make sure I was laughing too.

He said, 'I love this. It's funny.'

I said, 'It depends what you call funny.'

I looked at the desk and saw a thin, alert man with prematurely greyed hair and sharp eyes which told me he wasn't thinking about wrestling.

'Turn it off, Jacko.' His right hand made the motion of turning a knob. His eyes didn't leave my face.

I walked over to the television set and turned it off myself. The fat guy on the sofa blinked at me. From behind the desk Tommy Endell pointed a sharp forefinger at me. 'Police?'

'Does it show that much?'

'Does to me. Smell 'em a mile off. Get out, Jacko.'

Without complaining the fat man shuffled to the front of the sofa and heaved himself up. The effort made him breathe harder. He waddled obediently to the door and closed it behind him.

Tommy Endell said, 'My cousin.' He said it as if everyone had a fat cousin who watched wrestling.

I leaned against the desk. For some reason Tommy Endell's hands went to the top drawer. 'What do you want?'

I said, 'I'm trying to find Medd.'

'Fucking coppers are always trying to find Medd. You think I'm his fucking minder?'

'I think you know where he is.'

'I don't, though. Not any more.' He underlined the negative with a sharp sideways movement of his head.

'Since when?'

'Since the last time I told you where he was. What happened then? Run too fast for you?'

I said, 'Last time we couldn't hold him. This time we can do better.'

Tommy Endell threw back his head and laughed. It was a scornful laugh that went on too long and started to sound forced about halfway through. 'Let him go, did you?'

I nodded. 'Do you know where he is now?'

The laugh fell off Tommy Endell's face as if he had pressed buttons and changed a channel somewhere. 'So you come back to me. Want another try, do you? 'Nother bite of the apple?'

I said, 'Something like that.'

Endell snorted. 'Don't know any more. I told you. Haven't heard of him since he was hanging round at Pike's place. Two, three days back. He dropped out of sight.'

'Where does Medd go when he drops out of sight?'

'Hell.' He cackled briefly to let me know it was meant as a joke.

'Does he have a place of his own?'

Endell regarded me suspiciously as if we were playing cards and he still hadn't worked out what I had in my hand. His hands were hovering around the top drawer again. 'Got a flat off the Old Kent Road. You won't find him there.'

'Why not?'

'Hasn't been there all week.'

'How do you know that?'

'I was told.'

I didn't ask who had told him. 'What's the address?'

Tommy Endell thought for a minute then pulled an envelope towards him and scrawled rapidly on the back of it. 'Won't do you any good.'

I said, 'Thanks, anyway.'

'What's it about? You going to hold him this time?'

'Maybe.'

'Send him away for something decent?' His sharp voice was bitter.

I said, 'What did he do to your brother?'

'No business of yours.'

I turned towards the door. 'Aren't you scared of Medd coming for you?'

'I want him to.' The little man's voice was bright and sharp. Instinctively his hands had moved back to the top drawer. I wondered what he kept inside it. 'Self-defence, then, isn't it? Won't be me who starts anything.'

The address scrawled on the envelope didn't have a street name, just the name of a council estate. I found the estate curled around some grass that was going bald in patches and a row of four unused benches. There were three blocks of flats and each one was named after a different flower, as if to make up for the bald grass. Long access decks were slung between brick stairs towers. Above a window halfway up Medd's block I could see scorch marks. The window was boarded over with plywood. On the fourth side of the square two left-over terraced houses still clung to the pavement like the last two teeth in an old man's mouth.

The stair to Medd's flat didn't smell of gardenias. I climbed it slowly and tried not to think of Medd climbing it every day. From the access deck, the ground and the open pavement beyond the terraced houses looked too far away to be any use to me. I kept walking past doors covered in steel plates and windows hidden behind grilles. Most of the doors needed paint; one had been changed for a panelled door with a brass knocker and a ceramic number next to it, as if there was a neat suburban house behind it and a patch of lawn at the back. No one else on Medd's deck was even bothering to pretend.

I stopped at the number on the envelope. There was a steel plate over the door which someone had started to paint green. Through the kitchen window I could see nothing but dusty glass. Out of the corner of my eye I saw a blind fall back over the window in the flat next door.

I raised my hand and knocked. It didn't sound loud, but maybe that was because my heart was drowning out everything else. I saw Medd's face in the battered steel panel. It looked at home there, as if it was made of battered steel itself – a rough piece of protection nailed over a human skull to ward off blows and keep the coppers out. I lifted my fist and knocked again.

There were faint footsteps inside and I heard locks turning. When the door opened it was stopped by a chain. Through the six-inch gap a girl's face looked at me from the height of my chest. It was thin and pale with dirty brown hair framing it and black rings about the eyes. Bright red lipstick still didn't make it look older than fourteen.

'Yes?'

'I'm looking for Medd.'

The face disappeared, leaving only a bony shoulder in the gap. She was wearing a white shift that looked like the night-gown in a Victorian nursery story. Thin white fingers gripped the edge of the door.

'He isn't here.' Her voice was so thin I could hardly make out the words, a child's voice failing to make itself heard in a grown-up world of access decks and steel doors.

'Can I come in?'

The face appeared again and stared at me. It didn't answer.

'Why not?'

'He said not to.'

'Medd?'

She nodded dumbly.

'Do you live here?'

The child licked her lips nervously. 'I'm waiting for him.'

'Do you know when he's going to come back?'

She shook her head again.

I put one hand on the wall and leaned down to her level. 'What's your name?'

'Tish.' She made it sound as if she only had one name.

'How long have you been waiting for him?'

She shook her head.

'More than a day?'

'Don't know.'

'Does he know you're here?'

Her eyes widened in fright. 'You won't tell him, will you?'

'Why don't you want him to know?'

She thought for a moment. 'I'm waiting for him.'

I looked at the thin white cheeks. Something other than Medd had painted those black bruises under her eyes. The greasy hair had left spots on her forehead and around her neck.

'How old are you, Tish?'

'I'm nineteen.' She was proud of the lie. Someone had taught her to say that to strange men who appeared at the door and asked too many questions.

'Are you his friend?'

She nodded, then fear came back into her eyes and she hid her face behind the door.

'Did he tell you to wait for him here?'

'No. I wanted to see him.'

'How did you get in?'

'I got keys.' Her accent wasn't London. I wondered what sad trail of broken homes and motorway cafés had led her to Medd's door in the first place.

'Did he give you the keys?'

The face appeared at the door again and moved nervously from side to side.

'You stole them?'

'Kind of.' It was a child's half-lie, begging me not to press the point.

I squatted down on the access deck, putting myself lower than her. 'When did you last see him, Tish?'

'Are you a friend of his?'

'In a way.'

'What's your name?'

I only gave her my first name. She hadn't realized yet that some people had more than one name, or more than one way of using it.

'I never saw you before.'

'No.'

She thought for a bit. She didn't want to leave the door. I wondered how long she had been waiting alone in the Medd's flat. As if she'd been thinking the same thing, she said, 'I'm hungry.'

'Did he leave you any food?'

'There were biscuits.' Her pale tongue felt her lips for the taste of them. 'I ate them.'

From the thinness of her arms I didn't think there could have been many biscuits.

'Don't you have any money?'

She shook her head.

'I'll give you some, if you like.'

A thin hand appeared at the door. I put a ten pound note into it and some loose change. It was all I had in my pocket.

'Thanks.'

'Will you let me in? We can talk some more.' Her face looked doubtful. 'You don't have to if you don't want to.'

The door closed. For a moment I thought she had taken fright, then locks turned and it opened fully. Tish was wearing purple velvet jeans under the white shift and no shoes on pinched feet that looked as if they'd spent too much of her short life walking. She turned and led me back down the hall. She walked with an affected swing of the hips that belonged to a woman twice her age, not to a child.

She led me into a living room with a tatty brown carpet on the floor and walls in the state the last tenant had left them. A television filled one corner. The floor was a mess of old beer cans and magazines. Tish didn't seem to notice the mess, or what kind of magazines they were. She stood in front of me, the tips of her fingers thrust into the tops of her jeans pockets.

'Have you been watching television?'

She looked at the blank screen. 'It's bust.'

'What have you been doing?'

She frowned as if she didn't know that people were supposed to do anything. 'Waiting.' She shrugged. 'I suppose.'

'Did anyone tell you Medd was going to come back here?'

'Course he will.'

'Do you know when?'

She shook her head.

'Do you know where he is?' She shook her head again. 'He didn't tell you?'

'I'm hungry.' She looked down at the money in her hand as if she knew it could lead to food, but didn't know how.

I went back out of the living-room door and found the kitchen. The smell of decaying rubbish came from a pile of dirty plates in the sink and a bin overflowing in one corner. The light switch produced a hollow click. I opened cupboard doors and found a tin of soup and a dented aluminium pan.

Tish watched me from the doorway with wide, scared eyes. 'He doesn't like me touching his things.'

'You can tell him I made it for you.'

She sat down eagerly enough when I took it back to the living-room for her. I left her eating from the pan with a spoon I had rescued from the debris in the sink. While she ate I went through the rest of the flat. It didn't take long. The cupboard in the bedroom was empty. Squares pressed into the carpet showed where hi-fi speakers had stood. I didn't think Medd was going to come back.

I went back to the living room and watched Tish scraping soup from the bottom of the pan. 'Does Medd have another place?'

'Only here.'

'Can I see your keys?'

She didn't want me to see them, but her eyes showed me where they were, lying among the magazines on the floor. I picked them up. The ring belonged to a car, but the two biggest keys matched the locks on the front door. Alongside them was a smaller one, new, with the marks of the maker's file still burring the edges.

'Do you know what this is for?'

Her eyes watched the key over the rim of the pan. 'The lock-up,' she said at last.

'He has a garage?'

'His friend does.'

'Why does Medd have the key?'

'He keeps things there.'

'Do you know where it is?'

'Downstairs.'

She looked into the bottom of the pan, as if she was searching for more soup.

I took the key off the ring and slipped it into my pocket.

Tish frowned. 'He'll be angry.'

'Then don't tell him where you got the keys.'

She nodded and frowned again, trying to memorize it.

I looked at her. 'Is there a phone here?'

'In the bedroom.'

I took a notebook out of my pocket and wrote something on it. Tish frowned as she reached for the slip of paper. 'Next time you get hungry, will you ring this number?'

She looked at the number and nodded. 'Who is it?'

'They'll help you. Just tell them your name and where you are.'

She nodded again and followed me back down the hall. The last I saw of her was a white face peering through the kitchen window.

The row of garages was beyond the last council block, five brick boxes in a strip of wasteland hemmed in by the block and a high brick wall with wire along the top of it. Nobody watched me try the first door. It was the wrong kind of key for the lock and I started to wonder whether I was in the right place at all. It was only when I went further along the row that I saw one lock had been changed. I glanced over my shoulder. Either nobody was watching me, or everyone was watching but nobody cared.

The key fitted into the lock and turned. I stooped and lifted the foot of the door. It squealed on its runners and the hollow clang as it hit the ceiling echoed back from an empty garage. A broken-down table stood at the back, limping on three legs with the fourth hanging in mid-air. Beneath it were cardboard boxes soft from the damp air. I walked towards them. The concrete floor was black with oil, and the smell of oil filled air which had been standing still for a long time. I pulled one of the boxes towards me and opened it. The only thing in it was a square of cardboard, a photograph.

It showed a girl in her twenties with her dark hair tied back and a slight squint where the light caught her in the eyes. In the right place, with the right music playing, she would have been beautiful to somebody. As it was she looked just like anybody else: quite pretty, quite happy, not ready to die.

32

The cherry trees were in full blossom outside Michael Harvey's house. They cast a gentle shade over the whole street, as if they would protect anyone who lived there from sun or rain; as if their lives would always be filled with flowers. Children were still playing in the back gardens. It was late in the afternoon, but these children had a future of cherry trees and expensive cars in front of them; they would live most of their lives in houses like these; they had all the time in the world.

Through the front window of Michael Harvey's house I could see the furniture that had belonged to his wife's family – the furniture an ambitious boy from the North had decided to spend the rest of his life with, and which had then made him homesick for what he had known before. The lights were not switched on in the big drawing-room. I heard footsteps inside but the door did not open. Instead, an Entryphone grille crackled next to me.

'Who is it?' It was Joanna's voice.

'George Havilland.'

'Oh.'

The door stayed closed. A faint hum came from the Entryphone but there was no voice behind it. I waited and watched a man in a city suit lock a big car and start climbing the steps to his house.

'Michael's resting at the moment.'

'I've got to talk to him.'

'Can't it wait?'

I said, 'No.'

A chain rattled and the big door swung open. Joanna Harvey was waiting for me behind it. I looked at her. Her face wasn't beautiful, I noticed; it was just faultless. The nose was the right length, the eyes as far apart as they needed to be. Her eyes were tired and faintly disapproving.

'He's very tired, you know. This *business* has exhausted him.' She stressed business as something foreign to her. It came from Michael's world of politicians and lawyers, not from her own.

'Have you had more threats?'

'They can *say* anything they like.' For a moment I heard Sam's voice: a little girl striking attitudes in a world far bigger than she realized.

I didn't want to think about Sam – not now and certainly not in her mother's house. I followed Joanna upstairs to the study. The hunting prints and the mahogany desk hadn't changed, but somehow Michael Harvey looked out of place with them. He was sitting behind the desk with a tense expression on a face which lack of sleep had bleached white. The tortoiseshell glasses lay on the desk in front of him.

'Couldn't it wait till morning?' He asked the question to Joanna. He sounded like a schoolboy trying to get out of his homework.

I said, 'It can't wait.'

'Will this take long?'

'I don't know.'

Joanna went out and closed the door behind her. There was no sound in the room but the shouts of the children in the communal garden. Michael Harvey rubbed his hand over his face. That did something to give it back the clever, alert look I had first met; but exhaustion flooded back into it even as I looked.

'I'm sorry. It's been quite a week.'

He heaved himself up from the desk the way a much older man would get up and went over to a drinks cabinet in the bookshelves. 'Can I get you anything?' He poured himself a whisky larger than a tired man should have been drinking and went back to the desk. The first sip brought artificial colour to his cheeks, like the colour a woman might fake with rouge.

'Well.' He looked at me with the first signs of a smile. 'What's happened?'

'We had a visitor yesterday.'

'Oh?'

217

'The same man you saw attacking June. The man you saw in the line-up the other day.'

'I told you, George . . .'

'It was because you wouldn't identify him we had to let him out. He put Mary in hospital. He left before I got there.' I nodded towards the window. 'He's still out there now.'

'George!' Harvey's thin face was shocked. 'I . . .' The desk didn't tell him what to say. 'I'm sorry. Dreadfully sorry.' He looked back up at me. 'Truly I am.'

I said slowly, 'I know why you wouldn't identify him.'

A faint crease appeared between Harvey's brows. It seemed to bother him, as if he couldn't work out who had put it there. 'I told you. I couldn't be certain. I wasn't going to identify a man that I wasn't sure . . . beyond reasonable doubt.'

'If Medd didn't kill June,' I said, 'that makes you a suspect your-self. You'll have some questions to answer if anyone else finds out you were her lover.'

Harvey flushed. 'They *mustn't* find out.' His voice was wretched. Doubt suddenly flooded his eyes. 'You don't think I killed her, do you?' Killed was a whisper going down into darkness.

I said, 'I thought that for a while. I don't any more. There was a time when I thought you'd paid Medd to kill her.'

Harvey bowed his face into his hands. 'That's horrible.'

I watched the top of his head. The silence went on for a long time. At last I took a sheet of paper from my pocket and dropped it on the desk in front of him. Harvey looked at it between his fingers, then slowly reached out one hand and picked it up. It took him time to read it and then to understand what he had read.

When he looked up his face was incredulous. 'Where did you get this?'

'It was in June's room. Is this what you wanted her to bring you?'

He nodded once. He was still reading the document.

I said, 'Peter Thacker called me up this morning. He had me followed – probably by Medd. He had an offer for me. I'll be promoted if this comes out the way he wants.'

'What does he want?'

'He wants that buried.' I pointed towards the paper. After a moment I said, 'Don't you want to know what I said to him?' I took the paper out of his fingers. He didn't try to keep it. His fingers were trembling slightly. 'If this went to the newspapers now it would kill the deal he has with Philip Lord. There's no way Lord could sell the Thackers nuclear power stations when that report shows what happened at Sizewell. With what you have as well it could bring out everything PTI have ever done. It would ruin Thacker and it would finish Lord. You wouldn't have anyone blocking your political career any more. What was it they were going to make you? A whip?'

He nodded without understanding what he was agreeing to. His eyes pleaded with my face.

'If I took this to the press today, would you help me?'

'No, George. You mustn't.' There was panic in his voice. 'I told you yesterday . . . You've had threats yourself. You saw what they did to . . . Mary. It's not worth the risk.'

'I don't think that's what you're scared of.'

Michael Harvey's lips moved but nothing came out of them.

I said, 'When did they get in touch with you? On Thursday morning? On Wednesday you weren't scared of threats and you knew who Medd was when I showed you his photograph. A day later it was too dark for you to recognize him and you weren't interested in exposing the Thackers. What happened on Thursday morning?'

'I don't know what you mean.' His voice had nothing behind it.

'I thought they'd found something good enough to buy your silence. I was sorry about that. I didn't think you had a price.'

Michael Harvey shivered suddenly, as if the cold evening had suddenly made its way into the room.

'They didn't need a price,' I went on. 'Everything was easy for them as soon as Peter Thacker found out about your affair with June. After that you'd do anything he wanted. That was what happened on Thursday.'

'No.' His voice was a whisper.

'What was the deal?' I asked. 'Do you get your career back? Are they going to stop passing rumours about you? Will Philip Lord give you a job in his ministry?'

'No.' His face was white. He put his hands over his cheeks as if to hide the whiteness.

'Peter Thacker told me a lot about you two days ago. All politicians are afraid of scandal. For you it would be worse. You owe your whole career to your wife. If she found out about your affair you'd lose everything. Is that what you were scared of?'

Michael Harvey took his hands away from his face. The expression of shock had faded from it. When he spoke his voice was flat. 'Yes.' He picked up his glass and took a gulp from it. The whisky didn't seem to do anything for him. He looked at it resentfully, then up at me. 'I can't go back, George.' It was a moment before I realized what he meant. In a lower voice he went on, 'You should see where Jo's parents live. Fifteen bedrooms. The park goes on for two miles.' He was a newcomer again, gawking at fifteen bedrooms and an estate. The remains of his Northern accent had become stronger. 'Where would I go back to? My mother does her ironing in the spare room.' For the first time he sounded bitter. He wasn't a bitter man, but he didn't want to be thrown out of the garden.

He raised his head. He sounded determined again. 'So you're right. They won. I don't like it any more than you do, George. I couldn't swallow how they work before, and I can't now. But I'm not going to throw everything away because of it. If I leave them alone now, I'll manage. I'll be OK.' His face twisted. 'You're right, Philip Lord is going to help me with a job. It's important to me. We might lose the election. It's important to have a foot in the door.' He wanted to share his humiliation with me; he was too proud to pretend it was anything other than humiliation.

I stood up. Outside the sky was growing dark over thickly massed trees. Children were no longer playing in the gardens. They had gone indoors to supper, and then to comfortable beds.

I said, 'After I left Peter Thacker I went to Medd's flat. He wasn't there but I found the lock-up where he keeps his things, a friend's place.' Michael Harvey's face was bowed towards the desk. He might not have been listening to me. 'I found a photograph of June Donaghy in the lock-up. The Thackers must have sent it to him. What June knew threatened their whole company. The only way to silence her was to have her killed. The photograph they sent is the same as her PTI security pass. I don't know why Medd kept it. Maybe he was planning to blackmail the Thackers. He didn't know anyone was going to see the murder take place.' I shook my head. 'The photograph might be enough to send Medd away, but only if you'll identify him as the man you saw attacking June. Without that it won't do a thing. Medd's a professional and Peter Thacker will pay him whatever it takes to keep his mouth shut. Unless you're prepared to bring forward what you know, there's no chance of jailing Medd and no chance of proving the Thackers were behind her murder.'

I stopped. Michael Harvey was leaning forward in his chair as if a crushing weight had landed on his shoulders. I went and stood behind him. There was sweat at the nape of his neck. 'The Thackers had June killed,' I said. 'The man who killed her is out on the streets now. He's already attacked Mary and he's probably looking for me. Peter Thacker wants me quiet. I need you to tell everyone the truth.'

'I can't.' Michael Harvey's voice was low and determined. 'I've told you I can't. You guessed why – that was very clever of you. But the reason doesn't matter. I can't say anything.'

'So the Thackers get away with it,' I said slowly. 'A murder. The deals they've made with Lord. Medd stays free – and all because you don't want to lose your career.'

'I know.' His hands lifted off the desk like birds taking to flight. 'I've thought it through. I've worked all of that out.' His lips tightened into a determined line. 'I've made my decision, George. I'm sorry.'

Quietly I said, 'Do you know where it leaves me?'

'I'm sorry about that too. About . . . Mary.' He shook his head. 'I can't change my mind now.'

'You might have to.'

I went back to other side of the desk and looked down at him. I knew where Michael Harvey had started from. It wasn't too different from where I'd started myself. He wasn't going to go back there, but nor was I going to go back to the basement flat with the map of my father's death on the ceiling.

I said, 'The Thackers aren't the only ones who know about you and June.'

Shock spread slowly across his face as if from a distant explosion underseas. 'George?'

'Peter Thacker silenced you by threatening to expose your affair.' His head was absolutely still. 'I can do that myself.'

'What are you saying, George?'

'If you don't bring forward your evidence – against Medd and against the Thackers – then I'll go to the press myself.' I shrugged. 'That's all.'

'You can't!' His voice was another explosion.

'Why not? I don't have any choice.'

'You could . . .' He looked around the study for my choices. 'You could do what Peter Thacker asked. What I did.' His lip curled, full of contempt for himself and me.

I shook my head. 'It's too late.'

'Please, George.'

I said, 'Medd's out there at the moment. I need you to move now.'

'I need time . . . to think about it.'

'I need an answer now. Are you going to tell the truth or do I go to the press?'

I watched the top of his head. It took him a long time to give me an answer. He was thinking about a small house in the North, and about the corridors of Westminster, his daughter, the photographs of Michael Harvey with his fists raised above his head in triumph.

When he looked up at me his face was cold and determined. 'No, George. I don't think you will.'

'I've told you I will.'

'You couldn't. Think what it would do to Joanna.' His voice trembled. 'To Sam.' I wished he hadn't mentioned Sam but I wasn't going to go back now. 'If you went to the papers with this . . .' His face screwed up in disgust. 'It's *dirty*. Peddling stories about affairs. You wouldn't do anything so dirty.'

I said, 'The whole thing's dirty.'

'Not like this.' Michael Harvey shook his head. 'No, George. You won't do it. Not you. The answer's no.'

I turned and walked out on him without looking back. I had his answer and I knew what I had to do. I didn't want to think about Harvey any more, or about myself.

I called Neil Hudson from the phone box on the corner and walked away from it quickly afterwards, hoping that no one had watched what I had done.

33

The girl on the hospital information desk looked tired. She had spent too long talking to people whose relatives were dying, too long giving bad news to people who didn't want to hear it. They were sitting on plastic chairs behind me, staring stonily at the flower shop or the mural of happy children. It was Saturday night and they should have been at home with their families, watching television or doing whatever families do. Instead they had the smell of disinfectant in their nostrils and they were watching an old man in a dressing-gown inch painfully across the lino floor on two walking sticks. The old man took every step as if it might be his last. His eyes were fixed on the flower shop, as if all he needed was a bunch of flowers and then he could die happy. Lift doors opened and closed. The woman in the flower shop poured fresh water over flowers that were wilting from the hospital heat.

The girl behind the information desk said, 'Princess Margaret. West Wing.' She frowned at the list in front of her. 'You're too late for visiting hours. Visiting stops at nine o'clock.' Her eyes went past me to the clock above the hospital entrance.

'It's important.'

'Are you family?'

I nodded. She gave me a tired smile that had been used too often that day by too many people. 'You'll have to ask the sister. Do you know the way?'

All I remembered of the way to the ward was that it had bright lights and seemed to go on for ever. I listened to her directions. 'Do you know which room she's in?'

'Number seven.'

I shared the lift with two doctors and a woman carrying flowers.

The woman had a bright smile on her face. She held the flowers in front of her as if they were going to protect her from infection, disease and other people's misery. On the third floor I went through doors until I found a corridor which looked familiar. There was nobody in sight. A pin-board on the wall told me about visiting hours, dental hygiene and what to do about back pain. I started walking down the corridor. Through half-open doors I could see the ends of beds, temperature charts, darkened rooms. A murmur of voices came from a larger room with curtains round one of the beds.

Ward seven was a dark room behind a closed door. I shut the door behind me and gave my eyes time to get used to the darkness. Mary's face was a pale shape on a white pillow. I listened to her breathing. She was asleep. Cautiously I felt for the chair next to the bed and sat down. Through hospital blinds I could see lights on the far side of the river. The River Thames was flowing beneath us. I looked down at the hand lying on a grey hospital blanket. Tonight Mary should have been singing the biggest date in her career. I put my finger on the blanket next to her hand but didn't dare to touch it. I had to think of something so I thought about the first time I'd heard Mary sing. I'd never seen anyone put so much into their music. Even the Sunday pub audience had noticed. Just for a few minutes they'd stopped chewing peanuts and scraping chairs, and listened to what was happening around them. When the old jazz musicians heard something that was right – right not for any reason you could say, but just because it caught the right moment – they called it truth. That was what Mary had. She didn't have the biggest voice you ever heard, or the smoothest. But her singing found your hand and took you along with it. Just for a moment you couldn't hear the till ringing or the sound of the traffic outside: you knew you were listening to truth.

Mary's breathing changed and she sighed something in a voice I hardly recognized. I looked down at the pillow. Her eyes were open.

I said, 'Mary?'

The breathing stopped. It stopped for what seemed too long, then started again. She didn't say anything.

'Mary.'

Her voice said, 'You can turn the light on if you want.'

I didn't turn the light on. I moved to the edge of the bed. She had turned her face away from me, towards the wall, and didn't move to make space for me.

I said gently, 'How are you feeling?'

Mary twisted her face towards me. 'My head hurts.' After a pause she added. 'It's all right when I don't think about it. I've been trying to listen to music. Charlie brought me some tapes.'

My finger kneaded the blanket. I said, 'I've got to talk to you.'

'Does it have to be now?' She was speaking with an effort, as if speaking took her away from fighting the pain in her head.

'Yes.'

She twisted her face away from me again. For a moment she didn't say anything. Then she said, 'What about?'

'Us.'

Her body went rigid on the bed beside me. 'You pick your moment, don't you?'

I knew it was the wrong time, but if I didn't tell her now I never would. And that would be worse.

She drew in a deep breath and let it out again. 'Go on, then.'

I couldn't look at her face. I looked at her shoulder and told her shoulder about Sam Harvey. I said everything I could think of, sticking to what had happened and not why, or why it wasn't my fault, or why things like that ever do happen.

I didn't expect her to forgive me. As I brought it out I could feel the air souring between us, as if the words themselves had turned sour waiting inside me and now they were poisoning everything around them. I remembered whatever lies I had told her and brought them out too. It felt as if I was emptying out a cupboard in a house I was about to leave.

When I finished there was a long silence. Outside I could hear a trolley rattling along a corridor.

Mary's shoulder moved. 'Is that *all*?' The laugh she attempted turned into a gasp. Her fingers gripped her head.

More silence: not an empty silence, but a living darkness full of creatures I had stirred up. The lies were moving of their own accord now, flexing their limbs, testing their strength. I was no longer in control of them.

Mary sighed. 'Are you saying you want to leave me?'

'No.' There was something constricting my throat. 'I just wanted you to know what happened. You have to know.'

'Why? Why do I have to know?' She stopped and groaned. After a moment she said, 'You lied to me.' She said it matter-of-factly. I had expected anger. This was worse.

'Yes.'

'Have you often lied to me?'

'Not until this.'

'You did, though. You said you'd stop chasing after those people who threatened me. That was a lie as well.'

'Yes.'

There was a long silence. The noises of the hospital seemed far away. Everything seemed far away, as if we were alone on an island together with dark water all around us.

Mary moved on the bed. 'What was she like?' Her voice was bitter. 'Was she a good f . . .' She bit her lip. After a moment her voice said, 'Better than me, anyway.'

'No.'

'Did you compare us? Did you . . .'

I put a hand on her shoulder.

'Don't touch me!'

I took my hand away and looked down at it. The fingers were trembling. It looked like somebody else's hand.

Slowly her shoulders relaxed. 'You'd better go away now, George. I need to rest.'

I said, 'I'm sorry.'

She took time to think about that. When she spoke her voice sounded distant, as if she was looking down at me from the rail of a departing liner. 'I'm never sure what that means. What difference does it make, being sorry?'

'I love you,' I said.

'Stop it, George.' She moved again, as if no position was comfortable. 'Don't bother. It's a waste of time. I'd rather you just went away.'

227

I stared down at her figure on the bed. I didn't know what to say.

'I ought to be angry with you,' she went on. 'I'm too tired.'

'Can we talk tomorrow?'

'No.' She moved on the bed. 'I don't want to talk about it. I just want you to go.'

'We should talk.'

Her breath sounded irregular and too deep. She sighed. 'Go away, George. I don't want you any more.'

A door swung open outside in the corridor. A voice shouted for a nurse.

Mary stretched. 'I need to rest. I want you to move out of the flat. I don't want to see you again.'

I stood up. If she had shouted at me I could have said something back, or waited until the anger died down. Silence was too much for me: I couldn't climb it or see a way through it. There was nothing more for me to say.

I left her lying the way I had found her. The nurse was pushing her trolley from room to room, marking notes on the back of a chart. She frowned at me as I walked past. A clock above the lift told me it was almost midnight. Down in the hospital lobby the early editions of the Sunday papers had just been delivered.

I stopped. Michael Harvey's face stared out at me from the front pages.

34

I walked home slowly. There didn't seem to be anything to hurry for. Mary's voice followed me. It hadn't been like her usual voice. It was flat, weary, as if something inside it had died. In Kennington Road the tarmac was wet behind the road cleaners. At St Mark's church I turned left, into dark streets of sleeping houses and empty pavements. Taxis queued outside a nightclub, the drivers dozing behind their steering wheels. On Brixton Road two coppers were pointing at something in a shop window. By the time I reached home dawn was starting to come up.

I dug the key out of my pocket, felt for the light switch in the hall. It clicked uselessly, reminding me again that I had never changed the bulb. The ambulancemen had carried Mary down these stairs just two days before. There was a scratch on the wall-paper which might have been made by the stretcher. I felt my way up to the front door and found it hanging open. I must have forgotten to close it when the ambulance left.

The flat smelled of Mary's perfume. I stood in the hallway for a moment without turning the light on, and let that sink into me. I couldn't imagine living without that.

Something hit me hard on the side of the head.

I reeled over and felt carpet under my hand. I didn't know what was happening. A weight was crushing my arm, tearing at my jacket. I couldn't see anything, just felt hands tearing at me out of the darkness. A hammer crashed into my right knee.

I kicked out hard and rolled over, trying to protect my head. It felt as if the building had collapsed on me, or a sea wall had given way and the pressure on my chest was the weight of water rushing on top of me. I scrabbled with both hands, felt something hard and dug my nails into it. Somebody grunted in surprise. There was a man in the darkness, perhaps more than one man. Hands were gripping the collar of my jacket, feeling their way towards my throat.

I gripped the hard object with one hand and lashed out at it with the other. I could feel my knuckles tearing. The voice grunted. I did that again, then brought my head up hard into darkness. It felt as if I had butted a wall, but the weight was gone from my chest. I kicked backwards, pushing open the living-room door. In the orange glow through the windows I could see the doorway in front of me.

Medd's voice came through the doorway. 'I'm going to kill you, copper.'

I didn't have time to stand up. A black shape came at me in a rush. It hit me in the stomach, taking my breath away. My head struck something hard. The hands were struggling with my throat again. I opened my eyes and saw Medd's bulk above me. He was kneeling on my chest, arms at full stretch to hold me down. From his mouth came a low grunting, like the sound of someone making love.

I twisted my head around and bit into his wrist. Hair filled my mouth. It felt as if I was biting leather; I could taste his sweat on my tongue. Above me was a screaming noise, like an engine running out of control. I tried to ignore that. I tried to ignore the pressure on my throat. I kept my eyes closed, my teeth clenched on the hair and leather. My mouth was filling with something wet and foul-tasting. Suddenly something tore in my mouth; my throat was free. Medd was crouching on the carpet, clutching one hand.

There was a constriction in my throat. Breathing hurt. I tried to cough, but before I could get upright Medd was on his feet. I backed towards the wall. My eyes were used to the dark now. I could make out Medd's face. It wasn't enraged, but intent: the face of someone concentrating on a job he had to do. He was staring at a spot just below my chin. From his right hand dangled a soft black shape.

I felt the shelves behind me. My hand scrabbled on the top shelf, found a glass. When Medd charged me I brought it down on the top of his head. The glass splintered in my hand. I ground my hand against Medd's short hair, feeling my own fingers tear. I was being lifted up, forced back against the wall. Suddenly Medd took a step back. One hand was on my chest. The black shape in his hand swung lazily upwards, hung for a moment. I felt a crushing weight on the left side of my head. It drove out every thought. I was falling, falling down a lift shaft or from the edge of a building. My knees hit the carpet. In front of me I could see Medd's knees. His hand was touching my forehead as if he was blessing me.

I rolled just before the next blow came. Maybe that was instinct, or maybe I was about to fall over anyway. Medd grunted; the hand disappeared. I gripped the rough material of his jeans and threw my own weight forward. Medd was still off balance from the missed blow. He went backwards, not falling but staggering, with me crawling across the floor after him. When he hit the table his knees jack-knifed and he went over with the table alongside him.

His fingers were locked in my hair. I fell on top of him and felt my elbows jar on something hard. I could no longer see his face now. It was no longer Medd beneath me but a thick, foul-smelling darkness. Under my hand I felt something heavy. Its shape was familiar; I didn't know what it was. I raised it and brought it down into the darkness. It hit something hard, jarring my arm. When I raised it again it was lighter. The room was swaying about me. I slashed again at the darkness, and then again. I didn't know any longer whether there was anything beneath me or not. I was just slashing at darkness.

Suddenly I realized that I was sobbing. Whatever I was holding dropped out of my fingers. I crouched over, burying my face in my hands. My hands felt sharp: there was glass protruding from them. I didn't mind that. I pressed them into my cheeks and felt blood mingle with my tears.

I crouched there for a long time.

It was pain which cut through the fog in the end: a blinding pain like a bright light shone into my eyes. Slowly I sat up. The room was light. Underneath me, Medd was a dark shape. He wasn't moving. I wanted to get off him but as soon as I tried to stand up my head began to spin. The room was in chaos, furniture upturned, broken objects lying on the carpet. I tried to move again.

A noise made me look round. A man was standing in the doorway. He was a young policeman in a helmet with a white shirt unbuttoned at the collar. One hand was on his radio. His face was shocked.

He lifted one hand towards me. 'All right. Take it easy.' Tension made his voice shrill.

He didn't know who I was. He thought I was a killer and that I would probably try to kill him as well. The thought of it made me want to laugh. That didn't seem to calm the policeman's nerves. Behind him Don was peering out from the hallway.

Don said, 'I knew something was wrong. I heard a noise.' His voice was in shock.

'Take it easy.' The young copper was moving slowly towards me, one step at a time, as if I was a dangerous animal he had been sent to tame.

I said, 'It's all right.'

The young policeman blinked uncertainly. Suddenly his radio whined. Don took a step forward into the room. He couldn't take his eyes off what was beneath me. I looked down at Medd. His head was a mess of blood and soaked hair. There were shards of glass sticking out of it. Blood had run down over his ear and soaked into the collar of his jacket.

The copper said, 'Is he dead?' He tried to make it sound as if dead was normal, but his voice went high-pitched at the end.

I reached down and touched Medd's cheek. It was warm. His eyelids flickered. 'He's not dead.'

The copper was talking to a man on the staircase behind him. I heard words. Some of them made sense, others might have been in another language. I didn't want to move. I wanted to lie down where I was and sleep. Distantly I could hear footsteps, voices, the metallic crackle of a radio. When I opened my eyes two policemen were standing over me. One of them had a sergeant's stripes on his arm.

'What is this?' His voice was harsh, peremptory. He wanted to take control.

I said, 'Call Detective Sergeant Baring at Kennington. Tell him Medd's here.'

It was too much effort to look up at his face. Over my head I heard voices, more radio, the sound of argument.

'Who are you?' The peremptory voice again.

I felt in my pocket; my fingers touched my ID. Someone took it out of my hand.

There was hurried muttering, a hand on my sleeve. A voice said, 'Are you all right, sir?'

I didn't answer that. There were more questions, but I didn't have any more answers. More footsteps came into the room. A siren sounded briefly outside. A woman in a white jacket was sitting next to me on the sofa. There was a case open next to her.

'This will hurt.' Her voice was matter-of-fact. She was doing something to my hand. She was right about it hurting. For a while pain blocked out everything. The woman's voice said, 'You'd better come along with us.'

I shook my head. 'I'll be all right.'

They were lifting Medd on to a stretcher. A voice said, 'Skull like a fucking elephant.'

The young policeman was staring at me open-mouthed.

'You'd be better off in hospital.' She was winding bandage around my hand. Slowly the flesh was disappearing in a soft white cocoon.

I said, 'I want to sleep.'

'We ought to clean up your head first.'

The police sergeant was kneeling on the carpet in front of me. His voice was hushed. 'Sergeant Baring's meeting us at the hospital, sir. He said he'd take care of it.' The sergeant nodded at the stretcher being manoeuvred out of the door. 'What did he do, sir?'

'He killed a girl.'

'Nearly managed to kill you as well, sir.'

There were more questions, too many of them. The splash of cold water on my head didn't do anything to clear the fog inside it.

Falling on to the bed was like tumbling into a deep pit.

35

I woke to the feeling of something shaking me. I opened my eyes. In front of me my hand lay on the bed in a vast swaddle of white bandages. Pink fingers protruded helplessly from the end of it. It looked like a baby in swathing bands. I liked that idea. I remembered the crib we had had at home for Christmas. Ralph broke one of the kings so we had to double up with a US cavalryman that came from the fortress our uncle gave us.

The hand shook my shoulder again. 'Excuse me, sir.'

'What is it?'

'There's someone who wants to see you.'

'Tell them to go away.'

'They won't go away, sir.'

'Who is it?'

'It's a woman, sir.' He sounded embarrassed.

I had a last look at the mound of bandages. After a moment I closed my eyes and swung my legs off the bed. The room lurched around me, then gradually settled down. I opened my eyes.

Sam Harvey was standing in the door to the bedroom.

She was dressed in a stylish grey coat and black velvet gloves. A black leather bag was slung over one shoulder. To start with I thought she looked tanned, then I realized the colour was make-up. The make-up was neatly painted over her mouth and eyes, concealing any expression she might have had. Her hair was brushed sideways from her forehead. She might have been on her way to a society wedding.

She said to the policeman, 'Can you leave us alone, please?' Her voice was brittle.

The copper glanced nervously at me and went out of the room.

Sam's gaze flickered. Suddenly she seemed to notice my hand. Her mouth fell open. 'What happened?'

I said, 'There was a fight. The guy who was threatening to kill us. You don't have to worry about that any more.'

I stopped. Sam wasn't listening to me. Her breath was coming in shallow gasps as if there was something in her mouth she wanted to swallow but couldn't.

She said, 'Have you seen this?'

From her bag she pulled out a folded newspaper. She dropped it quickly on the floor as if it was something dirty that she didn't want to touch.

Harvey's face stared up at me. The headline above it told the story.

'How could they? How *could* they?' Her lips were starting to tremble. A streak of mascara hovered just below her eyelid. 'It's all lies. How *dare* they?'

I closed my eyes. Pain throbbed in my arm, but I had to ignore that. 'Have you asked your father about it?'

'I tried.' A sob broke from her. 'I called them up. He said . . . He said it was all very complicated. He made me speak to Mummy. She was crying. I've never heard her cry before.' The tears were running freely down her cheeks. She wiped them angrily away with the back of one glove. 'There were reporters outside my flat. Photographers. I didn't tell them anything. I put on make-up before I came out. I don't believe any of it.' She prodded the newspaper viciously with her toe. 'It's all a story made up by that *whore*. She must have written it before she died. It's all a lie. They called me up at the flat this morning to ask questions. I wouldn't tell them anything.' Her voice changed suddenly. 'And you haven't been here.'

Her blue eyes were staring at me. Suddenly she looked too small for the smart coat and the gloves. She looked like a little girl who'd just found out that Father Christmas didn't exist.

'Where have you been?'

I said, 'Looking for Medd.'

'Is he the man you had the fight with?'

I nodded.

'You should have called me,' she said. 'I haven't seen you since . . . You could have left a message, at least.'

'There's something you've got to understand . . .' I began.

'About you?' She shook her head. 'I don't mind if you've got someone else. I don't care. It's not as if you ever lied about her. I just need . . .'

'It's not about me.' I nodded towards the newspaper. 'About your father.'

Sam scowled. 'I don't want to know.'

'You've got to. It wasn't June who told them that story. It was me.'

I made myself look at her when I said that. Behind the make-up her face turned slowly to a deathly white. The make-up looked like paint smeared on to a doll's face. Her mouth was shapeless.

'Why?' she whispered.

'Your father ought to tell you that.'

'Why? You mean . . .' She stared at the newspaper on the floor. 'Is it *true*?'

'Ask him.'

'No.' She shook her head wildly. 'Why would you tell lies about him? Was it because of me? Was it because we slept together?' Her voice trembled. 'What have we done to hurt you? Daddy liked you. You liked him – you told me.'

I said, 'That's nothing to do with it. Your father can tell you the rest.'

'No.' Anger was starting to flood in to her voice. '*You* tell me. Why won't you tell me?'

'I'm not the right person,' I said. 'I'm sorry.'

'What do you mean?' Her voice was beginning to turn shrill. 'Was this revenge? Was there something I did? Do you think it was my fault your relationship broke down?' Her voice broke into a wail. 'I thought you cared about me . . .'

I said, 'I did care about you. I wish I hadn't.'

'And then you did this to Daddy.' She was leaning away from me now, as if she was afraid of me. Suddenly her face dissolved. She screamed, 'You *bastard*!'

She yelled at me then. She used words I couldn't have imagined her using, words that didn't sound right coming from her mouth. Her face seemed lopsided, as if the anger was twisting it out of shape. I watched her shouting. Sam had been caught in the middle. She'd never wanted anything wrong or foolish, anything she didn't deserve. But both the people she trusted had turned out to be liars.

When she had finished I looked down at her sleek black head. Her shoulders were still shaking.

I said, 'I'm sorry.'

'Don't be.' Her voice was furious. 'Don't be sorry for me. I don't want you to be. I never cared about you. Do you understand? You were just someone to go to bed with. I never cared about you.'

I didn't say anything.

'We slept together because I wanted to. You thought I was just a little girl . . . You did what I wanted, all right?'

'If you like.'

She rubbed the back of her hand angrily across her eyes and stood up. Her voice was no longer shrill. 'I'd probably have gone to bed with you even if I'd known what you were like. Even if I'd known you wanted to destroy my family.'

Her eyes were bright. She was trying to behave the way she'd seen women behave in movies but she didn't have any practice at it. 'You probably thought I was just a spoiled brat, is that it? A spoiled little girl who you could impress. It wasn't like that. All right?'

I said, 'I didn't think it was like that.'

'That's why Daddy wouldn't talk about you last night.' Her voice was breaking again. I saw the effort it took her to get back under control. She picked up the leather bag. She said coldly, 'I'm hope you're pleased with what you've done.'

I didn't say anything to that. I listened to her quick footsteps fading downstairs.

I wasn't pleased with what I'd done.

36

Don made me coffee and fed it to me through the side of my mouth. They took me back to Kennington Police Station to answer Baring's questions and to evade Mason's. That took most of the morning. As soon as they'd finished with me I made excuses and went upstairs.

I closed the door to my office and sat down heavily behind the desk. On Kennington Road Sunday morning was unfolding in the usual way. An unshaven man walked along the pavement with a carton of milk under his arm. A woman came slowly out of the newsagent reading a paper. At breakfast tables everywhere people were finding out about Michael Harvey's affair with a secretary: another MP looking grimly out of the front page; more journalists jostling visitors to his house; but a wife, this time, who would not stand by her man, and a lover who was dead.

I looked at the pin-board over my desk. It stayed out of focus until I put my hands up to squeeze my eyes. What I wanted more than anything was to sleep, but there wasn't time for that yet.

Miles Davis stared back at me out of the pin-board. I reached forward and took the picture off the board. Nothing had changed for Miles; his life was easy. All he had to do was blow his trumpet and let the truth speak for itself.

I looked at the picture for a long time. Then I crumpled it up with one hand and dropped it into the bin.

No one answered the phone at the Harveys' house. That didn't surprise me. I could picture the scene outside. Cars would be blocking the road, photographers clinging to the railings under the cherry trees. I opened the file which contained the first statement he had made to me. A second number was written under the first. I reached for the phone again and dialled it.

A man's voice answered. It was smooth, well-bred, slightly wary. 'Hello?'

'Can I speak to Michael Harvey?'

'This is Mr Harvey's solicitor.'

'Is he there?'

'He's not available for questions at present.'

'I'm not a reporter. Tell him it's George Havilland.'

The voice went away. In the background I could hear slow footsteps, a door open and shut. It seemed too normal for what must be going on in the house.

'Mr Harvey has asked me to take a message.'

'Doesn't he want to speak to me?'

'Not at present.'

I thought for a moment. 'Tell him I'll be waiting on Lambeth Bridge in an hour's time. Tell him to be there.'

'Mr Harvey isn't making appointments for today. If you'd like . . .'

I put down the phone.

Lambeth Bridge was empty except for a few tourists pointing cameras at the Houses of Parliament. The river slid below me, a brown current tugging at the piers of the bridge. Downstream a barge strained at its mooring buoy. Saturday afternoon strollers ambled along the embankment past St Thomas' Hospital. In the middle of the river a police launch circled fussily across the current, throwing up spray. A policeman in the stern was holding a line which ran overboard into the depths of the river.

I looked back along the bridge. There was still no sign of Harvey.

Big Ben struck four o'clock. I had been waiting an hour and a half. A tourist boat began to turn just downstream of the bridge. The wind carried the metallic voice of the commentator towards me without making sense of the words. The tourists were bundled up in anoraks and scarves. Below me the policeman in the stern of the launch was shouting instructions at the helmsman. There was still no sign of Harvey.

A few cars passed behind me: somewhere a light must have changed. I thought of the first time I had seen him, sitting behind the desk in his study. A lot of people had envied Michael Harvey. The glittering career at college; the legal high-flyer with only one cloud, a rumour, to mar his reputation; the seat in parliament and the beautiful family. I wondered how much of it he had planned in advance, how much he had dreamed of when all his friends were heading off to jobs in local businesses or to shops in the High Street. The photographs in his office had been a triumphal progress, a record of success. That was less than a week ago.

A taxi was drawing up on the other side of the bridge. I turned and watched it. The far door was opening, the taxi driver craning round to accept money. A man got out. The door slammed; the driver put the cab into gear.

Michael Harvey stood watching me from the other side of the road. He didn't move. He just stood watching me with his hands in the pockets of a black overcoat. His face was quite blank.

Cars passed between us. When they were gone Harvey started crossing the road. He walked stiffly, as if the last two days had aged him. The police launch droned behind me.

'Hello, George.' His voice was soft, as if he was recovering from a long illness.

He didn't put out his hand. He leaned beside me on the parapet of the bridge. I saw that he was breathing fast, as if the short walk across the road had been too much for him. 'I had a job getting here. They followed me. I had to slip into Smith Square . . .' His thin face turned bitterly towards me. 'And out the back way. I suppose these are the sort of tricks you learn.'

I didn't say anything. Harvey turned and looked quickly up and down the bridge. 'It's like being hunted. Tony Hughes took a cab off in the other direction. My solicitor. I think they went after him.'

I said, 'You should have believed me yesterday.'

Bitterness didn't suit Harvey's face. It looked uncomfortable, like a new jacket that didn't quite fit. 'I never thought you'd do anything so *dirty*, George.' His fingers gripped the parapet of the bridge. Looking away over the river he went on, 'Jo's going to leave me. She's on her way to her parents' place. I thought if I could only keep her in London I might persuade her, but . . . I got a call from her *solicitor*.' The words were stumbling out faster and faster, as if he was having to run to stay ahead of tears. 'I can't get hold of Sam. She walked out on me. I suppose . . . I suppose you feel *pleased* with yourself . . .'

He leaned his forehead on the back of his hand and breathed deeply for a few moments.

There was no point in my saying I was sorry. It wasn't my fault that Harvey's life was collapsing around him, but I was the one who had kicked away the props. I said, 'Are you going to make a statement against the Thackers?'

Harvey turned his face towards me slowly. His expression was incredulous. 'Is that why you asked me here?'

'Partly.'

'You think I'm going to help you *now*? After what you've *done*?'

I said, 'You'd be helping yourself too. Everyone's going to ask if you killed June Donaghy. You admitted you were with her when she died. Everyone knows you were having an affair with her.' I shrugged. 'If you identify Medd now there's still Jimmy Bolan's first statement to corroborate it, and the picture I found in his garage. You can show why the Thackers would have wanted her dead.'

'Where is Medd?'

'In hospital. He tried to attack me last night.'

For the first time Harvey seemed to notice the bandage on my hand and what Medd had done to my face. His lips trembled a little, then he shook his head. 'I'm not going to help you, George. You destroyed my family. I'll never forgive you for that.'

'What if they start to investigate you?'

'I don't have anything to hide. I didn't . . . kill her.' He swallowed when he said kill and looked down into the brown water where June Donaghy had ended up. 'I got a call from Peter Thacker this morning. After the paper came out.' His lips tightened. 'After the journalists woke us up. He offered to get me a job back in the City. His solicitors . . . the ones who work for him now . . . They're looking for a junior partner.' He grinned at me but the smile didn't mean he was happy about anything. 'It's the only option I've got, isn't it? I don't have any choice. There'll be plenty of work to do, in any case. After they announce the deal tomorrow . . .'

I said, 'There isn't going to be any deal.' Harvey stopped. His mouth was open. 'If you bring forward your documents we can stop PTI ever making deals like that again. And Philip Lord.'

'But I'm not going to, George. I already told you that. Didn't you hear me?'

'I'm not giving you the choice.'

Something was twisting Harvey's face, something more than the cold wind down the river. 'How are you going to make me? Have you got any more sordid little stories to tell? Any more . . .'

I said quietly, 'You killed Sarah Rider.'

Harvey's face froze. There was a long silence. From behind me I could hear the police launch drone. Spray was whipping over the passengers on the tourist boat.

Harvey laughed suddenly. I'd never heard him laugh before, and it was the wrong time for him to start. A clenched muscle turned his forehead into white stone. 'This is absurd.'

The laugh didn't last long. Harvey frowned suddenly, then tried to look outraged. His expression kept changing, as if he was no longer in control of it.

'I don't think you meant to. But Sarah Rider told you that she had done the one thing you feared most. She'd told the Thackers about your affair with June.' I watched his eyes blink desperately as if he was shuffling through a pack of cards, looking for an expression to counter what I was saying. 'She was the only one who could have told them. You and June kept your affair secret from everyone except her.'

'Why?' It sounded like a voice he had borrowed from some-body else. 'Why would she?'

'For money. I don't think Sarah was vindictive. She didn't like you but I don't think she would have hurt you because of that. I'm only guessing but my guess is that she came to you after June's death and tried to blackmail you. She had some letters of June's; she knew what they would be worth to you. You refused to pay her anything. You didn't think she'd do it . . . You didn't think people did things like that.' I remembered Sarah's hard, determined face: *When do I get my share?* She had thought her share had finally arrived. 'When you turned her down she sold them to the Thackers instead. She knew they would be worth something to them because of what her sister and you had been planning. She probably didn't know how much. I don't know how much they paid her.

'But by then you were having second thoughts. You must have called Sarah on Wednesday morning to say you wanted to meet her. That was when she got in touch with Jackie and asked if she could use his flat. She wanted him to be there as well. She wanted protection . . .' I shook my head. 'She still thought she could get some money out of you. Maybe she had an idea the Thackers weren't going to use the letters in the press, and that would be worth something more from you. Either way, she was expecting money. That's what she told Jackie . . .'

Harvey interrupted, 'It's not possible. I wasn't there that night. I was . . .'

'You said you were working late, trying to catch up. Was there anyone in the office with you?'

Harvey wasn't looking at me any more. He gripped the bridge with fingers that were white at the knuckles.

'I don't think you meant to kill her,' I said quietly. 'I don't know what happened . . . a struggle, an accident. I guess you must have lost control. Maybe that never happened to you before.'

Harvey's whole life had been kept under control: a career planned years ahead, a wife whose every action he could predict. When he could see all of that disappearing, then the control which had won it for him had snapped. Sarah Rider had not been killed coldly and ruthlessly, the way Medd would have killed her. For a moment I saw Harvey panting, appalled, staring in shock at the woman lying on the floor in front of him; around him, the tatty wallpaper of Jackie's flat; the voices of strangers upstairs.

'I didn't . . .' He hesitated and the hesitation turned his denial into a lie. He knew that. His eyes were no longer shocked; they pleaded with me. 'I didn't *mean* to.' He covered his face with his hands suddenly, either to hide it from me or just to block out everything except the smell of his own hands. He didn't seem to like the smell of his hands. He dropped them to the parapet as if he was throwing them away from him.

I watched him standing with the river behind him. A man who only a week ago had had everything and had just lost the last support he had left.

'It was like you said. I lost . . .' He shook his head. 'I don't know what happened to me.'

For a long time he was silent. I gave him the time he needed. Below us the policeman in the stern of the launch was pulling his rope in hand over hand. The launch's engine growled against the current.

'What are you going to do?' His voice sounded hopeless.

I said, 'That depends on you.'

Harvey turned towards me. His eyes were intent. 'What do you mean?'

I took a deep breath. 'I could arrest you now. You're a killer.' He winced and lifted one hand off the parapet, as if to protest. 'The trouble is . . .' The fight with Medd seemed suddenly to have caught up with me, or else all the painkillers had worn off. My head was spinning. 'If you're convicted of Sarah's murder, then what chance do you have of being believed as a witness against Medd? Everyone knows you were having an affair with June. They'll know you killed her sister. It will look as if you killed June and set Medd up as a fall-guy. You could have killed her for the same reason you killed Sarah – to keep the affair quiet. You can bring forward your evidence against the Thackers.' I shrugged. 'What good will that do? The evidence will come from a murderer, someone who told lies.'

'What are you going to do?' Harvey's voice came from the mouth of a cave.

I put one hand out to steady myself. The wind seemed to be trying to pull me off the bridge. 'At the moment no one's looking for you. They might start to make connections if they think you killed June, but they won't think that so long as you identify Medd and show why the Thackers would have wanted June killed. At the moment everyone's looking for Jackie – Sarah's husband. He was a junkie and she died in his flat. It's the most obvious thing. Besides, the timing stacks up against him. He turned up after Sarah's death and after you were gone, but Jackie isn't the sort of person anyone's going to believe. Apart from anything else, he's half convinced that he killed her anyway. He was supposed to be there to protect her and he didn't turn up.'

'Have you spoken to him?'

I nodded. 'Two days ago. He was in a bad state.'

'What are you saying?' Harvey's voice trembled.

'I'm saying that I'm the only person who knows you killed Sarah Rider. I don't have to tell anybody about it.'

Cars passed behind us. From further up the river the wind brought us fragments from the sound of Big Ben and carried them away again, upriver towards the darkening west.

Harvey's face looked as if he no longer understood anything, was no longer sure of what he knew. 'You mean . . . you'd let Jackie Rider . . .'

'You'll have to take a chance on it. I'm not running the investigation. All I'm saying is that I won't come forward and tell them what I know about you.' I shrugged. 'I don't have a choice. I might be letting you off, but unless I do that, then Medd will get away with what he did, and the Thackers as well.' It wasn't a choice between black and white. It was a matter of which compromise to choose.

'I . . .' Harvey choked suddenly. His hand was clamped tightly over his mouth as he stared downstream. The wind tore tears out of his eyes and ran them sideways across his cheek.

I took a card out of my pocket and put it into his fingers. 'Call this number and ask for Mason. Tell him everything you've told me.'

'If they find Jackie?' Harvey's voice was a whisper.

'You'll have to take your chance.'

I turned around and started walking. The wind tore at my back. I only looked round once. Michael Harvey was slumped over the parapet of the bridge like an old man or a drunkard vomiting into the swirling current.

Behind him the Houses of Parliament were stretched out against the skyline.

37

There was light in the wired-glass window over Neil Hudson's door. I found him tapping furiously at the computer keyboard, with newspapers spread out over the floor around him.

'George!' He gave me an excited grin which turned to shock when he saw my arm and the face that went with it. 'Sit down.' He swept papers off a chair. 'Can I get you something?'

I shook my head. 'I can't stay long.'

'What happened?'

'A fight.' I didn't want to tell him about it. 'It doesn't matter.'

'Are you OK?' he glanced over his shoulder at the screen. 'Thanks for the story, George. I never thought . . .' He stopped.

I said, 'Nor did I.'

'Dailies are picking it up tomorrow. Fall-out. Harvey's future. They're saying he's got pressure on him to give up his seat. Act quickly, try to limit the damage.' He stopped when he realized I wasn't listening. 'You look terrible.'

I shook my head. 'I'm OK. You know what else is happening tomorrow?'

'Announcement on the nuclear power stations. This'll knock it off the front page.' He made a face. 'Worst luck.'

I reached into my pocket and drew out a folded sheet of paper, handed it to him. I didn't have the energy to watch while he read it. From a long way away his voice said, 'Where did you get this?'

'It doesn't matter.' With an effort I lifted my head. 'PTI are going to win the bid for the power stations.'

'PTI?' He frowned. 'I didn't even know they were bidding.'

I nodded. 'I saw Peter Thacker yesterday. And Philip Lord. I don't know what they're paying Lord. I can't prove they're paying him anything. But if you call Michael Harvey he'll give you evidence of how they got the Sizewell deal in the first place. That ties Lord to the Thackers. You shouldn't need any more than that.'

'Michael Harvey?' Neil shook his head. 'I don't understand. George?'

The room swayed as I stood up. 'George?

I said, 'Nobody understands.'

People were coming out of an evening service as I approached Brixton Road. There weren't many of them: some old ladies, a man walking on crutches, a black family in neat clothes. Apart from them, the street had a Sunday evening stillness. I had lived here for eighteen months and already I felt like a stranger. It felt as if I had stepped off an aeroplane and I was walking around a city I had never visited before. I thought of the hotel room I had slept in two nights before: the empty wardrobe, the dirty towel which the chambermaid would leave on my bed. That was my home now.

I climbed the stairs in darkness and stopped. There was light under the door of the flat. Tentatively I knocked.

Mary opened the door. She had to use it to keep herself standing as well. She looked as if she hadn't slept for a year. The skin was pinched around eyes from which the shock and pain had still not faded. That was what I had done to her.

'What are you doing here? Why aren't you in hospital?'

'I made them let me out.' Her voice trembled, as if it was a newly set leg she hadn't walked on before. 'An hour ago. I couldn't stand it in there.'

'What did the doctor say?'

'He wanted to keep me in. There's nothing wrong with me. I just need to sleep.' She frowned. 'What happened to your hand?' She was looking at the white mass of bandages on my hand. The frown grew deeper. 'What happened in here? There was a policeman on the door. I've just been trying to clean up. What happened, George?'

I said, 'There was a fight. Medd was waiting for me.'

'Oh.' The corners of her mouth turned down. 'Medd . . . ?'

'The man who attacked you. He's been arrested now. It was Medd who killed June Donaghy.'

She made space for me to get past. The living-room furniture had been pushed back against the wall. A hoover was propped up by the sofa.

'Are you all right?' Her voice was studied. We'd got over meeting and now she was trying to find a new voice to talk to me with – the voice she'd use for an old friend.

'I'm fine.'

'Your hand?'

'It'll heal.' I looked at her. 'What about you? You should be lying down, at least.'

'Oh . . .' She shook her head. ' My head hurts, that's all. I keep taking aspirin. I'm tired.'

I looked around the room. The only sign of my fight with Medd was the rug on the floor. Mary had used it to cover the place where he had been lying.

Mary said, 'A girl came to see me. She was looking for you.' Her voice was uncertain. 'She had a grey coat. She said she'd been here earlier and said the wrong thing. I don't know what she meant. Was she the girl . . . ?'

I said, 'Yes.'

'She was pretty.' Mary's voice was neutral. She might have been commenting on someone we'd seen in a crowd.

'Yes.'

'I can see why . . .'

I said, 'Stop it.'

Mary bit her lip angrily and looked away.

'I came to get my things.'

She followed me into the bedroom and watched me pulling out trousers, shirts, shoes. Neither of us spoke.

After a moment Mary said, 'I'm going to move out of here. I can't sleep. I keep thinking he's going to come back.'

'He's not going to come back.'

'I know that. It's the feeling. When it's happened once.' She shivered. 'I suppose you stop feeling safe.' She paused. 'Charlie brought me home.'

'Yes?'

'Ronnie Scott's have offered us another date. In the autumn.'

'I'm glad.'

'Yes.' She sounded uncertain. 'It doesn't seem to matter so much now.'

I finished with my clothes and looked around the bedroom. There wasn't anything I needed to take: some books that didn't matter; a pair of shoes that needed replacing anyway. Mary followed me through into the living room. This was the bit I'd found hard last time: the bit I'd imagined if I ever thought of our relationship ending. One by one I turned over familiar covers: Ben Webster, Art Tatum, John Coltrane. I couldn't remember any longer which had once been my records and which were Mary's. They were part of both of us, the story of a life together. Dividing them into two piles was like tearing ten years in half.

Mary watched me from the sofa. I started with the easy ones. The old recording of Louis Armstrong's All Stars had been a present from Ralph on my seventeenth birthday. I pulled that out and dropped it on the carpet. Behind me I heard the scrape of a match, smelled burning sulphur. Nina Simone had been a present from a previous girlfriend. I pulled that out, and a battered copy of *Birth of the Cool* – I knew we had two of them. The pile on the carpet was hardly growing.

Mary's voice said, 'She'd been crying, the girl who came here. Have you had a fight? What have you been doing to her?'

'It's too hard to explain.'

'Maybe you're just good at making people cry.'

I said, 'I thought you didn't want to talk about it.'

'Maybe it would help,' Mary said defiantly. 'She wanted to talk about you. She said . . . What did she say? She said it was interesting to meet me. How old is she? She didn't look more than eighteen. I suppose everyone looks eighteen when you're my age.'

'I don't know how old she is,' I said.

'She was classy. God knows where you managed to find her. You're going up in the world, George.'

'Stop it,' I said.

'Why? A woman likes to know who's taken over from her.'

'It's not like that.'

Mary didn't say anything.

I said, 'Nothing's happening with her. It was just a stupid fling.'

'That's not what she seemed to think.'

'I told her that.'

'You should have said it before . . . before you had the fling. You can't just pick people up and drop them, George.'

'What did she want?' I asked.

Mary's voice was bitter. 'You.' There was a pause. 'She looked dreadful. You must have got under her skin. That's what you do to people, George. You get under their skin.'

I turned round. Mary wasn't looking at me. She was holding the cigarette in her mouth, looking out towards the windows. She swallowed and drew angrily on the cigarette.

I turned back to the shelves. CDs stretched either way in front of me: songs we'd listened to together, albums we'd bought in Pie's jazz shop in the Portobello Road. I pulled out the Five Blind Boys from Mississippi: Mary never listened to gospel. I tried to picture the stack of records at my old flat, before I moved in with her. All I could think of was an empty room, a room I didn't want to go back to. A tattered Oscar Peterson LP joined the pile. I'd bought it on a trip to Chicago before I ever met her. I looked at the heap of plastic and cardboard on the carpet. That was all that was left of my earlier life: the only part of it I could disentangle from Mary. It didn't add up to much.

Mary's voice said, 'Why did you tell me about her last night? Why couldn't it wait?'

'I needed you to know.'

'That was *honest* of you.' Her voice was bitter. 'It happened on Thursday night, didn't it? The night I came back from Jack's. Is that why you did it?'

'What do you mean?'

'Because I went off to Jack.'

'Of course not,' I said.

'I shouldn't have gone. I only did it because I was angry.' She gave a jerky laugh. 'It seems so stupid now. I was angry because you wouldn't give anything up for me. I thought I was more important than that.'

'You . . .'

'Don't lie, George.' I heard her blowing out smoke. 'You made your decision. Most people don't have to make decisions like that. It was just bad luck. Most people can compromise.'

Names blurred in front of my eyes: Coleman Hawkins, Lester Young, Earl Hines.

'Jack kept wanting to talk about you. He thought I was going to go to bed with him. He kept saying . . .' Her laugh was shaky. 'I kept trying to defend you. I was angry with you but I didn't think anyone else was allowed to be rude about you. I thought that was my job. So I came back. And you . . .' There was a pause. 'You didn't waste your time, did you? I'd only been gone two days. Even if you're bored of this girl, you'll find someone else, no problem. I know half a dozen people . . .'

I said, 'I don't want anyone else.'

There was a pause. 'I don't know what that means, George.'

I didn't say anything.

Mary's voice said, 'I ought to hate you. I *want* to hate you. It wasn't fair, what you did. You lied to me.'

I tried to shuffle the records into a pile. The face on the top cover blurred. My fingers were clumsy. A stack of CDs slipped and clattered sideways on to the carpet. I put one hand on the floor to steady myself.

There was a long silence.

From behind me Mary's voice said, 'Don't go, George.'

The face on the cover was black: a man holding a trumpet. He stared back at me, then blurred, dissolving into red and brown shapes.

'I don't want you to go. I don't want to have to start over on my own again. It's too late for that. I want to be with you.' She sounded angry. 'I'm not brave enough.'

I turned round. She was leaning against the back of the sofa, her face covered by one hand. 'We've done too much together. It isn't worth throwing it away – do you see? I don't care what you think of me.'

She took the hand away and stared defiantly at me as I came towards her. 'I don't *care* what you think of me. Maybe I'm a coward.'

I knelt in front of the sofa. Mary took my club of white bandages in her hands and gently touched my fingers. She was frowning. She said, 'You're crying. I've never seen you cry before.'

Slowly her fingers moved up to my face.

Late that night I woke up. Mary was sleeping next to me. Her hands were clasped around the bandage on my wrist. Outside, Brixton Road was silent.

For a moment I thought of Sam Harvey: her white body curled up against the beanbag. Mary and I would always have something between us now. Slowly time would grow over it, absorbing but never dissolving it. It would be somewhere under the surface, painful when you touched it but otherwise no more than a dull ache. That was the compromise Mary had accepted. What we had was damaged, but it was better than not having anything.

I thought of Jackie Rider hiding somewhere in the city's labyrinth, and of Michael Harvey. In whatever direction I looked there seemed to be nothing but compromises. The truth was a distant ring of mountains on the horizon.

Mary stirred beside me. Her lips nuzzled my shoulder. She was only half awake.

She whispered, 'We should move out of here. Find somewhere new.'

Before I knew it I was asleep again.

38

Kennington Police Station was crowded on Monday morning. There was a whole weekend's debris to clear up, a whole week of trouble to look ahead to.

Mason waited for the noise of feet on the stairs to die down before going on. 'Heard it on the radio as well. Announcement delayed for another month. Philip Lord can't be a happy man this morning. It's always the ones you don't expect, isn't it? My wife always liked him. She thought he looked the sort of chap you could trust.'

Under his breath he was humming a tune I couldn't make out. His fingers danced on the edge of the desk. Suddenly his face broke into a delighted grin. 'Philip Lord won't be the only one with things on his mind. I wouldn't want to be John Harlow this morning, either. Not after what you told me on the phone last night.' He wrinkled up his nose. 'I never did trust Johnnie Harlow, you know. Ever since I first met him. I always thought there was something funny about him – never managed to put my finger on it before. I was on the phone to Scotland Yard this morning. Blokes up there running around like blue-arsed flies. They need to – got some explaining to do. Thackers thought they were well in, didn't they? Suddenly they don't have any friends any more.'

I said, 'What time did Michael Harvey call you?'

'Six o'clock?' Mason frowned. 'I feel sorry for Harvey in a way. Poor bastard. I'm not saying I like what he did to his wife. All the same . . .' He looked across at me. 'Did you see her family on the news yesterday? His wife's family. I wouldn't want to fall into their hands.' Mason sighed. 'Harvey'll find something. He's a smart lad, the type that picks himself up. You never know, he might even get himself another seat. Didn't sound too good on the phone last night, though. I made him come in, make a statement. Just after nine o'clock. Gave me time to get some boys from the Fraud Squad down here.' Mason shook his head. 'Couldn't believe what I was hearing. Boys from the Fraud Squad were lapping it up, I can tell you. Looked like the cat that found the cream. Ted Baring was here, too. We must have got warrants for the Thackers about midnight.'

Mason looked across at me. His face showed concern. 'You might look a bit happier about it, George. I suppose it's the reaction. How's the hand?'

'It's fine.' My hand would heal. I wasn't sure about the rest of me.

'That was quite a scrap you had with Medd. You should see what he looks like.'

'Has he made a statement yet?'

'He can't – not with his face the shape it is now.' Mason grinned. 'Won't either, not Medd. He's a pro. I wouldn't worry about it. With Harvey as an eye-witness and what you found in his lock-up, he doesn't have a chance. Soon as he realizes that, he'll put the finger on Peter Thacker.' Mason laughed suddenly. 'You hear what happened when they went to Barney Thacker's house last night? Surrey Police. He went ape, apparently. Tried to bite a copper's nose off. He's a nasty piece of work, that one.'

'Barney didn't even know about it. It was Peter who set up June's murder.'

'You think?' Mason raised his eyebrows. 'Peter told us it was all his brother. Smooth bastard, by the time we turned up he already had his lawyer there. Camped out in the hall. Statement typed out with names, dates . . . blamed the whole thing on his brother. Halfway through, cab turns up to take his wife to the air-port. There's one girl who isn't going to stand by her man.' He chuckled at the memory of it. 'Even if Peter Thacker gets away with it, there won't be anything left of his business. Not after what the papers said this morning. He won't get away with it, either. Soon as we nail Medd, Medd'll bring the others down with him. The whole thing depends on Harvey's word against Medd.'

Mason looked across at me and his forehead creased with

concern. 'I'm sorry, George. I'm running on. Are you all right? You look all in.'

'I'm fine,' I lied.

'You don't look it. You need some time off. Get the hand sorted. Look after Mary. Ted Baring can finish off with Medd. You've done good work, George. No one's going to take it away from you this time. It's what you always wanted, isn't it? You got some of the big boys. All the ends tied up so they can't get out.'

'Not all of the ends,' I said.

Mason frowned. 'What do you mean?'

I said, 'There's still Sarah Rider.'

Mason frowned at me for a moment, then his face cleared. 'I forgot to tell you, didn't I? Had too much else on my mind. I'm surprised you even remember that one. You've had your plate full enough as it is.'

A dull weight seemed to have lowered on to my head. It was crushing me, pressing me down into the chair. I fought against it, forced myself to my feet. 'What's happened?'

'You remember her husband? The musician – the one who killed her?' Mason shook his head. 'Found him last night up in Camden Town, didn't they? Overdose. Friend of his called the ambulance but they were too late to do anything. Better, in a way, after what he'd done . . .' I saw his face darken suddenly. 'George? Are you all right, George?'

I walked quickly out of the room, along the corridor, down stairs crowded with laughing policemen. The desk clerk stared at me. Outside, Kennington Road was filled with voices, heels scuffing the pavement, the roar of traffic. I kept on walking; I didn't want to stop.

The sweet, reedy tone of Jackie Rider's saxophone pursued me. It rose up from hidden crevices in the pavement and windows open on to the street, drowning out even the noise of traffic. The melody followed me all the way to the tube.

> I see skies of blue and clouds of white
> The bright blessed day, the dark sacred night
> And I think to myself
> What a wonderful world

PREVIEW PATRICK DILLON'S

TRUTH

Police Detective George Havilland is also
featured in Patrick Dillon's first novel TRUTH, now
published in Penguin paperback.

The first chapter follows.

The last time I'd seen Joe Bates he was wearing a peaked cap and a grey suit and leaning against a dark green Rolls-Royce with shaded windows. Maybe he'd wanted people to think the Roller belonged to him, or maybe he'd thought it would fall over if he walked away. Today he was wearing a denim jacket with three holes in it and something that looked like a black scarf but wasn't. It spread all over the pavement around his head, as if he'd wanted to use it as a cushion.

He was lying with his head by a row of parked cars and his feet by a brick shed full of dustbins. Beyond the parked cars was an expanse of paving and a dead tree with someone's initials carved on the bark. Tower blocks looked down at him from every side. It wasn't the sort of place you'd choose to die in, but Joe Bates hadn't been given the choice.

I said, 'Who found him?'

Cayman nodded towards a fat man sitting on a wall at the back of the pavement. The man's face was the colour of old paint and there was a pool of vomit on his shoes.

'Time?'

'Six.'

'What was he doing?'

'Walking the dog.'

I said, 'Where's the dog?'

No one knew where the dog was.

I bent down and examined Joe Bates. From the front he looked as if he'd just felt tired and lain down for a nap, except the parking lot between two tower blocks was a funny place to take a nap and his eyes were open. He had handsome eyes, model's eyes, and a long handsome face to go with them. If it wasn't for the three holes in the back of his neck you could have put him on the front of a magazine.

Cayman said, 'His name's Joe Bates, sir. He lived in one of the blocks. They must have got him on his way home.'

I didn't say anything.

'There's every chance he's got a record,' Cayman went on, 'living round here. We can check it back at the station.'

'He didn't have a record,' I said.

Cayman looked at me in surprise.

'They let him off.'

'Did you know him, sir?'

I said, 'He was a friend of Hill's.'

A man in uniform got out of one of the cars parked behind the ambulance at the kerb. He came towards us, stooped down and started to draw a chalk line around Joe Bates's body.

'How was he killed, Sergeant?'

'Three bullets,' Cayman said. 'One in the neck, two a bit lower down. The damage to his head must have been when he fell over.'

There was a pause. Cayman was looking at me as if I was supposed to give him a prize for working that out by himself.

I said, 'Did anyone hear anything?'

We both looked up at the towers. Above us were tiers of access decks. The parapets were lined with kids' faces staring down at us in silence. As far as they were concerned, it was just another show, better than a crazy old woman, not as good as a fire. The faces had the cruel look of spectators at a circus.

Cayman said, 'We've done the two far towers. We'll be through any time.'

'That's too slow.'

'I'm doing the best I can, sir. I —'

He was about to tell me something about too few officers covering too much ground. I cut him off. 'All right.'

'Anything else you want, Chief Inspector?' Cayman's voice was tight.

'No.'

'All right, then.' He wasn't looking at me.

'You can send anyone back who isn't needed,' I said. 'Get an incident room set up. You'd better stay here with me.'

He grimaced and went over towards one of the police vans. Cayman was ten years older than me and two rungs back down the ladder. The last time we'd worked together that hadn't mattered. We were never going to like each other but at least he'd respected me. That was before Hill.

I watched the policemen coming back from the two further

towers. I didn't think they'd have learnt anything, and I didn't think they'd learn anything in the low-rise blocks either side of where Joe Bates lay. In Chelsea we'd have had neighbours running out of the front doors to tell us what they saw, or heard, or dreamed. Round here people kept the doors closed and televisions turned up high. If they heard shooting they turned the volume up even higher to drown it out.

A white car drive up to the kerb with its light flashing. Three more uniformed men got out. Cayman spoke to them and they spread out, one to each of the stair towers on the nearest blocks. There was a stampede of children's feet. Suddenly the access decks were deserted.

Cayman said, 'How much do you know about him, sir?'

I sighed. 'Do you remember Paddy Moran?'

Cayman didn't say anything. I knew he remembered Paddy Moran.

I said, 'Bates was driving the car when Hill killed him.'

'That was your case, wasn't it, sir?' Cayman knew it was my case.

'Bates has been following Hill round for years,' I went on. 'I don't know what else Hill used him for. Some time back he was charged for splitting open Tim McCreedy's knuckles with a monkey wrench. GBH. They let him off.'

'Why?'

'Hill paid for the lawyer,' I said.

There was a pause.

Cayman said, 'Who would have killed him?' He nodded towards what was lying on the pavement.

'Who do you think?'

'Would Hill do this to one of his own friends?'

I said, 'Hill doesn't have any friends.'

There were people coming out of the flats now on their way to work. Some of them walked past with dead eyes and some of them wound up against the barrier staring, as if we'd staged the whole thing just to cheer them up. One of them, a little braver than the others, came across the pavement towards us. He was an ordinary man in the sort of coat you wouldn't remember anywhere.

Cayman looked at him and said, 'Back, please.'

'What's happened?' The man's eyes were glued to Joe Bates's outflung hand.

'There's been an incident. Could you get back, please, sir.'

'What sort of an incident?'

'Somebody's dead,' Cayman said flatly.

'Dead?' The man nodded vaguely as if he'd heard somewhere about people dying but couldn't remember where. 'Was he killed?' He already knew the answer to that. If Joe Bates had died of a heart attack there wouldn't be two vanloads of policemen crawling all over the estate.

Cayman snapped, 'Back, mate. Behind the line. Now.'

There was a gleam in the man's eye. Dead was boring but killing woke something up in him. The animal knowledge that one day, if he got tired of working and watching TV, fucking, voting or drinking soapy beer out of tins, he might just kill someone himself – or get himself killed by someone. And that felt like a relief. His focus skewed over the body. He almost looked as if he was laughing.

He said, 'Shot, was he? Or was it a knife?'

Cayman shouted, 'Everyone back *now*. Get behind the line and stay there. And that includes you.'

The man turned and trotted back towards the line: the line that keeps all of us in and thoughts of murder out, that keeps us working and drinking soapy beer and still not killing anybody.

Cayman said, 'Fucking vultures. Sorry, sir.'

The fat man at the back of the pavement stood up. His belly was hanging out of the top of his trousers and his mouth was open.

He said, 'Do I have to stay?' It sounded like his tongue had suddenly become too big.

I looked at him. A trickle of grey sick clung to his collar. For a moment I almost felt sorry for him. He was just an ordinary man who loved his dog and didn't like finding dead people on his morning walk. He had swollen tears running down his fat cheeks and was staring at me with a heartbroken look as if there was anything I could say that was going to make things right.

'Has anyone taken his statement yet?'

'No, sir.'

'Why the hell not?'

'There hasn't been time.'

'Make time. Do it now.'

Cayman's lips tightened but he didn't answer back. He called two policemen over and spoke to them. They lifted the man up by the shoulders and carried him towards a car.

They needn't have bothered. I could have written his statement for him:

One morning I was going for a walk near where I live. I was thinking about my breakfast, and whether to get the car serviced, and what the teacher said about my boy's homework, when suddenly I saw a man lying on the pavement. It seemed to me strange that he wasn't moving and that blood was coming out of a hole in his head. Then I started screaming. After that I stopped screaming and was sick. I am making this statement in a state of what the doctors call shock. Next week I will be talking about it too much, and the week after my family will be bored, but I still won't be able to sleep without seeing dead people. The only dead person I saw before was my grandmother who was eighty years old and had no hole in her head. Signed . . .

It would only tell us what we already knew: that somebody had killed Joe Bates in a council estate just of Kennington Lane. But because we were policemen we wouldn't believe it was true until we'd typed it out on a form and lost it in some filing cabinet. In six months' time we'd find the fat man again and put him in court, and he'd testify that he was indeed whoever he said he was and he'd seen the dead man with his own eyes, but he still couldn't sleep at night and his wife had now left him because she didn't like him talking about dead people, particularly just before breakfast.

I watched them help the fat man into a car and drive him off towards the station. Cayman was still hovering about, watching the policemen move along the access decks.

'Do we know anything else about Bates, sir? Was he still working for Hill?'

'I don't know. He used to make money on fashion shoots until he found out he could make more money hanging round Hill. The past few months he's been working as a chauffeur. He was supposed to be going straight.'

'What about Hill – what's he been doing since Paddy Moran?' Cayman wouldn't meet my eye.

I said, 'Killing people.'

Somebody's radio squealed, spat static and said something about a road accident at the Elephant and Castle. A blue Astra drove up behind the ambulance and a small man got out holding a silver photographic case. The rows of kids' faces were back on the access decks.

The small man came up to us, unlocked the case and started screwing together an aluminium tripod. He had a leathery, sly face and patter that was so old and smooth he couldn't even hear himself say it any more.

'Lovely day for a picture.' He didn't laugh; nor did anyone else. He screwed the camera into the top of the tripod and pointed it at Joe Bates.

'Any sign of a gun?' I asked Cayman.

'Not yet, sir. If he's got any sense he'll have dropped it in the river by now.'

I nodded. 'We'd better go through the bins. Keep them cordoned off until forensic give us something to go on.'

It was a routine, as pointless and automatic as checking the tower blocks.

Cayman turned to talk to a policeman standing behind us. The photographer was peering through his camera at Bates's body. He said, 'Smile for the birdy.' Nobody laughed.

'We've got his wife down at the station,' Cayman said, turning back to me.

'Clare,' I said.

'You know her, sir?'

'I interviewed her in the Moran investigation.'

'What's she like?'

'Better than him,' I said. 'She thought he was innocent. I didn't know they lived here.'

'Number twenty-nine.' He pointed towards the block nearest us.

'Have you taken a statement yet?'

'We were waiting for you.' His voice was tight.

I said, 'Was she in a state?'

'Quiet, they said. She's got a kid – two years old. Bloody hard.'
I said, 'Isn't it?'

The photographer snapped his tripod shut. Two men in green overalls who'd been lounging against their ambulance came to life. They pulled a stretcher out of the back and carried it over to where Bates lay.

I looked round. The morning traffic was snarled up behind us on Kennington Lane. Faces looked down from the top deck of a stationary bus. Something to tell them about at work: a blanket with a man's hand sticking out of it. Something to think about in the middle of the night, and make them get up and check that the doors were locked and the gas switched off. Police vans, a crowd of people, a shape under the blanket that was at the same time familiar and as strange as anything ever could be; the same shape their husband made under the blanket at night. I wondered how many of them had seen somebody dead before. A woman with thick forearms leaned on the access deck above us and peered down as if she was looking into a pit.

I said, 'Wait a minute.'

I stooped, and rolled Joe Bates over on to his side. His head sagged to one side and came to rest. The handsome blue eyes stared past me through hooded lids. His sneering, hard man's mouth was an ugly purple line split by teeth. Stubble covered his jawline and cheeks. Joe Bates needed a shave but he wasn't going to get one.

I felt in his pockets. In the side pocket of the jacket there was a Rolls-Royce key ring with two doorkeys and the keys to a car. I found a half-pack of Marlboro in the other side pocket along with a cheap lighter and another key, not on a ring. I gave all the keys to Cayman and told him to try them on Bates's front door. Then I rolled Bates over on to his side again and felt his back pockets. One of them was empty.

From the other I pulled out a roll of green banknotes tied up with a rubber band.

One of the stretcher men whistled. He was going to say something, then caught my eye and didn't.

The notes were fifties. I started to count through them. The stretcher men picked Joe Bates up and lifted him on to the stretcher.

265

His body was stiff, as if he didn't want to go wherever it was they were taking him. His head dropped back, bumping once on the pavement.

I was still thumbing through the notes when Cayman came back.

'The two Chubbs open his front door, sir. The separate one . . .' He shrugged. 'Doesn't seem to belong. Maybe it was from his office.'

There was a roar of car engines starting up behind us. One by one they were pulling away from the kerb. The photographer drove off; the ambulance gave one shriek of its siren, to move the kids, and nosed its way towards Kennington Lane.

Cayman said, 'Are we quite sure it wasn't just a mugging, sir?'

I opened out the roll of banknotes for him.

Cayman whistled. 'Keep him in fags for a bit.'

I didn't laugh. 'We need to find Hill.'

We turned towards the car. One of the policemen who'd been knocking on doors was waiting for us.

'Old lady in thirty-six,' he said. 'Light sleeper. Heard three shots about one o'clock. Thought it was the television. Then she heard a motorbike drive off.'

'Immediately?'

'She said immediately.'

'Is she making it up?'

The policeman shrugged.

'A motorbike,' I said.

Cayman said, 'Not Yardies. They use four wheels.'

I looked at him. 'Bring her in for a statement.'

We got into the car, slamming doors. Behind us two policemen were unrolling red plastic tape across the pavement. There are 150 murders a year in London and most of them start something like this, with two coppers unrolling red tape across a pavement. The kids were still looking down from the access decks, staring at the chalk mark where Bates had been lying, as if it was about to get up and walk away. An old drunk was staggering around beyond the cordon, shooting people with his forefinger and laughing. Like I said, it wasn't the sort of place you'd choose to die in. But Joe Bates hadn't been given the choice.